THE
JADE
TIGER

E. W. COOPER

INK DOG PRESS

978-1-7352449-0-7 (paper)
978-1-7352449-1-4 (Kindle)
978-1-7352449-2-1 (EPUB)
978-1-7352449-3-8 (WebPDF)

INK DOG PRESS

742 E. 20th Street, Unit 350
Houston, TX 77008

Cover design and illustration and interior design by Lindsey Cleworth

Printed in the United States of America

For
My family, who never once told me I was crazy
and
Jessye Norman, who sang Carmen *slow and hot*

1

THE LETTER ARRIVED IN THE MORNING MAIL. Heavy linen paper supplied an ample canvas for sweeping handwriting, which wrote, *Mrs. Penelope Harris Ambrose; c/o the Excelsior Hotel; New York, New York.* Then, in the return address, a name well known enough to give her pause. Wasn't he on tour with his protégé, the soprano? She turned the envelope in her hand and tried to remember. Wasn't he? What was her name? Penelope stared at the handwriting for a moment. Her heart beating a little faster.

There had been invitations from lesser-known vocal teachers. Society photographers appearing at the exact moment the instructor threw her out on her ear. Penelope couldn't ignore the coincidence. "All publicity is good publicity," the social editors told her when she called to complain. "Girlie, you sell newspapers!" Free advertising for an instructor looking for new talent wasn't too shabby either. After the last invitation resulted in a snap of Penelope with an unattractive gape and a double chin front and center in the *Evening Standard*, every invitation to sing went to the Excelsior incinerators with the rest of the trash—with no regrets.

But this one . . . Signore Avenetti. Penelope held the letter in her hand, weighing the consequences of another appearance in the society columns. She checked the postmark— October 11, 1928—only two days before. Had the Signore's precious soprano ditched him for a French conductor after her Parisian debut? Could the Signore be looking for another student? Someone to fill her place? Penelope stood stock-still, allowing the dream of a career on the stage to press in around her.

"What's that?" Her older brother, James, emerged from his bedroom, a heavy bathrobe lashed to his wiry frame, blond hair ruffled, glasses on the tip of his nose. Plucking the letter from her fingers with one hand, he adjusted his glasses with the other and said, "Love letters? So soon? We've only been in New York two months!" He waggled a finger in her direction. "Keep your nose clean, Penelope, or high society will cut you dead!"

"As if they haven't already!" she sniffed. The letter appeared smaller in his hand, less consequential. She remembered the photographers when the steamer had stopped in Liverpool, the newspaper headlines, relentless publicity. Then again in Boston. And again in New York. Kinkaid Ambrose had been a terrible husband in life. In death, he had been worse, killed in an alley behind the notorious Jade Tiger, a gambling casino of the very worst sort. A man like the Signore wouldn't—no, he couldn't be interested in a student who might put him on the front page in all the wrong ways. It simply was not possible.

Penelope was crisp. "High society wouldn't have me before I got married. Why on earth would they have me after I became a widow? Anyway, it isn't a love letter. Give it here." She stretched out her hand.

"What on earth is keeping the paper?" A tallish woman stood in the doorway to the living room. "James! Just look at yourself! If you are going to join us at breakfast in your bathrobe, you could at least comb your hair." She turned to Penelope. "Is that the paper?"

"Here it is, Mother." Penelope handed her the bundle. "There are two letters for you."

Eleanor took the paper and then eyed the mail. "Most likely your uncle Harry instructing me to remarry. It positively offends me to even think about it. Your father has hardly been dead a year!" She looked over the letters and added with some relief, "These are bills. You can tell by the handwriting; it is distinctly prim."

"What does this letter's handwriting look like, Mother?" James held up the envelope.

"Setting aside the fact that the letter is addressed to your sister and not to you, I would wager that it is definitely not a bill."

"I think it's a love letter," James said quickly, holding the letter up and away from Penelope where she could not reach it.

"My darling boy," Eleanor cocked her head to see the envelope better, "that is not a love letter. The handwriting is far too musical. I'd wager it's another audition." She returned to the letters in her hand.

"Then it goes in the trash." Practical facts filled Penelope with resolve. "Just another musical tutor looking for his picture in the paper."

"My dear, how can you tell?" Eleanor looked up. "It could be a legitimate invitation. The flourish on the *H* is very promising. You should go. Your father would have wanted you to continue your studies."

Would he? Penelope wasn't as sure. Before he died, her father hoped selling his company would produce enough to live comfortably in America. But he couldn't have realized how reduced the trip across Europe would make them. Nor how expensive the expert doctors in Munich would be. Her scar, which started above her ear and continued in an arc across her neck, was almost invisible, thanks to them. But at what cost? There was no money to attend the academy and continue her vocal studies. Not anymore. There was enough to see James through medical school and settle her mother in an apartment near her brother Harry—but none for singing. It didn't bear thinking about. Even if she could afford it, no teacher would want her. She thought her father would have understood. Especially now that the press was onto her past. Her mother needed an apartment. Her brother needed a career. Penelope did not deserve the money.

She imagined the Signore pointing to the exit in a grand, dramatic pose, his favorite student at his elbow, a newspaper photographer in a funny squashed hat shouting, "Mrs. Ambrose! Smile for the camera!" as he jumped out from behind a potted plant. It was easy to imagine. The circumstances had repeated identically four times in the previous six weeks. Penelope straightened. "Even if it was the genuine article, I don't need an audition—I need a job." She took the letter from James's fingers and dropped it onto the table next to the telephone in a single fluid movement. "I won't have any students at all if I get my name into the papers one more time." Penelope stuck out her chin. No more auditions. No more fools' errands. It was time to get down to real work—if she could find it. Time to give up on childish ambition.

Two hours later, with James on his way to campus for a lecture on the Spanish influenza and Eleanor off to the library for a new book, Penelope opened the letter and read it. The thought of her father haunted her. He could be in the living room reading the paper, he felt so close, the scent of his pipe drifting through the morning sun. A year of grieving hadn't made the loss any easier. She missed him dreadfully. Would he have approved of her giving up? The man who told her she always had to try? Fifteen minutes later, she was in a cab headed uptown in the best disguise she could put together on short notice: an old dress, her mother's second-best wool coat and gloves, a faded brown cloche pulled down over her hair and halfway over her eyes. With any luck at all, the press wouldn't catch on. So far she was sailing free of them.

Penelope allowed a dangerous glimmer of hope. The city passed by the windows in a blur as she dreamed.

2

Blackened by exhaust from the street, and leaning slightly to the east, the apartment building looked like a penniless drunk propped up by a barstool, good humor, and gasoline masquerading as a cocktail.

"Hey lady, you want me to stick around?" The cabbie leaned out of the window and looked up at the building. "I can wait for a minute or two if you were just delivering a letter." He nodded to the letter from the Signore.

Penelope stared up at the building and wondered what she had let herself in for. Children played up and down the street, a number of them camped out on the front steps watching her with the cabbie. At the corner, a group of men turned to look her over. "Yes," she said finally, "better wait." She crammed the letter into her pocket, adding, "I'll pay you for your time."

"That wasn't why I offered, lady." The cabbie sat back, offended. "You shouldn't be on this side of town alone. There are rough types." He nodded his head toward the men.

She didn't like to admit it, but he was right. The street was too loud and unkempt for someone like the Signore. He'd live on the park or near the opera house on Thirty-Fourth. Looking down the block, she could see the men on the corner were no longer talking to each other. They watched her. Penelope made up her mind. She reached for the door, her head down in case a photographer jumped out from between the cars.

"Don't worry about her." The voice, low and predatory, came from the top of the steps. "She's got friends."

Penelope froze, her eyes traveling past the children and up the steps to the vision standing on the top step. Covered in a luxurious mink, a red dress winking through the heavy fur, the woman hit upon the inappropriate. The men at the corner stared.

Renee Strong came down the stoop, her movement slow like she was coming down a steep hill. Penelope recognized the too careful slowness without a thought—Renee was drunk. "My car's coming up now," she said without the hint of a slur. "Mrs. Ambrose and I are old friends. I can give her a ride home. Isn't that right, Penny darling?"

With a shuddering advance of fear, Penelope realized the trap Renee had set. She should have listened to her instincts and stayed away. The cabbie gave Penelope a quick look, uncertain. If he stayed, it would only mean Renee had an audience for whatever malicious terror she had planned. Penelope couldn't take another witness. Her mortification was already excruciating. She nodded, unable to look him in the eye. The cab went into gear, leaving her alone with Renee.

"Here for an audition?" Renee swayed, looking around herself.

Penelope hid her shaking hands in her wool coat, pushing the letter deep into her pocket. What a fool hope had made her! She replied too quickly, "I'm here to see a student. I teach now. Music, singing."

"Oh?" Renee pushed back the fur to put one hand on her hip, exposing the deep-red dress. "I thought you might have been here to see Signore Avenetti." She met Penelope's eye directly. "No, huh? That's interesting. The letter I sent you was specific about the time. I guess you forgot. Did you forget?" Renee smiled, her red dress vital and alive against the drab street.

"Was your point," Penelope whispered loudly, "to embarrass me? Humiliate me?"

A car pulled up to the curb, announcing its arrival with a horn. The driver rolled the window down and gave them both a watery leer. Renee continued, "I had to get you to leave your apartment, darling. For a little chat. You've got the bridge up. No visitors. Even if I got past the front desk, there would be your mother to contend with. Speaking of which, I didn't think you could afford the Excelsior these days. Are you just keeping up appearances? Should I feel sorry for you? Or did your father have a secret drawer of cash you found after he died?"

Penelope just managed to keep her hands inside her pockets. She was itching to slap the smile off Renee's face, just once so she could know what it felt like. "As it happens, I worked for that money."

"Halfway around the world in a gambling hell." Renee smiled. "Of course, everyone knows that already, don't they? I saw it in the *Times*. Why don't you get in the car? We can catch up. Girl talk."

"Did you pay for that dress yourself?" Penelope asked. "Or have you sunk your claws into some poor fool who doesn't know any better?"

"See, Mikey?" Renee reached through the window to tap the driver on the shoulder. "Isn't she a pal? It only took her twenty seconds to call me names! You wouldn't know it, Mikey-boy, but take it from me—Mrs. Ambrose's got a temper like a rooster in a cockfight."

"Harris. It's just Harris now." Penelope considered how much force it would take to knock out a couple of Renee's white teeth. "What do you want?"

"How about we just sit in the car for a minute." Renee leaned toward the door. "Get out, Mikey. Us girls need to talk."

The driver raised his voice. "But it's cold, Miss Strong," he protested. "I just got in from it!"

"Didn't you build up your strength to that kind of thing in the prison yard, Mikey-boy?" Renee's hand darted through the window and pinched his ear hard, leaving a bright red mark.

"Ouch!" Mikey slapped his hand against his neck. "What was that for?"

"That was for not listening, you overgrown punching bag. Wait on the sidewalk. I'll call you if I need you." Renee opened the door to the back seat with a fluid movement, curling herself inside the car like a cat. "Don't sulk," she said as she settled in. "No reason to freeze while we catch up.

"No." Penelope took her hands out of her pockets and crossed her arms, leaning against the side of the car so she could watch Mikey as he walked. She kept her eyes on him until he was leaning against an empty storefront facing away from them. Penelope turned her attention back to the woman in the back seat of the car. "What do you want, Renee?"

Renee clicked her tongue. "Don't jump the gun. I've been looking forward to this for such a long time."

"You have ten seconds to give me a reason to stay."

"Why, the Jade Tiger of course. What other reason would there be?"

"Is it blackmail?" Penelope almost laughed. "Because I don't have any money, not anymore. It took almost everything just to settle Kinkaid's debts, not to mention the cost of getting out of China." Penelope willed herself not to think of Kinkaid's face or his perfidy or his lurid extramarital affairs, in which Renee figured prominently. "There's nothing left." This was almost the truth. At the very least it was the truth brandished by every English-speaking newspaper experiencing a slow news day from Istanbul to Hoboken.

"Blackmail is just what liars call the truth, Mrs. Ambrose." Renee slid closer to the open car door, draped her arm across the front seat. "They'll pay plenty to keep my mouth shut about it. Plenty."

"The poor bastard." Penelope recognized something in

Renee's tone that made her hair stand on end. "I hope he's got enough money to keep you happy."

A flawlessly drawn eyebrow lifted. Renee looked as content as a purring cat. "He doesn't, but his family does. They'll pay to keep me clear of the papers because of what I know. Five thousand dollars to see the back of me. They're good for it if they pull together. I'm rather proud of myself. I've never done a job like this one. I've got the whole family by the short hairs, all in one go."

"Then it's blackmail after all."

"No, darling. You always think so small." Renee smiled. "This is revenge."

"Revenge?" Penelope resisted the urge to shudder. "I didn't think you let anyone get close enough to warrant that kind of attention. For what, may I ask?"

"So high and mighty." Renee's eyes narrowed. "Queen of the Jade Tiger is what you thought you were. You couldn't stand the fact that your husband loved another woman. Couldn't take it that he was going to leave you."

"No chance he was running away with you, Renee. Kinkaid hadn't finished robbing me blind yet. Without me, there was no one to finance his operation. Besides," Penelope uncrossed her arms, "you were welcome to him!"

"Run away? Ha! We weren't running anywhere. We were going to stay right there in Shanghai." Renee gritted her teeth. "You found out. You couldn't stand it. Everything you had would have been mine. The nightclub, the gaming tables, the Jade Tiger—all of it, mine!"

"Everything he had?" Penelope snorted. "You mean he was gifting you all the markers he put down between Joffre

Avenue and Bubbling Wall Road? And the Jade Tiger? That was leveraged months before he died. He lost the value of the Jade Tiger three times over in a single game of craps. Of course, maybe he didn't tell you that his money came from me. That the only interest he had left in the Jade Tiger was under my name."

"That's a lie!" Renee's shout traveled.

Mikey looked up from the trembling paper of his hand-rolled cigarette, meeting Penelope's wary eye.

"Why don't you write Dai Li and ask him about it? He took on Kinkaid's share personally. I'm sure he'll be happy to hear from you." Penelope felt the men on the corner taking more of an interest. Mikey lit the cigarette, palming it against a breeze. "You should have gotten what you could from Kinkaid before he died."

"You killed Kinkaid. I know you did." Renee's face twisted with fury. She struck the seat with her hand and shouted, "We were happy, and you couldn't take it!"

"Kinkaid was killed in a robbery, Renee. Some roughs jumped him in the street thinking he had the night's take on him. Everyone said so—even the commissioner." Penelope kept her eye on the street. Even the children had stopped jostling to listen.

"You've got them all wrapped around your little finger. God knows how you did it. Well, you won't get away with it this time. Everything is all set for the party tonight . . ."

"What do you mean? What party?" Penelope felt a sharp jolt of surprise.

"Darling, you're in America now. Everyone who is anyone knows your cousin Mary is throwing a society party tonight."

Penelope relaxed. "I won't be there to see whatever it is you have planned. I wasn't invited, and I have no intention of going even if I was."

"Not invited? That's a good one! On the outs with the family? Well, my dear, you had better sort out a way to get an invitation. You don't want to miss these fireworks." Renee paused, a smile crawling up one cheek as her eyes narrowed with sadistic delight. "On second thought, maybe it's better if you wait for the papers. They're sure to cover the news I've got." She giggled as she waved a hand to her driver. "Come along, Mikey-boy. Time to earn your money. We're going uptown."

As the salon car went down the block, Penelope began the long walk back to the Excelsior, the echo of Renee's laughter ringing in her ears.

 **3**

"PENELOPE," ELEANOR DROPPED THE PAPER on the floor and stood up, "where have you been? I've been worried sick!"

"I went out for a walk. It was perfectly safe."

"Safe? You didn't tell me where you were going, didn't leave a note at the front desk. I didn't have any idea where you were. Can you imagine how worried I was?" She crossed the room quickly, throwing her arms around Penelope. Holding her by the shoulders, Eleanor searched her daughter's face. "Why, you're freezing! You must get into warmer clothes! What possessed you to go out in my old coat, I'll never know!"

Penelope turned on her heel and headed to her bedroom.

"Honestly, Penelope!" Flushed with irritation, Eleanor followed her, picking up clothes and shoes and anything else in the bedroom that gave her hands something to do. "You could have a little consideration next time you decide to go out for a walk."

"I went to the audition."

"The letter! I knew you couldn't resist." Eleanor straightened and put her hand to the collar of her blouse. "Did you sing? What did he say?"

Penelope had debated telling her mother the truth all the way from Forty-Third. On the one hand, Eleanor had so much invested in her daughter's vocal training that any stumble or rejection hurt her more than it ever could hurt Penelope herself. On the other hand, Penelope knew she couldn't lie— not like she once could. The Jade Tiger had wrung the skill out of her. Now hope stood out so clearly in her mother's face that she regretted her lost ability. "It wasn't really from the Signore, Mother. The letter was a forgery."

"A forgery?" Eleanor said the word as though she didn't understand what it meant. "A trick? Were there photographers there?"

"No." Penelope slipped her coat from her arms and laid it across the bottom of the bed. She stood still for a moment, looking from her window down into the street, where the traffic queued for a policeman in a blue uniform. She was cold all over. How had Renee known about the party? If Renee meant to make a meal out of humiliating her, it would only be the beginning. Had Mary handed out too many invitations? Penelope had been insistent about privacy, and Mary had agreed. Hadn't she? Lost in thought, she heard herself say, "Renee was there . . ."

"That woman?" Eleanor took a step forward. "I knew it. Say no more—I know the whole story. That . . . that harlot!"

"Please don't shout." Penelope sat down on the bed. "I don't know how she knew, but she threw Mary's party in my face like she was invited."

Eleanor struck her fist against her hand. "The gall of that woman! To travel halfway around the world just to persecute you with her sordid lies about Shanghai and that dreadful casino . . . the Red Cat—"

"The Jade Tiger, Mother."

"It's all the same! What did she say?" Eleanor flapped a hand. "Never mind! You don't have to tell me!" She gasped. "She wanted to blackmail you! She's going to tell the world about that dreadful casino." She tapped a finger against her lip. "She'll try the newspapers next. Americans will print anything. You told her we don't have any money, didn't you?"

Penelope stood, gathering her mother's hands in her own. "She knew about Mary's party. I think she means to crash it."

"Crash? What on earth does that mean?"

"Attend without an invitation." Penelope dove for her bedside table and her address book. "I must call Mary."

"Oh dear. Remember what your uncle said? He was clear the newspaper coverage makes it impossible for us to attend. He will have business partners there and important people from the city. He was quite firm."

"I'm not going to go to the party. What on earth would I wear? Everything is over a year old and much too bold for a party." But perfect for the dim lighting in a casino. Penelope sighed. "I'm just going to warn Mary to have the porters check for invitations. Renee couldn't possibly have gotten one. Unless . . ." She paused.

"Unless Charles gave her one," Eleanor finished for her. They looked at each other in horror, Renee's plan slowly rolling out between them. Mary's brother wasn't known for much except his spotty taste in fiancées. There had been three since '27, if Penelope's recollection could be trusted.

"Mother," Penelope's words were quick, "this girl Charles is seeing, has anyone met her?"

The phone rang—two long rings and a short.

Penelope waved a hand. "That's the front desk, but which one does it mean? Does two shorts and a long mean a direct call? Or is it—"

The phone rang again. This time the two long rings were a little longer, the short barely longer than a single bell.

"Damn and blast!" Penelope picked up the heavy black receiver. "Hello?"

"Penelope, is that you?" Mary's high-pitched twitter was as the tinkle of glass. "Charles went and got himself engaged to a terrible girl, and I don't know what to do! You couldn't lend a hand, dearest, and come tonight after all, could you?"

"Who is this person, Mary?" Penelope held on to the last shred of hope she could find. Charles might fall in and out of love as quickly as a rabbit, but he did have some sense of self-preservation, didn't he? She tried to sound natural. "Does this one rouge her knees like the last one?"

"That was Dierdre, the one before last." Mary twittered. "The last one was nice, darling. You would have liked her too. She was always good for a laugh. I'd do just about anything

to convince her to come back, but she's gone and married a
financier from New Jersey. No, this one's named Renee."

Penelope's heart lurched at the name.

Eleanor leaned down. "What is it? What did she say?"

Mary continued, "She must come from money, the way
she knows how to spend it. She floats everywhere, doesn't eat
a bite, drinks like a fish, and complains of a perpetual headache, all while shod in nothing but the best Parisian fash-
ions. She says she knows you. Her name is Renee Strong."
Mary proceeded to describe her in unladylike terms. "Can
you come, my dear? I can't tell you how much I could use the
help. Papa will have histrionics all over the salmon when he
finds out they're getting married!"

Of course Uncle Harry disliked her! He had been one
of Renee's many Shanghai conquests. Penelope set her jaw.
Renee knew exactly what to do with a weak-willed man like
Charles. Was he handsome? Oh my yes. But quick on the up-
take? Sadly not. The plan would be to marry quickly, before
anyone could make a move to stop them. Penelope thought
fast. "Does Charles have any money of his own? Enough for
them to elope?"

"You know he doesn't. Papa took it all away after he
sank Phillip March's motorboat off the cape last spring. He
doesn't have any cash except what Papa gives him and what he
manages to talk his tailor into putting on credit. Besides, he
wouldn't get married without me," Mary added indignantly.
"He knows I would never forgive him."

"Mary, I do know Renee Strong. I know her quite well."

"Who is she?" Mary's plaintive question was almost
childlike over the line.

"She was the headliner at the Jade Tiger—she sang." Penelope couldn't bring herself to list Renee's other talents: petty theft, picking pockets, extortion, blackmail.

"Your casino? In China?" Penelope could practically hear the furrow in Mary's brow. "But what on earth is she doing here? And with Charles of all people? You know I love my brother to the end of the earth, but he isn't exactly Valentino!"

"I saw her this morning." Penelope met Eleanor's eye as she spoke. "She was crowing about being engaged to a rich man's son." Even as she said it, she felt the weight of certainty—Renee would never give up. Her hooks were in. It would be a fight to get free.

"Charles has about as much sense as a pair of stockings, Penelope. We can't leave him to a wolf like her," Mary protested. "He'll never stand up for himself. Is there any kind of choice in the matter? What on earth will I do? Could I pay her?"

Penelope guessed her cousin had easily spent a thousand dollars on food for the party, let alone the extra footmen to check invitations and serve champagne. "Maybe. If it's enough." A thought occurred to her as she said the words. Was this what Renee had in mind all along? She had to admit, the plan—if it was a plan—was simple and clever, especially if Renee and Charles had already married. Divorce was still enough of a novelty to fill every courtroom with benches of newspapermen and photographers. Renee had known Charles's family would pay—she'd said so right to Penelope's face not an hour before. But perhaps she hadn't meant blackmail—she had meant alimony.

"I have two thousand set aside in case we needed a bootlegger," Mary offered. "Come a little early and I'll pass it to you

in a purse. You know her, so you can convince her to take it."
Mary's words were filled with a certainty Penelope did not feel
herself. She considered the dress, jewelry, and fur Renee had
worn that morning. Two thousand would never be enough.

"All right," she said. "I will be there."

"Oh," Mary blurted out, "and bring your brother too! I'm
short of attractive men who know how to dance. Tell him he
can bring a handsome doctor or two if he knows any." Mary
rang off.

Penelope returned the phone to the cradle. She looked at
her mother.

"I hope you didn't just promise your cousin we would attend that party tonight." A furrow of concern appeared on
Eleanor's brow. "You know Harry and I don't see eye to eye.
He never approved of your father. All he ever talks to me
about is remarrying. We won't go, and that's all there is to it."

"Mary needs my help. Charles has gotten himself engaged again . . ."

"It's her, isn't it? Renee Strong?" Eleanor's logic leapt
ahead, as Penelope knew it would. Whether it was because
she had the keenest hearing of anyone Penelope had ever met
or the sharpest mind, Penelope couldn't say. "Don't tell me
he's gone and asked that harlot to marry him?"

"You don't have to go, Mother. This is because of me. It's
my problem to solve."

"You can't carry the fault for what that woman is or for
what she does. Leave it to Harry. Charles is his son. Surely the engagement is his responsibility? Stay out of it. Stay
clear away." Eleanor prattled on, her words buzzing in the air
around them as Penelope thought.

What did her uncle know? All of it? Part of it? What he had read in the paper? Harry had been there the night Penelope met Kinkaid at her debut. It came back to her in a flood of odd detail: her white dress, the Hong Kong evening dark and cool with just a whisper of a breeze, the crowd of people filling the grand ballroom of the Repulse Hotel. Her father must have invited every expat in Hong Kong the dance floor was so swollen with people.

It was a magical night, a triumph. Every door open to let in the night air, the band playing popular jazz for the young people while her father and uncle talked business with the investors from London and New York. Eleanor sailed proudly through the crowd of British and French socialites who made Hong Kong their temporary home, meeting every eye with a generous smile. She twittered with her friends from the Kowloon British School about the number of available men from the consulate. James hid on the outdoor balcony drinking champagne and smoking cigarettes with the chaps from the cricket team.

Penelope danced all night long, the floor light beneath her feet. The invitation to study at the Royal Academy in London was on her night table in her room, the girls from Kowloon were adequately jealous of her party, and her mother hadn't objected once to the jazz the band played so well. When Penelope took the stage to sing the aria she had prepared for her audition with the Royal Academy, her heart was full of happiness. Perhaps that was why she couldn't forget when she first caught sight of Kinkaid, leaning casually against a door frame, his coat cut to flatter his athletic build, his unblinking brown eyes watching her from across the room as though there were only the two of them. Six weeks later, instead of boarding a train to England, Penelope and Kinkaid took a train south to Shanghai. They were married in the dining car by a priest on his way to his mission, his disapproving frown an uncomfortable portent.

Penelope shut her eyes tight. All of this her uncle would know, but the rest? She couldn't be sure. She took hold of herself. "I'm not going to let Mary down. She's never met anyone like Renee before. She can't know what she's in for. I'm going, and that's all I have to say about it."

Eleanor frowned. "Then we all go. I'm not letting you step a foot inside that house without your brother and me there to see you through it. That woman!" Eleanor turned on her heel and disappeared into her bedroom.

4

"LISTEN, BUB." THE CAB DRIVER hooked his arm over the front seat. "I'm all for waiting in line, but you'd have a much better chance of getting to that party tonight if you got out and walked."

Lund had to agree. Limousines and cabs lined up a block away from the Staughton house, and a crowd gathered on the sidewalk in front of what he presumed was the residence. He opened the door and stood in a single fluid movement. "Keep the change." Lund passed some money through the window.

The cabbie sped away, leaving Lund in the street. He

stood for a moment, looking down the street, then moved to the corner. James had said it would be a small party, but the line of women in evening gowns and men in boiled suits stretched down the house steps and into the street, at least thirty people waiting around the front door. The crowd continued to grow, taxis expectorating guests. It began to drizzle.

Lund lit a cigarette, not wanting to rush. He was still thinking it through, still telling himself he had a chance to walk away. At odds with everything from the fitted tuxedo to the damp creeping up through the soles of his shoes, he tried to think of a good enough reason to counter his promise to James. No matter how hard he tried, his confounded brain would always arrive at the same question: Would she be very changed?

The Staughton house stood open to the city. Every window cast light into the street, revealing the rooms inside. Beautiful women dressed impeccably wandered past the glass, casually looking down at those outside who stopped to stare. Lund had the impression of an audience and a stage complete with curtains, lights, and symphony. Guests passed the windows in groups, laughing, talking. He wondered if he would see Penelope there, in a moment or two. Dancing past on another man's arm. The quick pull of regret made him certain it had been a mistake. He was unable to stop looking for a glimpse of her.

"Thom!" James Harris, tall and blond, jogged through the traffic, the streetlights reflecting off his glasses. James looked so like his sister through his eyes and nose, Lund would have known him anywhere. "I'm glad you decided to come."

Lund was surprised. Had there been any doubt? He was

certain of his attendance at the party as soon as James promised Penelope would attend. "I said I would."

"Listen, Thom, could you take Penelope along for me? Mother's arguing with the cab driver, and I don't like to leave her alone with him or she's liable to end up with a charge for assault."

"Did he overcharge her?" Lund couldn't help a smile.

"No." James's face brightened. "She can't understand a word he's saying." He looked over his shoulder. "Penelope is over there. There's a good chap." James rushed away.

Lund lifted his head and wondered how he could have missed her. Penelope was directly across the street from him, no more than twenty feet away.

Her hair was white in the dimness of the evening, her skin a bright shimmer against the shadows. The luxurious mink around her shoulders ended just below her knees, peeking blood-orange silk around her feet. Holding the dress in her hand, saving the hem from the damp, she looked up at the windows just as he had a moment before. Above the fur, he could see only the slope of her neck, an ear, and her hair, a white nimbus against the dim streetlight. He was astonished he had missed her. Even without seeing her face, he could see she was just the same. His heart beat just a little faster. He told himself he could leave now. He had seen her after all. Later he could tell James he had missed them in the swell of the crowd, seen them from across the room. Some kind of nonsense like that.

Instead, Lund crossed the street to get closer to her. He wanted to see her face, not just her shoulders. Every part of her made him thirsty for a little more. He began to move without thinking, through the headlights and along the side-walk. Jostled by a small crowd of partygoers, he ended up farther away from her than he had meant. As he came closer, he had a good look at her profile and her long neck as she watched the people through the windows.

"Mrs. Ambrose?"

Lund froze at the name, mirroring Penelope's sudden stiffness. The name of a dead man. Kinkaid's name. She turned away from the house and toward a figure coming up the sidewalk. Lund waited.

"Penny Ambrose?" the man prompted again. He took his hat off and stepped closer to her.

Penny? Lund bristled at the indignity. She was not a *Penny*.

"Jack?"

Lund still couldn't see her face. But hearing her voice, careful in the darkness, he knew it was her. He looked past her to the man, tall with dark hair and the puffy eyes of someone who drank freely and often. He took in the faded tuxedo, just a little too large, and worn shoes. Lund had last seen him wearing sailor dungarees and a pilot's cap tilted low over one eye. Jack Rollins was always covered in oil and muck up to his elbows. But not tonight.

"Mrs. Ambrose! Well, look at you!" Jack's smile revealed white teeth and a dimple where his mouth slid up into effort-less cheer. "Gee, it's good to see you."

"It's Penelope Harris now. I've gone back to my maiden name." Lund could see Penelope's discomfort from the angle of her head and hear it in her voice. "Jack," she said, "what are you doing here?"

"Looking for a friend." Jack shifted his weight to his back foot. "Actually, I'm not invited to this shindig, but I thought I would give the man at the door a try. There's plenty of opportunity in a crowd like that. Investment opportunity." Jack nodded toward the windows. "Could be a good night for doing business."

"If you have the nerve for it." Penelope tried to laugh and almost managed it.

"What are you doing in New York, Mrs. Ambrose? If you don't mind me asking. You aren't an American, if I remember right."

"But I am an American, Jack. My father was American, and I was born right here in New York City. I can't help it if I sound like a Brit. All the Hong Kong schools were British."

"I forgot. I've been away for a while . . ."

Lund's mind raced through what he knew about Jack's last months in Shanghai, smuggling guns to the revolutionaries in the northern provinces. He had been an excellent ship's captain and a terrible criminal. Caught speedily and banged up in a prison camp until his father had bought him a one-way ticket back to the states. The payoff must have been incredible. On top of all the other charges, Jack had killed a man in a bar. He had received a life sentence.

"My father passed this April. It was sudden. I expect that's how I would like to go, quick and quiet." Jack nodded, turning the hat in his hands. "Without an investor, the business is a goner. Not much cash these days." The speech had the air of repetition. Lund wondered how often Jack had tried the pitch on investors who hadn't known him.

Penelope's posture straightened. "I don't know what

you've heard, Jack. I had to sell the Jade Tiger after Kinkaid died. Settling his debts was just the beginning. When my father died, I used what was left to move my mother and brother west." She paused. "It bought us second-class tickets here and a year's lease at the Excelsior. If I had money to invest, I would. But . . ." She spread her hands and shrugged. "There's nothing left."

"Try that on the daisies inside."

Even with Jack's good humor coloring the words, Lund knew a threat when he heard one. Lifting his hands from his pant pockets so they swung free, Lund made his way toward them.

"I have a good memory," Jack continued. "By my recollection, Kinkaid wasn't the one with the head for business at the Jade Tiger." He smiled. "Look, I just want enough to save what's left of Dad's company. I'm not asking for much. You can afford it." He lowered his voice, reached forward to take her by the arm.

"Jack Rollins?" Lund stepped between Jack and Penelope so that Jack was looking down at the center button of Lund's tuxedo shirt. "Well, who would have thought it?" He put out a hand, forcing Jack back another step to shake it.

"Officer Lund." Jack licked his lips, looked away.

"Miss Harris?" Lund looked down into her face. Her blue eyes caught the light as they swept up to his face and did not look away. A year of heartbreak. He couldn't help himself. Could it be this easy?

"Thom! What a surprise!" Penelope offered her hand, and Lund found himself bowing over it like he was a bloody teenager. Penelope shifted, allowing him to take more space between her and Jack. There was a hint of a smile. Lund couldn't tell in the dark, but he thought there was a growing flush on her neck. "Mary didn't mention you were coming."

Lund looked around himself but could not find James. Damn the man! He nodded toward the street and said, "Your brother invited me. He said there wouldn't be enough men."

"Oh, that man!" Penelope spoke with the rapid approbation of a sister. "You have no idea what it's like to have a brother who believes torturing his sister is amusing. Don't have enough men!" She laughed. "Can you imagine?"

Now this was more like it. Lund couldn't resist the happiness that slipped past his reservations. This was the woman he remembered. It was as though time had not passed.

"Did you come from China, Officer Lund? Just for a party?" Jack's words sliced their sudden connection in two. Penelope's smile faded, replaced by a politely blank expression. Lund straightened, letting go of her hand.

He turned his shoulder into Jack, forcing him just a little farther away from Penelope. It was the politest way he could think of, short of knocking the man down. "Just regular Thom Lund now. I'm not a policeman anymore. I work at New Amsterdam Bank." Lund relaxed. "My brother Matthias and the bank president are old friends from the war. When he needed someone he could trust, he sent for me. I moved here a year ago next month."

"A year ago?" Penelope asked. He could see her thoughts as clearly as if she were flipping back the sheets of a calendar. "What do you do there, at the bank?"

"A couple of clerks decided they could embezzle their

way out of debt. The president needed a man he could trust, and he knew I wanted a change. Once that cleared, it seemed like there was a crime around every corner. Tracking down fraudulent stock, investigating corporations to ensure they are what they say they are. Sometimes a private matter for the board or a bank customer. A man in my line barely has to look for trouble. These days it's everywhere I turn."

"Thom, thank goodness!" James appeared beside them. "I've deposited Mother inside, and I would suggest we do the same. Feels like it's about to rain any minute." James gave Jack a quick once-over. Pushing his glasses up, he asked, "Are you with our party?"

Penelope smiled broadly. "Yes, James, he can come in with us." She spoke to Jack. "You'll be my guest. I may not have the money to invest, but there are plenty inside who might give it a go."

Not to mention the access to the hot buffet, thought Lund. Jack did look down on his luck. It wouldn't be the first time a glass of champagne and a warm meal had made a difference in a man's life. Maybe Jack would find an investor inside, someone to share the burden of Rollins Shipping. Lund set his inner policeman aside. Give the man a chance to have a fresh start, he thought. We're a long way from China, and thank God for that. Penelope was already waving the butler over from the steps.

"Parker, this is Jack Rollins. He's forgotten his invitation, but he is my guest. Could you please show him past the footmen? I don't want him to be turned away."

Jack replaced his hat on his head. "Here, Mrs. Ambrose," he handed her a worn calling card, "in case you change your

mind. That's my number on the back. I'm there most nights."
He tipped his hat and disappeared with Parker.

Lund offered Penelope his arm. She took it with a hint
of a smile.

The evening began.

 **5**

"Penelope my dear! What on earth are you doing here?"
Penelope's uncle Harry squeezed every vowel until they
howled for charity. Smashed against his tuxedo, Penelope relaxed, even as his booming words attracted the attention of
everyone around them. Built like a bear, Harry had an enor-
mous chest and arms, with hammer-like hands that squeezed
out of the sleeves of his jacket. She drew a strange comfort
from him. Perhaps because he was just the same as when she
was a child, with his bushy black beard and twinkling blue
eyes. She found herself wishing it had been just the six of
them at the party, and not the social event of the season. A
servant lifted the fur from her shoulders, the cool air from the
open door cold against the plunging back of her dress.

"Papa, please! They can hear you in the street! I invited
them." Mary reached around her father to embrace Penelope.
"My dear, you look as though you have been dipped in red
gold!" Mary, as finely built as a small bird, looked Penelope
up and down, pausing to touch the glittering straps. "That
dress will be all anyone can talk about tomorrow!"

It was a wholesome view of the only almost-acceptable dress in Penelope's closet. The truth was much more shocking. Heavy persimmon-dyed silk flowed from the diamond clasps at her shoulders, the fabric pooling in a flattering train that pulled against her breasts, waist, and hips. The whole dress, cut on the bias, left nothing to the imagination but still flattered the whole of Penelope's body in the most meaningful way. It was the prize of her closet, one of the last dresses she purchased in Shanghai. Most of the women in New York still wore the dreadful dropped waist that did so little for the figure.

Mary's bright peacock-colored dress made her blue eyes sparkle. "I've counted three papers so far. They think I don't know who they are, but you can always tell the reporters." Mary whispered, "They make a straight line to the buffet." She babbled on, her neat head darting this way and that like a bird as she spoke. "The only person I absolutely will not allow is that Stone woman. She's such a wasp! She said unkind things about Perry Watkins after he got drunk on Mrs. Emerson's elderberry wine and crashed his mother's Rolls into Bunny Randolph's pool. It doesn't matter at all if they were true. I've got the staff keeping an eye out for her." She stopped to take a breath.

"Surely, she's not as bad as that, Budgie." Penelope laughed. She scanned the crowd of social matrons staring back at her around the foyer. She smiled. They did not smile back, but she took no offense. They were only there to get a good look at the woman who had once owned a casino and left a dead husband in China. Thirty minutes to have two glasses of champagne, an hour to show off Grandmother's coronet from the Continent, then it was back to the town-home and into bed until the next round of bridge with an earful of gossip to share.

"Leave it to you to come to a party with three of the best-looking men." Mary pointed across the foyer to Jack. "Who is that standing next to the butler?"

"Jack Rollins. Don't even think about it, Mary. He isn't your speed."

"Too fast?"

"No, Budgie dear, much, much too slow." Penelope glanced over her shoulder to be certain Lund couldn't hear her. "Darling, did James tell you he was inviting Thom Lund?"

Mary took more interest than Penelope would have liked. "Who? Which Tom?" Penelope was sure they had heard her all the way back in the kitchen.

"For goodness sake. Keep your voice down," Penelope whispered. "You're practically shouting."

"Just look at you! You're blushing!" Mary giggled, then whispered loudly, "All James told me was he was bringing a man from the bank. I said as long as he wasn't a creditor, he was welcome. Is he an old boyfriend?" She waggled her eyebrows. "A *new* boyfriend?" This was followed by a tittering that Penelope was certain someone would notice.

"Please, Mary! He's just a man." The heat seemed to be on, and it was intolerably hot in the foyer. It was hot enough to make a girl wish she had fan to wave about. And hide behind. Yes, Penelope thought, I would very much like to hide behind something.

"A very handsome one," Mary commented slyly, "that you have never mentioned before."

"I didn't know he was here! In America, I mean. He should be in China. Oh, hell!" Penelope stamped her foot. "I'm blushing, aren't I? I can feel it going up my neck!"

"You need a glass of champagne," Mary said, nodding somberly.

"I do," Penelope agreed.

"Good. Because we have a wine cellar full of it!" Mary waved a hand at a nearby footman, who deftly pivoted away from the dowagers to bring them a tray of full glasses. "Papa was so insightful. He ordered a whole boatful of champagne before Prohibition began. Such a relief!" She leaned forward and confided, "Renee is here. She appeared like the devil just when the footman was opening the first bottle of the '22 Bichat."

"Where is she?" An easy turn of the head revealed a dozen society stalwarts, obvious with their ready furs and turned-up noses. But no Renee. She set the matter of Lund to one side. She had to cope with Renee first—preferably without a former policeman in tow.

"In the parlor," Mary indicated the room with a slight tilt of her head, "holding court. Here it is."

Mary handed the clutch to Penelope with the subtlety of a rhinoceros. Penelope wished that her cousin's reading had not included so many illicit mystery novels. "I was only able to get two thousand. It will have to be enough. I will keep your mother here until it's done." Mary winked, a drawn-out affair that made her entire face compress and expand like a vaudeville comedian. Penelope just stopped herself from laughing.

"Whispering, whispering." James put his well-coiffured blond head between them. "Mary, what will your guests think?" Mary giggled as she turned back to stand next to her father. James took Penelope's elbow with the grace of a dancer and turned her toward the parlor. "I've sent Lund to find some champagne. Judging by the crowd, we have at least ten minutes before he finds his way back to us. Let's go and see Charles about this dog. I believe she's in the parlor."

"James, someone will hear you!" Penelope hissed.

"Chin up, Penelope. Don't let a society bitch get you down. All that's next is to send her straight to her kennel." James led her on across the crowded foyer, debutants and society grandes dames shuffling aside.

"Why did you invite Thom Lund?" Penelope kept her voice low. "Of all people!"

"Oh, him? You thought well enough of him while you were in China, didn't you? He was a particular friend, slept on a cot by your bed in the hospital. Stayed right by your side until Mother and I could get there."

"James, you never told me that!"

"I suppose I thought you already knew." James looked down at her. "I thought it would be a pleasant surprise. Are you very unhappy?"

Penelope glanced across the room at Lund's back. "No," she said slowly. "But next time, a little warning, please?"

"Next time? How many old boyfriends do you have?" He continued earnestly, "I have to admit it something of a cramp on one's style having an ex-policeman about. How did you work that one out? Back in China, I mean. Kinkaid had at least a dozen criminal activities on the go at any given time. How'd you square having a policeman about?"

"Not so loud! I don't know why I tell you things," Penelope

complained. "You make such a production of it. You could have warned me, at least!"

"And have you avoid attending the party altogether?" He patted her hand. "I'm looking after you, my dear. It's my loving nature. Everyone deserves a little happiness. I had the distinct impression he had given you a bit of it back in China, when it was hard to find. Don't worry. You'll find a way to thank me." He led her through the open doors to the parlor.

Penelope thought of a parlor as a small room, cozy. The Staughton parlor had a sixteen-foot ceiling and a fireplace three times the size of the modest grate at the Excelsior. On either side, facing each other, were two leather couches large enough to seat an army. Six east-facing windows bracketed two tall French doors, which led out to a stone balcony overlooking the street. This single room easily dwarfed her house in Shanghai and made every feature of their three-bedroom apartment-suite at the Excelsior appear modest, even shabby. It only took a moment to understand why Renee had thought there was cash to be had. Either her uncle was living much farther beyond his means than Penelope had first thought or his decision to leave England to speculate on the American stock market had paid off.

"Well!" James stopped and looked around the room. "I expect Mother is off somewhere giving Uncle Harry a lecture about his spending habits, wouldn't you say? I knew he made a packet on the market, but this is something unexpected." The room was packed with people, many turning to take an interest as Penelope entered on James's arm. She recognized only a few people, mostly friends Mary had introduced her to at tea parties and fashion salons. The majority were strangers who did little to hide their curiosity. A small clutch of guests stood near the radio without turning to take note, their laughter a little too loud, their drinking just a little too messy. That's where Renee would be, all right—in the middle of everything, at the center of the music, where the chaos always began.

She saw her cousin right away. Charles stood near the radio, his dark hair ruffled, an unlit cigarette held between his fingers. He appeared to be singing along to "Muskrat Ramble" without knowing any of the words. He was still a fool. Penelope shook her head. Some things never changed.

"There he is. I'll just go say hello," she whispered.

"Remember what I told you: leave the men's stuff to me," James whispered back. "Your job is to root out the dog."

"James!" Penelope protested. "I do rather resent your language!"

Penelope scanned the room behind them, catching Lund's eye as he pursued a waiter with a tray of coupe glasses. The knowing smile he gave put a girlish color in her cheeks and a flush in any number of unseen places. If she wasn't careful, she'd be giggling next. The hand holding the two thousand dollars tightened.

"Penelope!" Her name drew more attention from the crowd as Charles broke free from tuning the radio and came toward her. "My word!" He took her hand in both of his. "Jolly good to see you." His eyes sparkled with laughter as he dropped her hands to embrace James. "Mary said you were coming. Been looking forward to it."

She took Charles in now, from the scuffed shine of his best black shoes to his cockeyed tie. "I've never turned down an invitation from my wonderful cousins, and I never will."

"Capital! What a girl you are!" Charles embraced her, impulsively kissing her cheek.

The crowd near the radio laughed a little louder, a few of them craning their necks to get a good look at Penelope and James, then bursting out in undignified giggles. Someone turned up the music just as the broadcast from the Cotton Club began. A woman sat on the arm of a chair with her back to the room, her lean body draped in rich black silk velvet, her back framed by a shockingly low cut. Penelope found it hard not to stare. Damn Renee's dressmaker.

James had to pitch his voice louder to be heard over the radio. "I heard around the club that you are preparing to stride down the aisle, Charles. And here I thought you a terminal bachelor!"

Charles shifted on his feet, drawing Penelope's attention. He glanced across the room to his father, who was pouring himself a drink. "I say, don't mention it in front of the old man, would you? He's rather touchy on the subject."

"Then it's true!" James yelled his ear. "I didn't think you had it in you!"

Charles swayed with the rhythm of a man who has had too much to drink. Penelope had spent hundreds of nights on the floor of the Jade Tiger watching men like him consume liquor they shouldn't, drinking until they were indecent. "You might know her, Penelope old girl. From Shanghai. Name's Renee."

It had taken Penelope a good deal of thought to decide what to say in the circumstances. She worked the words free, shouting them over the radio. "I did know Renee in Shanghai. I should like to talk to you before you make any definite plans." It took a great amount of effort to control her temper as she said it.

Charles shuffled uncomfortably. Putting one hand in his pocket and stepping away, he said loudly, "Renee told me about her past, cousin. She also told me you might be a bit upset, given your trouble." A few heads turned.

Penelope felt a warm flush begin at the back of her neck. "What do you mean 'my trouble'?" The tinkle of glass followed by a burst of laughter brought her to a quick halt. She fought hard to keep her eyes straight ahead, away from the cluster of people by the radio.

"Well, you can't expect a girl like Renee to keep quiet when a man takes advantage of her, can you? I mean the poor girl could only take so much!"

Penelope took a swift a step toward him, her skirt swirling around her feet. "What are you talking about?"

Looping his arm through her elbow, James said under his breath, "Steady, old girl."

Charles put a hand on her shoulder. "It wasn't your fault that your husband was a bit of a cad. But if he takes advantage of a girl, people should know! She told me how you covered up for the blackguard. My dear, there is a limit to human decency."

Penelope couldn't put the words together. Kinkaid taking advantage . . . of Renee? It was a joke—it had to be! Their love affair had been the talk of Shanghai, hardly a secret at all! They had gone to the theater together, gone dancing together, even kept a house together! Kinkaid had hardly come home the last few months, and had Penelope cared? It had been the most peaceful time in her marriage by far. Kinkaid taking advantage of Renee wasn't hard to imagine—it was impossible. Her temper sparked. "Now see here, Charles—"

"My goodness, Penelope," the cool drawl cut through a lull in the noise of the room, "you have to be careful not to let your temper fly." Renee slid between Charles and James. "You never know what people might think."

6

JAMES CLEARED HIS THROAT. "Listen, Charles. I think you've gotten the wrong end of the stick here." Their voices died away as James led Charles out onto the balcony that skirted the west side of the house. Penelope watched them go, hoping James could talk some sense into their cousin. As drunk as he was, there was no way to know if Charles would even remember the conversation.

Renee considered Penelope, one hand resting at her waist, the other holding a cigarette between bright red nails. A diamond bracelet flashed as she flicked her cigarette ash. A fortune nestled serenely around her neck. Penelope was glad James had dragged Charles away. It had saved her the control required to keep from slapping him. What Renee wore in diamonds was worth more than what the Jade Tiger made in gambling receipts for a month. Not to mention the way her dress clung to every curve.

Renee smiled as Penelope looked her over. "See anything you like?"

"Not especially."

Renee looked around, meeting the eye of anyone who still had the nerve to stare. After a moment, the chatter of the crowd resumed as more guests pressed into the room. Renee's slow appraisal of partygoers stopped, and she stiffened. Penelope turned to look and found Lund staring back at Renee, his expression hard as he came through the crowd with two glasses of champagne.

He was a handsome man. How had she forgotten? Because she had made herself forget. Because she wasn't his and couldn't ever be. The answer was quick and stung. Lund held out a coupe. Penelope took it politely and hoped he did not notice the flush of warmth at her ears and neck.

He took up a comfortable position next to her. Penelope imagined she could feel his heat on her bare skin. He looked down at her, amused. "Miss Harris."

He couldn't know what his smile did to her, could he? "Mr. Lund."

The crowd pressed around them, people moving closer and closer together as more guests entered the parlor. Renee stepped closer to Lund until she was near enough for the fabric of her dress to touch his sleeve. "Officer." There was a lurid suggestion in the flat delivery that set Penelope's teeth on edge. Renee's necklace seemed to glow against the black velvet.

Lund shifted with an almost imperceptible question. "Mrs. Strong."

"Soon to be Mrs. Staughton. Didn't Penelope tell you we're going to be cousins?" Renee smiled with her teeth, a languid glance from Lund to Penelope and back, connecting the three of them. "I've just about made it to the altar."

"But not quite." Penelope glanced over her shoulder. She could just see James's back and a ruddy pink profile belonging to Charles.

"That's right." Renee raised a carefully drawn eyebrow as her head moved. "Not quite."

A flash of blue-green near the door caught Penelope's eye. Mary's dress flitted between the guests as she made her way through to them, struggling through the crowd as they watched.

Renee's eyes focused with the bored concentration of a well-fed falcon. "Oh dear." She exhaled smoke. "Something has gotten up your dear cousin's nose. Again."

"You!" Mary stopped at their group, every inch of her sparking with indignant outrage.

"There's a bit of a crowd on your doorstep, my dear." Renee gestured with her cigarette at the crowd. "Are you sure you have enough of your lovely champagne?"

"Gate-crashers!" Mary fumed. "Chorus girls, gangsters, bootleggers—God knows who! They're your friends, Renee! I know they are! You must ask them to leave." The crowd around the radio turned their heads to watch. A few laughed. The music surged, and a couple began to dance.

"Why don't you ask Charles? They are his friends too." Renee gestured vaguely toward the balcony.

"I'm sorry, Penelope. I need your gentleman friend." Mary fumed as she turned her back on Renee. "Mr. Lund, I realize we just met, but I have lost track of my brother and I need a set of strong shoulders. Could you please join me in the foyer?"

"Is there trouble?" The word had the air of the familiar when Lund said it.

"Only what you'd expect with gate-crashers!" Mary's hands clenched at her sides. "Parker found a couple upstairs making intimate use of my bedroom. A complete stranger just put one of Grandmother's silver spoons in her garter. And someone calling himself the Amazing Gilberto is in the music room abusing the piano like a camel in a bathhouse." Her voice rose steadily as she spoke, her cheeks shining bright pink in the dim light. "I don't know any of them, and even more are at the door." She huffed as she spun on Renee, forcing her to take a step back. "They *all* have invitations, and they *all* seem to know you!"

"Charles suggested I send a few of my own. I thought, why not?" Renee pivoted to look around at the crowd. The swing of her hips made every move seem inevitable. "Your friends were invited."

"Our friends? These aren't Charles's friends." Mary took a sharp step forward, the hem of her dress swirling around her feet. Renee turned her head, looking across the room, away from her. "Charles may be many things, but remember this: if you take me for a fool, it will be the last mistake you make!" There was a lull in the music, and Mary's sharp words filled the pause. Heads turned. Mary put her nose in the air. "Mr. Lund, if you would be so kind." Someone near the radio laughed, and a few people in the room joined in. Mary led Lund toward the door. In a moment the music returned. The crowd of dancers swallowed them both.

"I haven't seen Lund in a tuxedo before." Renee was thoughtful. "Gives a girl ideas."

Penelope had not expected to feel so calm. "You sought Charles out deliberately, seduced him, just to strike out at me." Every word was steady, without a shadow of alarm or anger. "Since you can't squeeze me, your plan is to marry him and use him for everything you can get before you agree to a divorce."

"Is that what you think?"

"Does it matter?" Penelope placed her empty glass on the tray of a passing waiter and picked up a fresh one. She took a sip, watching the people around them over the rim of the glass. It was a rowdy crowd, gassed up with booze and God knew what else. There was a shimmer of hazard along the outline of the shadows. The room crackled with jazz. If they had been at the Jade Tiger, Penelope would have turned up all the lights and packed up the band to take the edge off the crowd. Gambling be damned. "I wouldn't think Charles was your type at all. Too decent, too dull."

Renee's expression froze. Something in it, a hardness that hadn't been there before, drew Penelope's attention. "You never did think much of me." Renee's words were brittle. She lowered her head, the blunt cut of her bobbed black hair brushing Penelope's cheek as she leaned close, her voice low and dangerous. "Now that I've got your attention, I want you to know. I'm going to have it all. Everything I would have had if Kinkaid had lived."

"You'll get nothing, then." Penelope's fragile temper snapped in two—she didn't care what anyone thought of her or what the papers printed. It would be a relief, she told herself. And if it weren't? Well, it was worth the satisfaction to show Renee there was a reality in which the money would never come, revenge wasn't so easy, and Kinkaid would still be dead. "He had already spent it all. He died broke, flat broke. Nothing is what Kinkaid would have given you, and nothing is what you will get."

"Are you so sure the Staughtons feel the same?" Renee looked around the room. "Just a few gate-crashers and your cousin thinks the sky is falling. When I'm done with them, you are going to wish you died in that alley instead of Kinkaid." Renee leaned closer, the smoke from her cigarette curling up between them. Her eyes slid toward the foyer, where Lund had disappeared with Mary. "Imagine Officer Lund showing up almost a year after Kinkaid died. Is it a coincidence you end up in the same city? What are the odds?"

Penelope thanked her lucky stars for the steely discipline her mother had drummed in about control on the stage. It took all her skill to keep her voice light and her hands steady. "I have two thousand in this purse. It's yours if you leave here tonight. Right now."

Renee considered her for a moment that stretched out between them. Penelope waited her out, the account balancing between revenge and greed. Renee's smile returned, her teeth bright against the red lip. Her words brightened, even if her eyes remained as hard as rocks. "Two thousand? Better make it ten, or I spill the works and take Charlie along for the ride of his life."

"Ladies!" A man emerged from the tangle of dancers with his hands outstretched to include them both. "Seeing you both there like that takes me back to Shanghai, yes indeed. Straight back to the Tiger, in all her glory!"

7

HIS WHITE HAIR AND MUSTACHE stood out in the dim light, the rest of his features receding behind them. Small black eyes appraised them both with a leer. Alfred Gott, failed stockbroker and by all accounts the black sheep of the extended Staughton family, reveled in Penelope's attention, his grin pressing the white mustache up into his cheeks. If she closed her eyes, Penelope could still see him strolling across the casino floor of the Jade Tiger with a pocketful of chips from her husband. With any other gambler it might have been a losing proposition, but Gott never won unless he was playing with his own dice. He would play until his pockets ran empty, then turn his attention to the girls in the chorus with varying degrees of success. He had his own money but never gambled with it. As far as Penelope could tell, it was the only glimmer of intelligence in the man.

Gott put a hand on her bare shoulder, his fingers squeezing lightly. "Don't you look lovely, my dear. No one would know you were flat on your back in a hospital just a year ago. Everyone thought you would die, but not me. Look at you now." His finger touched her neck. She flinched away from him.

"What nerve you have!" Penelope turned on Renee. Gott was an irrepressible lecher known throughout Shanghai as the scourge of the chorus. It had taken effort to convince Kinkaid Gott hadn't been a mark worth sweetening. "How could you invite him?"

"Don't look at me!" Renee complained.

Gott took Renee's elbow as she turned to leave, pulling

her close. "What's the hurry? I've been seeing people from China all over the room. A ship captain over here, an investor over there. Has the air of a reunion, doesn't it?" Renee started like a cat, then hid it so quickly Penelope couldn't be sure of what she had seen.

"What now, who's this?" James appeared beside Penelope, peering at Gott through his glasses. "What the devil are you doing here, Alfred? Has Mother seen you?" James looked around himself with alarm. "You'd better leave before Uncle Harry catches wind you're here."

"Just so happens he gave me the invite himself." Gott put one hand into his pocket. The other held fast to Renee's elbow. He considered the two women before him. "Light and dark, that's how I remember you. As different as night and day." He leaned forward into the light of a nearby lamp. "Did you ladies know there is a piano? Perhaps we could settle the rivalry once and for all?"

A brunette leaned over the back of the couch and called out, "What's this? A rivalry? Do tell, Freddy. Don't keep me guessing." Her navy dress cascaded in folds to the floor as she stood. Sharp interest made the woman's face bright. "Helen Mayfield, from the *Sentinel*," she added.

"Damn and blast, Penelope—she's the press," James whispered. "What's Freddy up to?"

Gott stroked his mustache. "What do you say, ladies? Shall I tell her?"

"No," Penelope answered firmly. As much as she would have liked to see Renee squirm, reliving those last months in Shanghai was much worse. "Shall we dance, James?" She took her brother by the arm.

Gott casually stepped in front of them, pulling Renee closer. He called over to Helen, who was now walking around the couch and coming toward them, "I knew both of these young women in China. Shanghai, to be precise." He pointed a finger at Penelope. "This one owned a casino with her husband, and this one," he looked at Renee, "was her headliner." He smiled, and his mustache crawled up his face like a caterpillar. "The Jade Tiger. Never was there such a casino before or since. Simply put, it was the ripest, drunkest, most illicit gaming house south of the Yangtze."

Helen focused. "Sounds promising. Do tell, Freddy."

Gott made a production of looking from Penelope to Renee. "I can't tell you from firsthand experience, because I wasn't there that night, but I heard these two had something of a falling out when Mrs. Ambrose took the stage to serenade her husband on his birthday."

Penelope concentrated on Gott. One wrong word and the world would know Shanghai had been ripe with rumors about Kinkaid and Renee. Their affair was so brazen and shocking that the magistrate himself had made it his business to bring it to Penelope's attention.

"I say, old man, keep it clean," James warned, the edge in his words as tight as a drum.

"Nothing wrong with singing to your husband," Helen commented coolly. "It's a well-known fact Penelope Harris has an excellent singing voice." She nodded at Penelope briefly and . . . was that a wink? It happened so quickly Penelope could hardly tell.

"That's true enough," Gott agreed. "What I'm talking about came from the other side of things. The audience began

requesting performances, calling out for her in the middle of
Renee's set. It would have been all right with another singer.
Not this one." He pulled Renee close and laughed.

Renee made no effort to smile. Putting either hand on
Gott's lapels, she pushed him away, disgust marring her beautiful red lips. "Do shut up, Freddy."

"I heard you at the Rutherford party week before last."
Helen cocked her head to one side and considered Renee.
"You sang 'Let's Misbehave' from the staircase. You were
good."

"I brought the house down at that party," Renee snapped,
"and you know it!"

Helen shrugged. "If you say so." She withstood Renee's
glare calmly. "I thought it came across a bit flat myself."

Penelope warmed to the woman. Sparring with Renee
was like hand-feeding a hyena—not many women had the
nerve for it.

"You can see how it started, can't you?" Gott chuckled.
"One would take the stage, and the other would wait behind
the curtain. By the end of August, the whole city was waiting
to see what would happen next."

August, the same month Kinkaid died. She didn't know
what Gott's game was, but knowing him like she did, it
couldn't be pleasant. Even Renee raised an eyebrow, and no
wonder. If Gott spilled all the juicy details to the press, there
would be little left to use as blackmail. Renee wouldn't come
out smelling like a rose either. The gutter press lived for sordid details like those of her affair with Kinkaid. Once he got
started on the story, Gott would go on until it was done. Hel-
en Mayfield would have every detail, right down to the damp,

stinking alley where Penelope almost died and Kinkaid was murdered.

"You should sing." Helen looked from one woman to the other. "Let your guests decide. You should sing!" She called over her shoulder to the crowd at the couch. "See who's best! Don't you think so? Sing!"

A drunk called out "Sing!" from a nearby couch. Then another, until a chorus of voices shouted out without the faintest comprehension of why they were doing it. Someone turned down the radio. The dancers stopped, searching out the cause of the interruption.

"Being a professional, I'm always at the ready." Renee put her nose in the air. "I understand if you aren't up for it. There's a difference between performing in a nightclub you own, where everyone can live in hope of a round on the house, and a party full of people who hardly know who you are."

Renee's insufferable arrogance did the trick. The audience in the Jade Tiger had been anything but easy. A pack of degenerate gamblers ready to behave badly where news wouldn't reach the long ears at home, attention-starved debutants, expats, cynics, newspapermen, good-time girls, and sailors. Not to mention the criminal element that followed Kinkaid wherever he went. Penelope had earned their applause.

"Is the piano in tune?" she asked with an innocent air.

"Don't try me, bug." Renee hissed. Shaking herself free of Freddy, she stared down Penelope with her hands on her hips. "I'm not afraid to show you up here or anywhere else."

"Cut the baloney, Renee. Are you going to sing or not?" Helen crossed her arms. "I'm beginning to think you might be yellow!"

"Yellow?" Renee's slouch disappeared, her height raising as she straightened. "Yellow?" Dropping her cigarette in
Penelope's glass, she exclaimed, "I'll show you yellow!" and
started toward the east parlor, the crowd parting ahead of her.
Helen Mayfield and an amused Alfred Gott followed in her
wake.

James pushed his glasses up to the bridge of his nose and
offered Penelope his arm. "This wasn't in the plan. Did she
take the money?"

Penelope looked at the clutch in her hand, the cash inside
bulky beneath her fingers.

"I see." James led her forward. "Poor Charles."

8

RENEE STOOD WITH A MAN by the piano, the picture of style
and sophistication. Penelope was sure that under it all, Renee
was seething, but she would never let on. It took someone who
knew her to recognize all the little signs that she was in a fury:
the handkerchief she gripped tightly in her hand, the fashion-
able slouch exchanged for a spine held as straight as a ruler.

Penelope felt a warmth near her back. She did not need to
look to know it was Lund.

"Will you sing?" he murmured, looking past her to scan
the gathering crowd. The sleeve of his jacket brushed against
the bare skin of her arm, raising goosebumps.

"If I don't sing, she can crow about it all over New York. And if I do—" She broke off and looked away.

"What becomes of Charles?" he finished for her. She glanced up at him. "James told me," he admitted with a faint smile.

Of course he had, the little squint!

"He wanted to know what the police might say. And of course, he was worried about you."

She crossed her arms, then uncrossed them, trying to contain her temper.

"You shouldn't pay her. A blackmailer will take everything you have." Lund's smile disappeared. "And of course, you remember what a dab hand Renee was at it."

"Are you telling me as a policeman? Or as a friend?" she fired back.

"I'm not a policeman anymore." He shifted his weight closer to her. They were almost touching. "I remember the first time I heard you sing. The whole casino came to a stop, even the roulette table." He grinned. "God help us if you had sung every night. The city would have worshipped at your feet. Kinkaid would have had to put the gambling tables away. When I heard you had come to New York, I was certain you would sing." When she did not reply, he focused on her. "I should have told James I wouldn't come. But you see, I had to see you. Just once more. It felt," he searched for the word, "harmless. Do you mind very much?"

"No, I don't mind." Penelope meant it. She could have told him she had missed him and meant that too, but she wasn't sure he would believe her. She had been the one to leave, after all. There had been plans, promises. She had left them all behind the night Kinkaid died. Kinkaid always knew how to ruin a good thing. He was still at it from beyond the grave.

"Why don't you?" Lund leaned a hand on the mantel behind her. The faint scent of sandalwood radiated from his skin.

"Why don't I what?" Penelope asked, watching Renee lean across the piano to speak to the man at the keys. Every time Renee opened her mouth, the rogue launched into a fanfare. Her face was turning pink with frustration.

"Why don't you find a shifty speakeasy and sing. You'd make a killing."

His words came all at once, too fast to choose just a few. The truth was it would be easier to find work singing at a club. Colleagues from Shanghai had reached out as she passed through Paris and London. She had been tempted but, in the end, turned them all down. The thought of her disapproving mother in the audience turned every daydream into a nightmare.

"I'm sorry. I didn't mean to offend. It's none of my business."

"I'm not offended." Words rose to the surface, words she was sure only Lund would understand. "The truth is I need work. I may end up in a nightclub somewhere, but I'd rather do that because I want to, not because I need to. And right now I'd rather do something else. Too many ghosts." She watched Renee preen at the piano. "Too many men like Kinkaid."

"Kinkaid is dead. His body's in a grave seven thousand miles away."

"Look around yourself. Kinkaid is right here in this room.

I'll never be free of him unless I make something different out of myself. I promised myself I would leave it all behind."

"All of it?"

Penelope looked up at him. Lund met her eye easily.

Across the room, the pianist played a jaunty fanfare.

Helen joined them, handing each a coupe of champagne. "Well, I can't guarantee he's sober, but the Amazing Gilberto can play."

Penelope sighed with relief, grateful for the change of subject. "The Amazing Gilberto?" The name conjured memories of magicians and the traveling circus. Penelope couldn't imagine either of those producing the quality of the music she heard. "I don't believe I have heard of him."

"Not sure why you would." Helen laughed. "Gil is always producing titles for parties like this one, thinks one will stick if he tries hard enough. But he can play, trust me on that." She put out her hand to Penelope. "Call me Helen."

Penelope took her hand with some caution. "Helen is a newspaperwoman, Thom."

"Say, no need to rub it in," Helen protested. "Sorry if I got you into the soup, sister." She gave a cheerful shrug. "If it's any consolation, I won't be writing about any of this in tomorrow's paper. This is one hundred percent for my pleasure. Since you know Renee, I'm sure you know what she can do to a man." She met Penelope's eyes. "Let's just say I've seen it and I don't like it. Will you sing?"

"No." As she said it, Penelope made up her mind. All it would do is further cement any rumors Renee had already started. Penelope put her chin out. "No, I will not."

"Up to you." Helen returned her attention to the piano.

"I knew I could get her to sing. Renee's been inflicting her vocals on every party between here and Fifth Avenue. Gott made it easy. Sorry you got roped in."

Penelope recognized the animosity only Renee could leave in her wake. The hard set of Helen's jaw told the story. Any number of women in Shanghai had seen their marriages ruined by the chanteuse. A few had even appeared at the casino, resolved to win their husbands back. They had all had the look of a boxer ready to go down swinging, the same look Helen had now.

The Amazing Gilberto bent over the piano keys with an exaggerated slump, his nose almost touching his fingers. A sauntering melody began to tumble from his fingers, rolling up the audience into a rapt silence. As he captured the listeners, the melody formed the swinging gait of a loping introduction, the notes coming together like a comedian gearing up for a punch line. Then, with a sudden swing of attention, the Amazing Gilberto drove the piano into submission with the total commitment of a swashbuckler at an afternoon matinee. His eyes rolled and his face screwed up like a comic book character as the fanfare came to a bursting end.

Penelope's jaw dropped. "Wait a moment. Is that Gilberto Ricci, the vaudeville star?"

"Now you know my secret." Helen winked. "He's a doll, Gil is. Not to mention he's sweet on me. Renee doesn't know what she's in for. Go ahead and tell her if you want. She won't believe you." Penelope was beginning to get the measure of Helen's plan. She almost felt sorry for Renee. Almost, but not quite.

Gil lifted his hands from the piano and shouted at Renee,

"Come on now, girl. Get to singing! We don't have all night!" There was a ruffle of restless laughter across the crowd. With the full attention of the room, Gil began the proper melody for Renee's selection. Next to the roaring introduction, the notes were empty, vapid. Gil played them that way, an air of tedious tolerance oozing from his every expressive grimace.

Renee turned her back to him and leaned against the piano, the white handkerchief clutched in one hand. Distantly, Penelope thought it was a nice touch, then began to wonder if she had seen it somewhere before. Renee began the song, a recent hit whose name Penelope couldn't remember. Renee's phrasing was slow and sweet.

Penelope's professional assessment found Renee sadly lacking. Her strength in Shanghai was her daring, which had as much, or more, to do with her popularity. Not one to blend in with the band, Renee smoked, swore, danced (sometimes on the bandstand, sometimes on top of the tables) while she belted out songs about sex, liquor, broken hearts, and booze. She was a force of nature that commanded attention. This version of Renee was too dignified to even be a relative of the wild woman who had stalked the stage at the Jade Tiger. This woman lacked guts. Penelope considered the white handkerchief and decided Renee was a hack.

At the bench, Gilberto rolled his eyes, mugging for the audience until they laughed. He then shut his eyes in a painful grimace as Renee plodded through the song, hitting every sentimental note with the precision of a watchmaker's hammer. He sped up the notes, then slowed them down. Turning her back to the Amazing Gilberto, Renee found Charles in the crowd and walked to his side, focusing all her attention on him.

"Indecent, isn't it?" Helen leaned over to Penelope. "Freddy told me they got married on the sly a few days ago. Is it true?"

It took effort not to show her dismay. Renee had already swung her final blow; they were married. Penelope stared straight ahead as Charles bent over Renee's hand to kiss it and generally made himself look like a staggering fool in love. "I wouldn't know." At least it was the truth. Penelope's temper rose, a head full of champagne fueling her rage. They were already married. If Helen had not forced the bet, Renee would already have the two thousand.

A hand reached over to take her empty glass. Lund whispered in her ear, "Are you all right?"

Penelope spoke through gritted teeth. "I could kill her. Does it show?"

"Get in line, sister dear." From the other side of Lund, James put a hand in his pant pocket and leaned an elbow on a chair back. "Get in line."

Renee struck the last note, and the Amazing Gilberto folded at the piano with dramatic relief. All eyes were on Charles, who turned to the room and announced, "My wife, fellas! That's my wife!"

"Not so fast, Charlie." Renee pushed him off and walked across the room to where Penelope stood. "Well, you can't do any better than that, and you know it. Might as well concede before you embarrass yourself."

Where no one could see, Lund's fingers found hers. "Go ahead." He whispered. "Show them."

Renee wanted her to sing? She'd give the woman what she wanted. "Hold this for me, would you?" Penelope handed her purse to Helen and set her temper free.

9

"*QUAND JE VOUS AIMERAI?*" Powerful enough to reach through the large crowd to the foyer, the voice struck all but a few in the crowd mute. She needed no announcement of quiet, no clap to silence the conversation. As Penelope cast her gaze across the crowded room, she captured their attention with a raw display of stage presence. Before their eyes, she transformed from a faceless member of New York society to a dangerous French street apache, from Penelope to Carmen. She stood with her hands loose, head bent low, eyes hidden by the shadow of her wild white-blonde hair. Her stance squared off with the crowd, facing them off as if in a knife fight. Though she sang in French, Lund heard only the English translation, as he did whenever he heard her sing *Carmen. When will I love you?*

"Dammit, she could have given me some warning!" James exclaimed. Hastily depositing his empty coupe on the mantel, he crossed the room in three quick strides, took the Amazing Gilberto by the collar, and roughly deposited him on the Axminster. Gilberto rolled over backward and sat up to stare at the wild thing at Lund's side. Penelope looked at him once and dismissed him entirely. Returning her attention to the crowd, she took them in as James's fingers found the right keys. The room was so quiet Lund could hear her footsteps on the carpet.

With imperious carriage of careening charisma, Penelope stepped forward, walking Renee backward across the floor until she was forced to move out of the way, almost tripping on the train of her dress. Charles caught Renee before she fell, never taking his eyes from Penelope. Renee's eyes followed Penelope with a dark hatred. And fear, Lund thought. Yes, that too.

Penelope reached the piano. *When will I love you? My word, I don't know.* Her eyes passed over the crowd, falling here and there with deliberate review. Penelope swayed, then laughed. *Perhaps never? Perhaps tomorrow?* She lifted her hands to the rapt audience as if to ask, then let them fall, disappointed. She stood back, her body relaxed, and her face appeared intent as she spoke the last line. It had the finality of a death sentence. *But not today, that's for certain.*

James picked out notes on the piano one at a time. Most singers rushed into the Habanera like mad dancers pounding their heels into the ground with the *click, click, click* of a rising tempest. Always there were drums and trumpets and loud clashes of cymbals. The beat of Penelope's Habanera was slow. She put one hand on the piano and began again to sing. The words came out like a jeering child at first, then dangerous, cooing, then seductive. She stared at Renee and smiled wide, her teeth white against her lips. Releasing Renee from her gaze, she found Lund.

Lund stared back. He forgot to blink.

She walked toward him as she sang. Her leisurely melody

was closer to the slow jazz of Paris than the discipline of the opera. Each note slipped together with the next. It made Lund blush with its lazy indiscretion. Soft with darkness that held the notes true, her voice hypnotized the crowd. The melody driving its purpose home like a stiletto finds its target in the dark.

Her voice stronger, she allowed the notes to rise into the disciplined vocal registers, more operatic in their fullness. The next moment, she dropped back into a breathy expression that was openly suggestive. She was before him now.

He offered her his hand, knowing full well what a fool he was to do it. But he couldn't seem to help himself, not with her.

Taking hold of his hand, Penelope stepped up onto the nearest armchair, its occupant amused by the sudden attention. She stood on the arm, Lund's hand in her own to keep balance, and gave a lesson in bringing the house down. Taunting, reveling in the attention, pulling back out of reach when her interest shifted, she drew out the last note with her head back and her back straight, her eyes fluttering shut as she held the final note against the long slow beat of the song with every sign of indecent ecstasy. Every head turned to watch, their attention rapt and breathless. She released Lund's hand, did a slow pirouette, and fell back without a glance, Lund catching her in a billow of flowing persimmon silk.

Penelope opened her eyes, found Lund's, and smiled. It took everything he had to place her down on her feet, his natural inclination to hold her tight and kiss her passionately. Something in the way she looked at him told him she wouldn't have minded. Enthusiastic applause washed over the room as

Penelope stood in the center and took a modest bow. The Amazing Gilberto crawled across the floor to kiss her foot.

"Well, that's torn it," Helen said somewhere near Lund's elbow. "Looks like I'll be writing something about this party after all."

"All of you, listen!" A man shouted over the applause, his words slurred. "I have an announcement to make!"

10

"GOOD LORD, JUST LOOK AT HIM!" Helen said with a degree of shock Lund thought unusual in a member of the press. "The man is smackered!"

Across the room, Charles wobbled unsteadily as he balanced on a Chippendale chair. "Everyone, everyone—" He tripped from the chair, falling to the floor with a loud thump. For the most part, the crowd ignored him, instead surrounding Penelope.

Lund was jolted from the scene by furious swearing at his elbow.

"Oh no, not again! I fired her last week!" Helen went stiff.

Following her gaze to the parlor door, Lund suppressed an irritated sigh. Mrs. Anthony Stone, gossip columnist extraordinaire, sailed into the room, resplendent in her furs and heavy rings. The hue of her cheeks and nose were a dead giveaway that the previous hours had been spent in deep contemplation of local hooch. It had been his ignominious pleasure to escort Mrs. Stone from the premises of the bank after she overdrew her account to the tune of three hundred dollars. He received several painful bruises on his shins to remember the woman by.

James put his arm around Penelope and kissed her on top of her head. "She's the social columnist for the *Sentinel*, my dear gypsy." He began to steer her away from the crowd, heading toward the doorway. "She's a menace!"

There were more people in the room than Penelope thought was possible. Every square foot seemed to be occupied by guests, all pushing past each other to get a better look at Penelope, pushing the dozen or so who continued to swarm around her as James led her along, pushing in closer until she could hardly move. A cacophony of voices rose louder and louder as everyone tried to talk over one another. Lund put himself between her and a man reaching to kiss her hand, and almost tripped over Gilberto, who remained on the floor at Penelope's feet, kissing the hem of her dress. "This is ludicrous!" Lund called over to James. "We must get her out of here."

"Friends!" Charles had returned to his position on the chair. Renee stood nearby, smiling like the cat that ate the canary. As the crowd jostled and laughed, Mrs. Stone began pushing through the revelers, bearing down on Charles and Renee like the flagship of the White Star Line. "Friends, I have an announcement to make." Charles could barely make his voice heard above the din.

"Renee Strong!" Mrs. Anthony Stone called out with command that only comes to a few. Nearly everyone in the room angled their heads for a better look at the grande dame of high society tittle-tattle.

Renee wore the vacant stare of someone trying to place the other person.

"My dear," Mrs. Stone began again as every ear braced for live theater, "I had no idea you were in New York! Why didn't you come and find me, your old friend Francine?"

"Hello there!" Charles put his hand forward to grip Mrs. Stone's flabby arm. "You know my wife?"

Mrs. Stone was only momentarily disoriented. "Which one is your wife?" She considered the crowd, studying their faces with the air of a connoisseur. Renee seized the moment to turn away from Mrs. Stone and begin to make her way to the door before Charles quickly caught her by the arm.

"This one, this one you pointed to." Charles turned her around and back into Mrs. Stone's line of sight. "This is Mrs. Charles Staughton!"

James hooked a foot on the banister and pulled himself up for a better view.

"No she's not," Mrs. Stone boomed. "That's Mrs. Roland Strong. She's married to one of the great Parisians, an artist named," she paused, "well, Roland Strong."

"I am afraid you are mistaken, madam." Charles's face grew red. "Roland Strong has been dead for some time."

Lund watched as Mrs. Stone clearly became more aware of the people listening as the audience's silence grew. She looked around the room, taking careful measure. Once certain that the throng would find the right side in an argument, she addressed her attention to Renee and Charles, giving them the famous eye.

Mrs. Anthony Stone had made much of her ability to suss out the truth with a good long look. She wrote about it often, and the partygoers delighted in seeing the woman's jaw set and eyes narrow at the couple.

"Well?" Charles asked, the drunken slur of his speech undermining his intended air of contempt.

"No," Mrs. Stone said, standing up a little straighter. Her voice rang out across the room. "That's Mrs. Strong, all right. A very married woman—to someone other than you!"

A sudden dissonance broke out in the room. Charles began shouting, with his mouth as wide as it could be, his face red, and spit flying in ungentlemanly arcs across the crowd. Renee relaxed as she watched them both, her mouth a bright slash of red. Charles leapt off the chair, only to land on a professional boxer protecting the rumrunner sitting behind him. The boxer's impact on the crowd as he fell backward caused a chain reaction of tumbling guests and spilled drinks that reached all the way to the piano. Gilberto, never one to miss an opportunity, returned to the piano and began an Irish jig. The guests surged together in an urgent rush for the door despite their insatiable desire to see what happened next. A small hesitation at the door caused another series of events that resulted in a glass of champagne spilling down the front of the rumrunner's best girl's lap.

"Oh, Jimmy," the girl squealed. "My favorite dress!"

Lund was hypnotized as he watched the rumrunner stand up, carefully take off his hat, place it on the piano, spit on both hands, and line up the perpetrator with a haymaker that would have rocked Hercules.

It was mayhem. Three or more fights broke out around

Lund and the Harrises, the closest averted when Lund reached out to pluck a partly empty champagne bottle swung like a bludgeon from the hands of a debutant in a ruined pink dress. Bottles were brandished, then smashed as reputations were forgotten and slights remembered. Pressing together, the rest of the crowd swayed back and forth as if it could not decide whether to separate the brawlers, join them, or watch them fight. Mrs. Stone, who had lost her wig to Charles's hand, yowled with the fury of an alley cat and prepared a mean right hook. Without her wig, the soon-to-be-retired gossip columnist reminded Lund of the cook from his boardinghouse. He warmed to her, the bruises forgotten.

The tremor of violence shook the room, a cacophony of noise and movement overwhelming his attention as he stooped down to stop two wrestling men from knocking Penelope over. When he stood, he saw Renee and Penelope standing toe-to-toe, each with a hand on Penelope's black clutch. He couldn't hear what they said over the sounds of the fighting, but their faces were bright with anger. Lund had never seen two women who loathed each other more. Then Penelope let go of the clutch, freeing her right hand, and gave Renee a sock on the jaw that knocked the other woman over.

"What's *this*?" Penelope's uncle Harry appeared in the doorway in full fury. "In *my* house?" He took a swing at the nearest combatant, his size and hammer-shaped hands making the work go quickly as he neatly dispatched brawlers to the nearby butler and footman. Behind them, the door to the street opened wide as the rioters were sent down the steps. Feetfirst or headfirst—it didn't matter.

Across the room, the rumrunner saw the wind shift.

Picking up his hat with one hand, he took his best girl's hand in the other and led her from the room without a word. He nodded once to Harry Staughton as he exited. "Nice party."

Lund shook himself free of the hypnotic free-for-all, reached down, and swept Penelope from her feet, carrying her from the room.

11

"CAN'T SAY I BLAME YOU," James said to Penelope with a languid smile. He and Lund had split up to look for Eleanor. After giving up the search, he found Penelope alone in the large coat closet, searching for her fur. "The party needed a little pep. But *Carmen*? Why? You should have known it would start a riot!"

She stamped her foot. "I was angry, dammit! I was angry! All I could think was, I'll show her! I'll sing!"

"Well, I don't know what Mother will say. You know it's the opera she likes least. I suppose I shouldn't ask if Renee took the money." He balanced on a stool between four racks of coats.

Penelope covered her face with her hands and groaned.

"I must say, there are more peaceful ways to deal with a dirty blackmailer."

Penelope straightened. "We must think of Charles. James, what should we do?"

James sighed and pushed his glasses up his nose. "Well,

my dear, he took that out of our hands, didn't he? He married the woman. The only remedy to marriage is death or divorce." He looked her up and down. "Where *is* your clutch?"

"She took it." She glanced at James and could tell he had seen her strike Renee. "She had it coming," she said quietly, and was only a little ashamed of herself.

James smiled. "I see. I've had a chat with Mary. She says that the footmen have things under control.

The tinkling of shattering glass from something a good deal larger than a champagne flute sounded over the rumbling of a discontented crowd. James opened the closet door to look outside and came nose-to-nose with an ample dowager trying the doorknob. "Cheerio. Done in a tic," he said brightly, and promptly shut the door in her face. He sighed. "All right then, what color is it?"

"Brown." Penelope put her hands on her hips and looked around herself.

"But, darling, they are all brown!"

They froze as the door opened, then relaxed again as Lund came through. "I can't find Eleanor."

"I wouldn't worry about Mother. I had a walkabout looking for her, and I'm sure she isn't here. She'll have stalked right out the front door, and no one would have stopped her. In fact," James gave Penelope a bookish glance over his glasses, "she probably left the moment you started to sing."

Lund addressed Penelope. "We need to get you out of here as soon as possible. There are photographers on the front step and a crowd. It will only get worse when the police get here."

"But my coat!" Penelope appealed to James.

The door opened again, and Mary peeked around the frame. "There you all are! Penelope, darling, you had better get a leg on. There are reporters just outside. I know how you hate them. Your only hope is to make it out the back door."

"But, Mary, your guests!" Penelope reached out, taking her cousin's hand. "I should stay and help."

Mary laughed, but there was no joy in it. "It's kind of you. But there isn't anything you can help me with—or even anything that can be done. Parker and the footmen are throwing out the gate-crashers. The rest of our guests are leaving in droves. The only ones that have remained behind are waiting for you to leave the closet so they can get their coats. Papa is having a grand time walking up and down the sidewalk roaring like a bear and making a spectacle of himself. There are only four photographers in front of the house, but there will be twenty in half an hour. You should go now."

"But I must stay." Even as she said it, Penelope felt her fear clinging to hope of a quick exit. She could imagine the pop and gasp of the camera, see the bright light just behind her eyes. "Mary, I can't just leave you here!"

"Mary's right," James added with a somber nod. "Renee is around here someplace. I can just imagine the scene if she has a chance to get at you with a photographer looking on."

Renee—Penelope had forgotten her in the mayhem. She raised her fingers to her mouth. "Oh, Mary, I am so sorry! I made a fool of myself at your party!"

"I certainly don't think that. I doubt anyone else does either." Mary was earnest. "I'd say it's Charles who deserves all the blame. He did take a swing at that columnist, after all." A furrow appeared on Mary's brow as she spoke. "Besides, there isn't much you can do to help other than keep me company. No, you should go home. Out through the back before the photographers realize they can climb the fence to the garden. Charles will turn up eventually. He's probably in the bushes being sick. And if you ask me, he deserves it!"

"I'll stay." James was firm. "Someone has to have a sober word with Charles when he reappears. Thom, could you take Penelope home for me?"

"Certainly." Lund had been so quiet she had almost forgotten he was there.

"But my coat?" Penelope gestured to the furs at their feet.

"Here, wear mine." Lund put his jacket over her shoulders and took her by the hand. Addressing Mary, he asked, "Which way is the garden?"

Mary led them through the maze of back hallways, up then down short flights of stairs, until they were in the kitchen. She stopped to speak to the cook, who was holding her apron to her mouth. Lund paused in the kitchen, turning his head as though to hear better what the cook had to say.

If there had been some new embarrassment, Penelope did not want to hear what it could be. It was already too much to know Renee had married Charles. Anything more would drive her past the point of tolerance. There wasn't another way to consider the situation—Penelope would have to pay to be free. Where on earth would she get more money? Renee had caught her in the trap, the screw slowly tightening. It was all her fault. All of it. She shuddered at the thought, turning away from the warmth of the kitchen and into the cool night air.

The small yard was exactly as Mary had described in her

letters, from the large vine terraces that covered the grey stone walls to the benches surrounding the decorative pond. A loud peal of laughter startled Penelope. On stone steps that led to the small courtyard balcony that followed alongside the west parlor, a few remaining partygoers hung over the balustrade to shout at someone in the street. Penelope turned back to the garden, shivering in the cold.

The house lights illuminated only part of the garden. She could just make out the butler standing next to a small pond, looking down at a figure on a bench. She came up alongside him and asked, "What is it, Parker? Is someone ill?"

Parker jumped when she spoke, his mouth opening soundlessly.

The woman was facing away from them on a small stone bench. Her foot rested awkwardly against the paving stones, an overturned shoe a few inches away. A fur coat swaddled the woman's dress so that all Penelope could see was the black velvet edge along the bottom. The woman's head and shoulders leaned into the wall, the coat covering her face completely.

"That's my coat!" Penelope came forward to touch the woman's arm, making quick sense of the black silk velvet and black hair she could just barely see. "Renee, you cat! You took my coat!"

As hard as Penelope tried, she couldn't make sense of the shoulders. It looked as though the woman had tried to curl into the coat, perhaps to sleep, but her shoulders appeared to be straight. Her head wasn't where it should have been. She stepped past Parker even as he reached for her arm to stop her. Penelope lifted the collar from the face and found herself looking down at the woman's neck, bent forward so far that it looked hardly human, the black hair spilling forward across the swollen face and open eyes.

The butler called out in near hysteria, "Her neck's broke!"

12

LUND CAME UP BEHIND PENELOPE, catching her just as she staggered. "Cover her face, Parker." Lund's voice was a low rasp in the darkness around the bench. Resting Penelope gently on the bench opposite the body, he knelt, holding her hands in his. "Can you manage it? Penelope?"

Penelope's hands clutched at the collar of his suit jacket, pulling it close around her with white fingers. "Thom, it's Renee."

"Penelope, I need you to walk back to the kitchen. Can you do that for me?" He shifted toward the sound of footsteps. "James!" He felt the relief acutely. "Take her into the kitchen and shut the adjoining door. We need to keep anyone from coming back here. You!" The butler flinched. "Pull yourself together, man! Stand over there and don't let anyone come back. Is there a way through the back?"

Parker nodded toward a dark corner. "There's a gate that opens to the private drive behind the carriage house. You can reach the stair from there."

"Can it be locked? Never mind that. I'll check and see."

"What—" The butler's voice failed. "What do I tell them?"

"Tell them a guest was ill." The words came quickly. "Get on with it, man!" Lund could see a few guests wandering down the stairs, looking for a back entrance they could use to avoid the photographers out front. He turned on his heel, covering the width of the yard in ten long strides. The gate swayed open with the touch of his shoe, the dark and empty drive just beyond the heavy wooden door. As it came back into the light, Lund could see the hasp hanging loose where it had been forced. He let it close gently and retraced his steps to the body.

James held the fur in one hand. The other was steady against her neck, looking for a pulse. "She's dead all right." James dropped his hand and took a longer look at Renee's face. "I can't say I expected any different. She was a nasty piece of work." He let the fur fall back over Renee's face and stood. His face was unreadable, his eyes hidden behind his glasses in the dark. "Penelope is inside. Cook is getting her some brandy."

Lund looked around the small yard. A short distance away from them he could hear Parker explaining that a car blocked the garden exit and that a guest had been ill in the garden. "James, we have to call the police."

"Already done, old boy. One of the footmen came through after you ran outside to say Uncle Harry had called the police to help see everyone off. He dashed back to the front of the house and—"

"What is all this?" Harry Staughton's voice boomed across the courtyard. James looked up to see his uncle taking the stairs down two at a time, a footman running to keep up. "Someone's sick?"

"Not exactly, Uncle. A little worse than that." James

pushed his glasses up with a light touch. "Dead, I'm afraid. Have the police come yet?"

"Dead?" Uncle Harry's face began turning red.

"Sir," Lund's words were quick and low, "if you could please lower your voice. It would be best if the other guests weren't aware until the police arrive."

"Police?" Harry compromised by lowering his voice to half its usual volume. Even with his effort, several guests turned their heads at the word while others began making their way back inside.

"Yes, the police," James said comfortably. "The lady has a broken neck. It appears to be murder, I'm afraid. They are already here, aren't they, Uncle?"

"Who is it, then," Harry stiffened, "the dead girl?"

Lund glimpsed a hint of curiosity in James's otherwise bland face. "Renee Strong." James's words had barely any expression at all.

Harry's reaction was immediate. Either hand reached out to take James by the shoulders, almost picking him up from the ground. "Are you certain? Have you checked?"

"Oh yes." James gently removed himself from his uncle's grip. "Best not to touch too much, but I did make quite sure. It is Renee. She is quite dead."

Lund had to reach out to catch Harry's arm as he staggered back. "Thank God! Thank God for that!"

"Mr. Staughton," Lund whispered, "you must go to the front of the house and wait for the police. James and I will stay here."

Harry ignored him. "You checked? You are sure? It's her? It's Renee Strong?"

"Yes, Uncle. It's just as I said."

Staughton swayed on his feet. "Come along, Parker," he said suddenly. "You can help me if you keep your head. Send the boys around with more champagne. That should keep the blighters happy for a while." Staughton looked at Lund as though seeing him for the first time. "You'll both stay, eh?"

"It's better that way, sir."

Staughton nodded once and left the way he had come, the crowd of partygoers on the balcony scattering in his wake. A few directed curious stares their way, with even more watching the fur-covered body against the far wall.

"You'll have to stay here with me, James." A grim smile spread across Lund's face.

"I think I know what you're on about." James removed his glasses, slowly cleaning the lenses as he looked from Lund to the body and back. "You don't have an alibi."

"No alibi," Lund sighed, "and one a hell of a motive."

 13

PATROLMAN McCAIN KEPT HIS HANDS in his pockets as he wandered through the party, his hat low over his closely cut white hair. He worked hard at being the type of policeman that went unnoticed, his uniform blending into the background like a fog. He was already halfway across the courtyard when the Danish bank detective noticed him. Lund stiffened when he saw the uniform, then relaxed noticeably when he saw McCain's face under the cap's brim. "Evening, Thom." Looking back over his shoulder to the house, Mc-Cain said, "There's a lot of illegal hooch in there. Either of you know about that?"

"It's all legal, Jasper. They bought it before Volstead." Lund's deep voice sounded rough in the dark. "Can't arrest them for planning ahead."

"Did Uncle Harry send you back?"

The young man had a familiar look about him, but Mc-Cain couldn't place it. Just in case, he gave the kid a smile. "The man with the beard? No, son, he was having a chat with a city councilman who was trying to leave with a silver candlestick under his vest. I showed myself around." McCain was just even with them now. His eye wandered across the courtyard, taking in the garden door with the broken latch, the pond, and the dead woman in the fur coat. "Something happen I should know about?"

"We found her about fifteen minutes ago. You didn't come from the precinct." Anyone just meeting the Dane might think he was calm because of his stillness, but McCain could read the nervous energy coming off Lund in waves. His feet were just a little too wide apart, his body a little too stiff. The man stood in the cold in shirtsleeves rolled up over his forearms, which were crossed as he stared into McCain with green eyes that gave little away. McCain had to wonder what had made the man so jumpy.

"No," he said, "just walking my beat."

"James, meet a friend of mine, Sergeant Jasper McCain. Jasper, this is James Harris." Lund gestured to the tall, thinn-ish man in glasses. "James was a medic for the navy in China, and he's examined her well enough to know there wasn't anything we could do for her." James nodded briefly.

"No need to promote me, Thom." McCain chuckled. "I'm just a patrolman these days." He nodded at the young man. "Anything else I should know?"

Lund lowered his voice. "James and I had a look around the garden, but we haven't found anything."

"Huh." McCain grunted as he lowered himself down on his heels and lifted the fur coat. She was dead all right. McCain took in the marks on her neck. "Maybe robbery, maybe not. We'll have to wait and see. Thom, I think you had better go inside and call my lieutenant. His name's Blake."

LIEUTENANT NATHAN BLAKE WAS THE type of officer who made a criminal check his sins at the door, or that's how McCain saw it. He had a way about him that made you feel that every wrinkle in your suit was a clue to all your secrets. That every man jack of your darkest sins was waiting to tumble out when Blake pulled the string. Men twenty years younger couldn't keep up with him when he was on the job, and it wasn't just his physicality. Blake was a smart policeman, might even make captain one day, and he understood how McCain liked to work.

The small crowd of policemen clustered around the garden straightened when they heard Blake's loud bark from the street. A few moments later, the old man (as some of the veterans called him—it was heartily unfair since Blake was

barely forty) was pushing his way through the guests standing on the balcony watching the courtyard. From his position
leaning against the garden wall, McCain watched the beat
cops straighten their uniforms, the air suddenly absent the
usual blue language that peppered an investigation. Blake had
come to the precinct a hero. Every one of them would rather
die than let the old man down, except for McCain. McCain
and Blake went too far back for either to feel the pinch of obligation. They were friends—that was all. That was enough.

It helped that McCain genuinely liked the man. Mc-
Cain had trained Blake on the beat seventeen years before,
and they'd worked together most of the years since, Blake
charging up through the promotions as quickly as a man could
those days. McCain had just made it to detective sergeant in
a precinct downtown when he caught a dirty little murder
that ended in a knife fight behind Grand Central Casino.
The captain had warned him the young suspect was a pal
of Mayor Jimmy's, but McCain couldn't let it go. Lord help
him, he had tried to arrest the kid. When McCain brought
his collar in with a murder charge, he took him to Blake's
precinct instead of his own. The precaution had been meaningless, though. The kid didn't spend an hour behind bars.
Before noon the next day, the monogrammed bloody knife
and the shirt the kid had been wearing were both missing.
(McCain guessed they were somewhere at the bottom of the
East River.) The girl who saw the fight recanted, and five
witnesses came forward to say the kid had been playing dice
in a basement downtown. It was a hard one to live with. A
month later, they found the witness dead in a flophouse. Coroner said alcohol poisoning, but alcohol hadn't had anything

to do with it. The kid ended up with a rich relative in Boston and working for a distant cousin. God only knew what kind of trouble he was getting up to there. McCain preferred not to think about it—the kid was Boston's problem now.

The ensuing scandal had been enough to bust McCain down to patrolman and move him to Hell's Kitchen, but not enough to fire him outright. Everyone, including McCain, expected him to die on the job, trapped in one of the Kitchen's warren-like speakeasies with bolt holes filled with dangerous men, poisonous alcohol, and innocent bystanders. By the time Blake pulled him out of Hell's Kitchen, McCain knew he was counting on his luck and his wits before some tough with something to prove put a knife in his gut. He was back to walking a beat; it was all Blake could do for him. It was better than ending up dead.

"Where's the medical examiner?" Blake's baritone growl filled the courtyard, causing all conversation to stop.

"Not here yet." McCain took his hands from his pockets.

"Where is she?" Blake could have been talking about someone who was still alive there was so much life in it.

McCain led the lieutenant across the courtyard as he spoke. "Member of the household found her here. According to the butler, there were over a hundred gate-crashers in addition to their folks. About a hundred and fifty or so total, I would guess. One of our photo boys was moonlighting for a paper tonight. I brought him back here to take some snaps before the scene got too cluttered. Fingerprint should be here in an hour or so. Looks as if our man used his hands." He nodded at the body.

Blake knelt on the ground to study the face and neck. He

pushed the fur collar back to look more closely, then sat back on his knee and asked, "Was she a guest?"

"Married to the son is what I heard. Husband's name is Charles Staughton."

"Where's the M.E.'s man?"

"Not here yet, Lieutenant."

"When was the victim seen last?"

"Nine or thereabouts." McCain licked the tip of his pencil. "She was found about an hour later."

"All right." Blake took the woman's right hand and then her left. He sat back. "Who found the body?"

"My sister did, Lieutenant. Penelope Harris."

"This is James Harris." Remembering what Lund had said, McCain snapped his fingers. "He's a doctor."

Blake looked at James in the half light. "Are you now?"

"Afraid not. I left before I could graduate."

McCain had the impression that Harris was cutting off half of a longer story.

"Oh yeah?" Blake stood, took a harder look at the kid. McCain returned to his notebook and listened quietly, careful not to break the lieutenant's thinking. "Couldn't hack it?"

"My father died, sir. Took all of us a bit by surprise. I had to take care of my mother and sister. My sister was ill. I gave up my studies to bring them back to the U.S."

"Did it work?" Blake asked. McCain had to give the kid credit. The jab hit James hard enough to turn the tips of his ears red, but nothing showed in his face. "Yes" was all he said.

"A doc, huh?" Blake frowned at the body. "You comfortable giving me an idea of what happened here?"

James pushed up his glasses and nodded. "Of course."

14

"HER NECK'S BROKEN." JAMES'S HANDS encircled the corpse's neck gently without the faintest hint of distaste. "Of course, you can see that clearly from above from the angle of the neck. There are marks here and here—could be from his hands. Looks to me like he was strangling her and broke her neck. Hard to say which killed her first." He turned her head to one side. Sitting up, he asked for a flashlight, then returned to the back of the neck. "There's a mark here."

Blake knelt beside him. "Ligature?" he asked.

"Must have been her necklace. It was a bloody great big one. Pearls, I think. Must have cost Charles a fortune." James was thoughtful. "They pulled it down." He put his hand on her neck and made a strong downward motion. "It cut into the skin, but she didn't bleed. Pulled off after she was dead?" He handed the flashlight back.

"You know what you're talking about, don't you, kid?"

James looked up at McCain. "I know something about it."

Blake straightened. "Anything else?"

James turned the corpse's head again. "The earrings were ripped off. Must have been after death. There would be blood on her neck if it happened while she was alive. The ear can bleed a lot when it's cut." McCain and Blake exchanged a meaningful glance, fluent in the language of policemen. The kid was making them nervous. They hardly ever got as much out of the coroner, no matter how much they pulled.

Blake pointed to the neck. "Could he have used the necklace to choke her?"

"No marks on the front of her neck. No, he worked with his hands. I'm not a medical examiner, but I would say he grabbed her from the front like this." He held his hands out in front of him.

"He was looking at her when he killed her?" Blake asked.

"That's right," James said.

McCain began writing in his notebook as Blake asked, "How well did you know her?"

"I met her in Shanghai." There was half a breath in James's words, almost like a skip in a record. McCain paused to listen without looking up from his notebook. "I like most people, Lieutenant. I'm a live-and-let-live kind of chap. But if you ask me, it doesn't surprise me Renee Strong was murdered, only that it took as long as this for it to happen." He looked away. "I am not myself tonight. You would think I had never seen this kind of thing before."

"Have you?" Blake asked genially. "Seen this kind of thing before?"

"I was on the Yangtze patrol for two years. There was quite a bit of this kind of thing."

"How long would you say she's been dead, Mr. Harris?"

"We found her at about ten o'clock. I saw her in the parlor a little after nine, so I would say somewhere in between. The body was warm when we found her."

Blake stood up. "You said 'we.' Who was with you?"

"My sister Penelope Harris and Thom Lund. My first thought was to get my sister away from the mob of people. We were sneaking out the back, I'm sad to say. Give the photographers the runaround if we could."

"That tells me what you were doing when you found her.

So why don't you tell me where you were tonight between nine and ten?"

"There was a fracas in the east parlor, I'm afraid. My uncle needed some help at the front of the house. I was there for a bit. Then I checked on my cousin Mary and went back to find my sister. She was hiding in the coat closet while I looked for Mother."

"And that took an hour." Blake's stance widened. He took his hand out of his pocket. "What else did you do? Have any idea?"

"I talked to Penelope for a bit. She had lost her coat. We looked for it."

"Ever find it?"

"Renee is wearing it. That's it there."

"The victim?" Blake turned to look at the body. "That's your sister's coat?"

"Well, they weren't exactly friends. But I hardly think Penelope would strangle the woman with her bare hands over a coat."

"I believe I'm the one who gets to decide that." Blake bristled.

McCain talked slowly, an old habit he relied on to keep things calm. "Did your sister know the victim?"

"Penelope's husband owned a casino. Renee worked there, for a time."

"Are they both here?" Blake looked around the courtyard. "I'll talk with them next."

"Penelope is inside the house. I'm sure she'd be happy to speak with you." McCain waited the kid out, listening. "Kinkaid—that was her husband—he died a year ago." There was something McCain couldn't place. The cool customer who had handled the body with ease was suddenly uncomfortable. James Harris was looking for an exit.

"Oh, that's too bad." McCain wore his sympathy on his sleeve. "Fever took a third of our crew while we were stationed there. Was it that?"

"Kinkaid and Penelope were injured during a robbery. My brother-in-law did not survive. My sister, only just." There it was. You could almost see the kid relax after he said it.

"How does the victim figure in that? Was she around to see him killed?" Blake leaned into the question.

"I wouldn't know, Lieutenant. I was in England when Kinkaid died. My father died just after that. It is a bit of a blur." James watched Blake without a hint of affectation. McCain couldn't tell if he was lying.

"All right." Blake cleared his throat. "McCain, get on the horn and tell Division we are looking for jewelry. Mr. Harris, if you could go with McCain and give him a description we can put out, it would be helpful."

McCain started toward the house with James in step beside him. Just before they entered the kitchen, Blake called the patrolman back. "Did he say Thom Lund?" McCain nodded. "As soon as you find Lund, bring him here. I want to talk to him."

15

PENELOPE SAT ON THE LEATHER couch in her uncle's office, her legs curled beneath her. Even with Lund's arm around her, she shivered. The cold seemed to come from somewhere inside her, rattling her bones until her teeth shook. Every part of her trembled. "I don't know why I am crying. I should be happy she's dead. I should be relieved. Why am I crying?"

"Shock. Takes some people that way." Lund put a glass into her hand. "Drink this."

Penelope took a sip, the burn of the whiskey warming her. "Thom, who could have done such a thing?"

Lund shifted farther into the shadow when she looked at his face. An inadequate lamp burned dimly on her uncle's desk, the rows of books and curios darkening the walls. He spoke. "There were quite a few people, Penelope. As I am sure you would recall. When you saw her this morning, did she say anything about trouble?"

The question cut through her shock. "You saw us?"

Lund nodded. "I've been following her. The bank I work for, they have some concerns that involve Renee."

"I think I can guess. May I?" Her voice carried a flinty edge. "Your client is being blackmailed. Some youthful indiscretion or amorous moment caught on film or in a snap. Am I close?"

Lund relaxed. A spark had livened her face with the sharp intelligence he remembered. "Don't let on to my management—you'll have my job." She smiled. He couldn't concentrate when she looked at him like that. "I've been following her and saw you this morning. It's none of my business, I realize that. When I saw you get out of her car, I wondered if she might have you in her sights."

"I hate her, even now that she's dead. But I feel sorry for her too." Penelope looked at him with bleary eyes. "She made trouble everywhere she went. I wanted to be free of her, but I didn't wish her dead. Not that."

"Where is everyone?" James shut the door carefully behind him. "I can't find a soul!" He kept his voice low, his steps soft.

"What on earth do you mean?" Penelope sniffed. "There must be fifty people in the parlor giving their names to the police."

James took off his glasses and rubbed his eyes. "I meant Mother, of course. What a ghastly night! Listen, Thom. I can't find her or Charles anywhere. I'd like to talk to both of them before the police do, make sure they understand what has happened."

Penelope lifted her head, "What about Mary? James, is Mary all right?"

Lund took her by the hand. "She's in the east parlor with her guests. She told me a good hostess wouldn't leave them."

"I should help her."

"I think the police would prefer you stayed here with us." Lund spoke quietly. "They'll want to talk to you since you knew Renee—perhaps better than any of us."

"I can't tell them that . . . I can't . . ." Memories from the Jade Tiger flooded back, and she felt her first stab of fear. What could she tell the police about Renee that wouldn't make them suspicious? How would she ever be able to avoid the newspapers slowly picking away at her story until the whole truth came tumbling out? Renee's face appeared in the disjointed memory, angry and watchful. "I can't tell them any of that, Thom," she whispered. "I can't . . ." His hand tightened around hers, anchoring her to the moment. Penelope clung to his fingers, swimming her way through the memory of Renee watching as she sang the Habanera, her dark eyes filled with cold rage.

"You can't hurt anyone by telling the truth," Lund said. She could have laughed out loud at the thought. Tell a newspaperman that, she almost shot back. Tell the police that!

"Thom," James pulled up a chair and leaned toward them both, "this man who they have in charge of the investigation, his name is Blake. Do you know him?"

Lund let go of her hand and sat forward so his face was in the light. He faced James. "I might. About forty? Bald, with a mustache?"

"That's the one. Listen, we must decide what to say," James said with an earnest certainty.

"Oh, James," Penelope laughed, "all the man has to do is wire Shanghai to get the whole story! Gambling, smuggling, even your time as a medical student. What isn't there for a policeman to enjoy?"

"Now listen to me, you two, and pull yourselves together." She could see her brother was right on the edge of losing his temper. "Penelope, you and I were hiding in that bloody closet looking for your coat while Renee was in the garden getting herself killed. We have an alibi. Lund doesn't."

Penelope straightened and looked at Lund, who was staring hard at James. She tried to laugh, only half managing it. "It doesn't matter anyway. None of us did it."

"It doesn't matter to me whether we did or didn't," James said carefully. "But the fact remains we've got a swinging big hole in our movements tonight. If Renee was killed after she sang, then any one of us could have done it. We all have motive, and we all had opportunity. We were all spread out over the house, inside and out, for at least twenty minutes. All this man Blake has to do is decide which of us he likes for the murder."

A seed of doubt settled in her gut as quickly as she rushed to denial. "You and I maybe, we've got motive. But Thom doesn't. It's a ridiculous idea!"

"Doesn't he?" James turned his eyes on Lund and took him in with a steady gaze.

Lund stood up and walked to the modest bar Harry Staughton kept on a bookshelf. She watched him go. "No, he doesn't! Thom isn't one of Renee's conquests, and if he won't defend himself, I will. I never saw them together in Shanghai. And if Renee had suborned a policeman, you can be sure she would have crowed about it from the rooftops!"

James sighed. "Honestly, Penelope, you can be quite dense. It wasn't Renee who stole poor Thom's attention away from his job. Think, woman! You used to have a brain in there!"

"I didn't kill her." Lund's voice came from the darkness, the words heavy. "But I could have." He looked at the glass in his hand and drank.

"Listen to me, Thom." James stood up and went to him. "Penelope lost her coat. You and I had a jape about it, all of us standing in the closet, hot as blazes as we listened to the crowd outside break the good crystal. We couldn't find the damn thing, so we went outside, all of us together. The whole time."

"You're a good man, James. I appreciate what you are trying to do, but I happen to believe in the law." There was a strange smile on his face. For a moment Penelope wondered if the man might be drunk. "It will be worse for you if they catch us in a lie. Plenty of people saw me walk through the house looking for Eleanor. I came through the kitchen on my way to see you. The cook saw me. I asked the butler if there was a back entrance when I saw him on the balustrade. He showed me the way to the courtyard."

The horror of it came to her quickly, all at once. "Oh no!" Penelope's hand went to her mouth. "Oh no!"

"You were outside?" James asked. "In the courtyard?"

"You really don't have an alibi." Penelope couldn't keep the tremor from her words. "They'll suspect you!"

"Regardless of what James thinks," Lund replied with a hard smile, "there are a dozen men who might have had a bigger motive to kill her."

"Charles, for one," James offered sagely. "A man didn't have to be drunk to understand he was embarrassed."

"The police will want to speak to him as soon as they can," Lund rumbled. "If he's lucky, he'll have a chance to sober up before they do. A murder like this one, at a financier's house with half of New York society in attendance, will have a quick resolution. The district attorney will want the matter closed as soon as possible."

A terrible thought began to take shape. "What about Shanghai? What if they find out about Kinkaid? James is right. We must say we were all together."

"One has nothing to do with the other, Penelope. We have to believe that. It's the only way." His voice was so low she could barely hear him. "What happened in Shanghai had nothing to do with this."

"I've read about the police," she began. "They're just as corrupt as the criminals! What if they're forced to arrest Charles even if he's innocent? What if they accuse some other person? What happens then?"

"You aren't thinking clearly." James sat next to her and put his hand over hers. "Someone murdered her. They have to investigate."

"But what if they dig and dig?" Tears were running down her face freely now as fear writhed around her heart. "What if they think one of you did it? What if they arrest you? James, we have to stop them. We have to make them stop investigating! What should we do?" she implored, her fingers tightening around her brother's.

"Do you mean to say we should bribe them?" James raised an eyebrow at the suggestion.

"Penelope, think it through." Thom put his glass down and came around to where she sat. "Don't make things worse by offering a bribe to the only policeman in New York who won't take one."

"I suppose you mean Blake." James crossed his legs.

"Evening, folks." A small man in a patrolman's uniform spoke from the doorway, one hand on the knob, the other in his pants pocket. "Now then, Thom," he swung his head toward the door, "the lieutenant would like a word."

"Wait a moment!" Penelope reached up and caught Lund's hand. "May I have a moment, please?" McCain nodded once.

She pulled on Lund's hand until he was close. "What if James is right? What if this Blake person doesn't believe you?"

"Then we will have to find the real killer, my dear. That's all there is to it."

"Please don't, Thom. James is right. Tell them you were with us."

"I can only tell so many lies, Penelope. I won't be long."

He left the room. The door swung shut behind him.

16

"I should have known you would be here." Blake put out a hand. Lund took it, matching the man's wringing grip. "What is it this time, business or pleasure?" They stood around the kitchen, hands in pockets, the lieutenant drinking from a hot cup of coffee.

"I know the family." Lund placed a hand on the countertop and leaned his weight down. He was tired. He could feel the hours all through his body.

"From Shanghai, you mean. When you were a cop."

Lund glanced at McCain, who shrugged. "Don't look at me. It isn't a secret."

"Yes," Lund said slowly, "from Shanghai. When I was a cop."

"And what did they get up to there?" Careful eyes watched him over the rim of the cup.

Lund smiled bitterly. "Not everything the papers would

like you to believe. The daughter, that's Penelope Harris, she owned a casino. There was the usual talk about it, but as far as the police could tell, the Jade Tiger was a legitimate business. James was in medical school. I suppose he told you that already. They had both lived there since they were children. The father moved the family to be closer to his shipping interests."

"Where's he?"

"Died last year." Lund crossed his arms and leaned his hip against the counter. "Heart attack."

"What about the victim? What do you know about her?" Blake asked.

Too much, he thought. Lund said, "Renee Strong had a visa from Canada when she arrived in Shanghai in 1923. She arrived with a little cash and a long letter of introduction from the Singapore police."

"Was she on the grift?" Blake nodded to McCain, who took out his notebook and a pencil stub.

"If she was, she got off to a slow start. Probably getting her feel for the place. She was like that—careful. Took her time with things. By the end of '23 Renee had been picked up for suspicion of petty theft and prostitution. We looked for evidence she was blackmailing some of her boyfriends. Nothing ever stuck. Just whispers. She was never formally charged before a magistrate." The only sound in the room was McCain's pencil moving across the paper of his notebook. "In late '24 she went to work at the Jade Tiger casino."

Blake's eyes narrowed. "Why is that significant?"

"You'd find out sooner or later." Lund's thin smile never wavered. "A good number of the people at this party were in and out of that establishment at one time or another. It was owned by Kinkaid Ambrose, Penelope Harris's husband—on paper at least."

McCain corrected Lund without looking up from his notebook. "Miss Harris's dead husband. She's a widow."

"Didn't I read about her in the paper?" Blake asked.

McCain paused his writing to look up. He recited carefully, "Miss Harris returned to New York about two months ago with her mother and brother. She's related to the Staughtons but is more like a poor cousin. Inherited some money a while back, her husband lost it in bad investments. Doesn't socialize, doesn't make waves. And definitely doesn't talk about owning a nightclub called the Jade Tiger." McCain gave Lund a long look. "My godson reads the social column to me every morning over breakfast."

Lund shifted uncomfortably. "Kinkaid, Penelope, and Renee became something of a scandal in Shanghai. Got a little wild."

"The kind of wild rich people travel to the other side of the world to get up to when they think no one is looking?" Blake intoned. "Or the kind the police might be interested in?"

"The kind that can't be proved one way or another in a court of law."

"So, it's like that?"

"Penelope's father didn't approve of the casino. Didn't approve of the husband either, if it comes to that. When Penelope and Kinkaid eloped, she went her own way. She had an invitation to study opera at the Royal Academy in London. She gave it up. Her father didn't like that. They didn't make it up until just before he died."

"Gave it up for love, did she?" McCain chuckled.

"Something like that." Lund paused, partly to breathe and partly to stamp down his anger. "Kinkaid had . . . other interests. Shipping mainly. He must have gotten in deep with his partners. Or he rubbed one of the gangs the wrong way. We never could settle what happened. The facts are these: In 1927 Kinkaid and Penelope were robbed as they were leaving the casino. Penelope survived. Kinkaid didn't make it."

"What did she have to say about it?" Blake stared at Lund without blinking.

"She couldn't remember enough to help with the inquiries. She doesn't even remember the attack." Lund kept his hands loose.

"Poor kid," McCain said. "She's got a scar under her ear." He pointed the end of the pencil toward his neck. "Was that from . . . ?"

"Yes." The memories were . . . difficult. He had been the one to find her, knew better than anyone what she had been through. Her ivory gown soaked in blood, her face so swollen from the beating he hadn't recognized her. He shifted his weight, tried to clear his mind. "We put a half dozen men on it but couldn't make progress. Closest we could figure, Kinkaid had rubbed someone the wrong way or welched on a deal or a bet. Who knows? It was an accident Penelope was with him that night. Bad luck. No one knew anything. The case went cold."

"What about our victim?" Blake asked.

"I can tell you this for certain: if Renee had anything to do with the robbery, it would have been Penelope who died, not Kinkaid. Renee wanted to be married. Wanted it bad."

"You mean this woman was having an affair with her husband and Miss Harris didn't say a word?" McCain lifted his pencil from his writing, his face screwing up with disbelief.

The lies were taking their toll on Lund. He could feel it acutely. A dose of the truth was necessary. "I think she was relieved, to tell you the truth. Kinkaid could be a brute. Any distraction that kept him away was welcome. And I already told you. Her family didn't care for the man."

"What about a boyfriend?" Blake asked.

"No."

"When was the last time you saw Renee before tonight?"

Lund welcomed the shift in questioning. "My boss was concerned about some regular withdrawals. For this particular account, management thought it might be money laundering. I agreed. I tailed him to a swank apartment and there was Renee. Wherever Renee goes, a blackmail racket is sure to follow, photos in the mail, cash in a drop box, that sort of thing. In Shanghai she'd set up a photo drop and bleed the mark dry. At first I thought our man was being blackmailed. I admit it: I was curious. I've been trailing her bagman for a week now trying to find where she's been holed up. Hasn't been easy to pin her down."

"What's the name of her bagman?" Blake asked.

"Mike Cernoch."

"Know him, Jasper?"

"Sure, Mikey-boy Cernoch." A wrinkle appeared between McCain's eyebrows. "He's an ex-boxer, got sent up for a racket for three to five. Must've just gotten out. Last I heard he was going straight."

"They all say that," Blake complained with a sigh. "What about the mark she was blackmailing? What's his name?"

"I didn't say he was her mark." Lund was still. "Hard to say what he was. Renee's never had a partner, so it couldn't have been that. I thought they might be keeping house. Renee hadn't struck me as the type to settle down, but for the right amount of money . . ." He shrugged.

"Blackmailer and a kept woman? Our victim was a real peach," Blake grumbled. "Was he a part of the blackmail racket?"

"Not that I could tell. But I'd only been following Renee for a week." Lund gestured for McCain's pencil and then extracted a card from his wallet and wrote an address on the back, handing it to McCain.

Blake leveled a stare. "So who was it, her paramour?"

"Alfred Gott. A stockbroker. Was just struck off for insider trading. He was paying her a mint."

"She see anything that might get her killed?" McCain lifted an eyebrow.

"Nothing like that." Lund made an open-handed gesture. "Renee hadn't been in New York long enough to make local enemies. She didn't have a connection to any of the outfits other than the cheapest muscle she could buy. She had a couple of boyfriends she met up with regularly away from her apartment, where Gott wouldn't know about it—stockbrokers mostly, bank people. She had a taste for finer things." Lund paused. "I don't know if this is important, but I had the impression that Gott didn't know there were other boyfriends."

"She was stepping out on him?"

Lund nodded. "Renee wasn't the sort of girl who settled down with one man."

"Prostitution?" McCain continued to take notes as he spoke.

"Nothing so sordid." Lund was quick. Singapore had been a difficult lesson. Afterward, Renee had known where to draw the line. "She wanted gifts: jewelry, furs, things like that. She wasn't interested in jail or bunking up with a madam who might leave her in the lurch. She only started blackmailing when they tried to break it off."

"Got any other suspicions you want to tell us about?"

Blake's tone, coupled with his folded arms, made Lund stop to consider. For a moment he had a wild fear that Blake knew he had lied. Lund took hold of himself, slowed down. By the time he spoke, his heart had stopped racing. "I'll let you know."

McCain licked the tip of his pencil and turned a page in his notebook. "Where were you between nine and ten?"

Lund ordered his mind. "There was a brawl in the east parlor. That was when I saw her last—Renee, I mean. I got Miss Harris out of the room and went back to help calm things down. Everything seemed under control, so I went around the house looking for Mrs. Harris, Penelope's mother."

"Where did you look?" Blake asked.

"Both the parlors, Harry Staughton's study . . ."

"Did you go outside?" McCain was letting Blake ask all the questions. Lund had to wonder if he had suspicions.

"I had an idea Mrs. Harris might have gone out on the terrace for a breath of fresh air. I had a look around there and came back inside."

Blake's eyes narrowed. "That runs along the side of the house, doesn't it? Goes down to the back?"

"It does. I saw the butler. He showed me where to go."

Blake straightened, looked from McCain to Lund. "Did you see the victim?"

Lund looked Blake in the eye. "I did not."

Blake laughed, a short, gasping thing with a hint of bitterness. "I suppose you know that puts you right in the cross fire, Thom."

Lund's heart didn't race. "It's the truth."

"We'll see about that. All right then. Let's talk about the other guests at the party. Why don't you tell me how many guests here might have known Renee Strong in Shanghai?"

Lund paused, gauging the risk. Say too much and risk Penelope, say too little and risk her again. He made up his mind. The truth was better. Blake would find out one way or another. "Harry Staughton."

"You mean Charles Staughton?"

"No, I mean his father, Harry Staughton."

Blake lowered his notebook. "You mean to tell me that our victim went and married the son of one of her marks?"

"That's what I'm saying."

Blake swore. "You think she was squeezing him?"

"I saw him meet with her, give her an envelope. Could have been money."

Blake swore again.

17

As soon as the door shut behind James, Penelope fell into a waking sleep, her thoughts unruly. Renee, the audition, her two young students from the Excelsior, Shanghai, the Jade Tiger—all overlaid in a surreal muddle of images and sounds.

It was then that she knew any real hope she had of singing opera was over. The papers would publish the story about the contest, the brawl, and Renee's murder, and finish her dream of a career. Then there would be more. A good journalist, perhaps even Helen Mayfield, would ask questions until stories about the Jade Tiger broke free. It could be hours or days, but eventually Kinkaid's death would find its way to the front page. Just as it had in Paris. Just as it had in London. New York had been her last chance to start fresh.

The dream was over.

The tide had changed so quickly Penelope could barely grasp it. Renee was dead. It didn't seem true. Part of her wanted to go back to the courtyard and look again. What if she had been wrong? Could it have been someone else? She closed her eyes, her consciousness trapped somewhere between her uncle's dark, book-lined office and a scandalous production of *Carmen* with tap dancers in revealing costumes made from wooden castanets. She was floating down into a deeper sleep when she was suddenly aware that she was not alone. Fear roused her awake, her eye opening to see through the dim light of the room to her uncle's desk, where a man stood trying the drawers.

He came into focus slowly as she woke, her heart beating so hard she was sure he could hear it. His white hair flew out around his head, the mouth below his mustache a distasteful frown as he fumbled through her uncle's papers, swearing quietly when the drawers would not open. With Lund's jacket over her dress and her head down low on the couch, he must not have seen her. Penelope prepared to lift her head and embarrass him in the act when the door opened.

"Alfred! What do you think you are doing?" Penelope was so relieved to hear her mother's voice she could have cried.

If only theater had been Gott's profession! Penelope couldn't think of another actor who could have the life scared out of him and still wear an endearing and believable smile. "Oh, my dear," he said with delight, "I am so glad to have found you, finally." Sadly, Gott was not an actor. He was, in her short but thorough experience, the most corrupt businessman she had ever known. Even her mother had accepted the fact, and her mother had known Gott all her life.

"Did you think I would be hiding in Harry's desk drawers?"

"I was looking for something to read. The paper. Harry always seems to have one about." Across the room, Penelope felt a stab of fear, his towering height made her mother look reduced and frail. "Such a nuisance, the police. Would you like to sit down? It's a cold night." Reaching forward, he covered her mother's hand with his own. "Are you unwell?" Eleanor appeared to flinch when he touched her, then straightened, her spine stiffening.

"You may release my hand, Alfred. I can manage perfectly well on my own.

"It will be in all the papers tomorrow, but I don't know a thing!" he declared. "I understand Penelope found the body, but I must confess, I don't know much, other than that. Who has died? You must tell me."

"Renee Strong."

"Not your nephew's wife!" He was pleased. Penelope could hear it in every word.

Eleanor looked Gott up and down. "Your sense of self-preservation has cut him off the family tree, has it? He was your second cousin, Freddy, in case you forgot."

"Still keeping your high opinion of our family, I see." Gott smiled, his face bunching up into a gruesome mask of shadows in the dim light. "What do you think the police will make of your daughter's performance earlier this evening? Have you considered what you will tell the press?" Gott strode across the carpet, standing so close to Eleanor she had to crane her neck to look up.

"If you intend to intimidate me, Alfred, I must remind you I am made of stiffer stuff than that. Kindly step back so I can see you properly."

Gott chuckled, pivoting so his back was to the couch.

"I already made a statement to the press regarding Penelope's performance. My daughter has an excellent voice and enjoys performing for family and close friends. That will be enough for now."

"Still quick witted, I see." Gott took her hand again, leaning over it. "My dear, have you given any thought to my proposal?"

"What cheek you have!" Eleanor removed her hand. "Offering your services for investment when you know very well there's nothing left! And more than one reason to believe you were the man who ruined us!"

"Now, now, Eleanor," Gott clicked his tongue, "don't lose your temper. I might take it personally."

"You forget, Freddy, I was there in China. I know you were the one who interfered with the sale of the business. You'll do anything to line your own pocket."

"Then tell the police, why don't you? If you think I have done something illegal," Gott waved a hand, "send me to jail."

There in the half light of her uncle's desk lamp, Penelope came to understand that Eleanor was a beautiful woman. None of the disadvantages, from her frightfully out-of-style Edwardian bun to the Victorian jet she wore to mourn the husband she had adored, could hide the bright light of intelligence in her face or the clever eyes that never missed a trick.

"Everything is gone. Even the accounting books were stolen. By your friend downstairs, if I know my criminal."

Gott stared at her a moment, then threw his head back and roared. It took several seconds for Penelope to realize the man was laughing. "You mean Renee, don't you? My friend downstairs!" He laughed heartily. "You should be careful what you say, Eleanor my dear. There are policemen about, you know."

"You knew what Kinkaid was up to, even went into business with him! Was it your idea they marry? Your idea that they buy the Jade Tiger?"

Gott sobered up quickly, his smile fading away to nothing. "You mustn't say things you can't prove. You'll get into trouble."

"I'll manage it one day, Alfred Gott! You were the only

person who could have told Kinkaid about Penelope's inheritance—as small as it was. The only one who could have gotten him an invitation to that party. I'll have the truth one day." Eleanor's hands balled into fists. "You can take my word on it!"

"It's an outrage how you treat your family, Eleanor! I'm your cousin! Your blood! I've only ever had your own interests in mind. Even your daughter pulls the wool over your eyes." Penelope stood as she felt her heart beat a little faster. Gott was so focused on her mother that he did not see her. "Do you know she paid that woman off earlier this evening?"

"You're no more family that that little policeman downstairs, Alfred. You're my second cousin by marriage. You aren't a Staughton!" Eleanor shook with suppressed rage.

"It hardly matters now. You have to keep me on your side or I'll spill everything to the police. The Jade Tiger, Kinkaid's murder—all of it. I wonder what the police will think when they hear how Kinkaid met his end?"

"That's enough." Her voice as smooth as milk and as sharp as glass, Penelope took Gott in from the tips of his expensive shoes to his white mustache. "You can tell the police whatever you like about my business. I've done nothing wrong." This was true. "I didn't give Renee anything. She took it from me." Also true. "And what's more, I'd like to see you prove what you say with evidence. Do you have evidence, Freddy? Or are you going off the word of a dead woman? How close were you, I wonder? Did you know she was getting married?"

Gott sucked in his breath and expanded. For just a moment, Penelope was sure the man was about to hit her. It took everything she had to stand straight and look him in the eye, until he suddenly turned on his heel and left the room, slamming the door shut behind him.

"What an odious man!" Eleanor declared. "Now, Penelope, you must tell me—why on earth must you insist on singing *Carmen* when you know I loathe it?"

18

"Officers." a young woman in a dark blue dress walked past the patrolmen at the door of the dining room. She extended her hand. "Helen Mayfield. I'm a journalist from the *Sentinel*." Long cleared of food, the room held the faint aroma of roast beef, reminding McCain he had missed his break and his evening lunch. At the very least, the butler could have offered them a plate before the staff took the food away. Not to mention turning on a few lights at the same time. As it was, with the candelabra on the table snuffed out and the overhead chandelier inexplicably turned off, the room was dim and inhospitable. Yet, the woman stood there with her hand out, as bold as midday.

Blake gave her hand wary consideration before he took it. "Miss, we are in the middle of an investigation. There's no way I can give you an interview right now."

"Wait a moment, you misunderstand. I was a guest at this shindig, which means you want to talk to me. Or at least you will once I tell you a thing or two." She put a hand on her hip.

McCain considered Blake. He wasn't an unpleasant man,

not by any stretch of the imagination. It was more a lack of flexible imagination that did him in. Whereas McCain felt a tickling curiosity when he saw Helen Mayfield spring through the door, Blake saw a girl working at a man's job. McCain was interested. Blake felt only pity. "What would that be?" McCain asked without looking at Blake.

"It's my employee, you see. You've asked to see her."

"We've asked to see a Mrs. Anthony Stone. Haven't we, Jasper?"

"Yes, that's right," she said cheerfully. "I am Mrs. Anthony Stone, but I'm not. Here, let me explain." Turning away, she went into the hall and came back leading a stout weeping woman dressed in an abundance of wine-colored rayon. Helen led the woman to a chair. "This is the Mrs. Anthony Stone you asked to speak to, but she is not a columnist."

"It was the booze that made me do it, Helen! It wasn't me!" the woman howled. McCain thought he could hear her stays creak as she sat. As she moved, her wig slid forward on her head. She reached up and straightened it until it was properly on top of her head but facing the wrong direction.

"Now, now, Francine. These are police officers. Let's not make a scene." Helen patted the woman's fat hand.

The woman formerly known as Mrs. Anthony Stone shifted on the edge of her chair and looked at Lieutenant Blake with wary eyes. "It wasn't all my fault," she said shyly. "The booze did have something to do with it."

McCain just managed to hold back a grin. The lieutenant was going to need help with this one. The reporter from the *Sentinel* noticed his discomfort and came up to put her arms around the other woman. "Come along now, Francine, let's put your wig on." McCain could see Blake's relief from across the room, grateful for small miracles.

They stood there and watched, one woman coaxing, the other sounding as though she was having a good cry. "I can't believe it," the older woman said. "She was so young and happy."

McCain opened his notebook.

"Now you sit right there and let me explain." Helen turned her bright eyes back to the policemen. "This is Miss Francine Turdik. I hired her about four months ago to play a part for me. She would go to parties and pretend to be Mrs. Anthony Stone." McCain thought of so many questions at once he didn't know where to start.

"You write the articles, she attends the parties?" he guessed.

"We both attend the parties, to be honest. I just sit up near the buffet and listen to all the old ladies go on about every shocking event of the week, and Miss Turdik here gets to drink as much as she wants and be the center of attention. No one notices me when she's at her job. Isn't that so, Francine?"

Miss Turdik burst into a fresh set of tears.

Helen continued. "You see, gentlemen, I don't want to be on the society desk for eternity. I want to write about real news on the city desk. But to do that, I can't be a celebrity. I need a face out there to help me stay anonymous so that someday I can do some real reporting."

Miss Turdik sniffed loudly and patted Helen's hand. "You're a good girl," she said. "You'll do just fine."

"I called my editor. He thought it best if you interviewed

us at the same time so I could explain." Helen smiled. "And perhaps you could give me an exclusive?"

"No." Blake looked as though he were staring down a man-sized Felix the Cat, fascinated and mortified at once.

"Well," Helen shrugged her bare shoulders, "you can't blame a girl for trying. I'm still going to write about it, just so you know." She nodded briskly and smiled.

Francine Turdik looked at Blake with glazed eyes, her respectable wig only slightly askew. "It's a bad business," she said carefully. "I knew Renee Strong quite well."

"Why don't we start right there, miss," McCain replied with a smile. "Can you tell me what you know about the victim?"

"It's missus, officer. At least let me have my dignity!"

McCain distantly wondered if the address was an honorific or a fact.

"Why don't you tell him how you met her, Francine?" Helen took a kindly tone. "That's as good a place to start as any, isn't it?"

Francine looked thoughtfully at a point in the middle distance, then down at her hands. An alcoholic blotch stood out brightly on each cheek and the tip of her nose. In her hands was a crushed hanky, which she flattened out and folded over and over again as she stared at it with tearing eyes. "We met during the war, of course. 1916. I went over to France to do my best as a nurse. I'm not sure that Renee got there the same way, or for the same reasons," she gave McCain a cautious eye before continuing, "but she was right alongside the rest of us trying to help out the boys. She did her part." Miss Turdik paused for a moment to wipe her eyes.

"How old was she then, ma'am?" McCain spoke to his notebook, trying hard not to break her concentration.

"About fourteen." Blake looked up sharply. She hardly noticed. "Renee had a uniform like the rest of us—God knows where she got it. She fit in. Renee was young, but she was game. Maybe too game. She married Roland when she was just fifteen. He was gassed at the front. The matron gave her away. I don't think she even remembered her father or his name—if she ever knew it. What else would you expect from a girl after that?"

McCain correctly judged the question as rhetorical.

Helen watched the old souse carefully but not unkindly. When Francine Turdik appeared to have stopped her narrative, she prompted, "Please go on. He needs to know."

The woman nodded remotely and began again. "Roland was her patient, and marrying him wasn't exactly the thing to do, but they were in love. Of course, we found out that she wasn't exactly a nurse either, but Roland was taking care of her, so that settled any trouble. We wished her well. It was a hard life. Roland was an artist, of course, and work was scarce after the war. But she was always a clever girl. I knew she'd land on her feet." Francine sighed. "Roland stayed in touch. We understood each other." She blushed. "I wasn't surprised when he told me Renee had taken the stage. She was suited for it. Renee didn't like being poor. And she didn't like the attention Roland got when people began to notice his sculpture. After the war, all anyone knew her as was Mrs. Roland Strong. Renee wanted more than just that." Francine looked up suddenly. "She had a child, did you know? That was the last straw. There wasn't nearly enough attention for her after she was born. And the baby was such a pretty thing. Roland doted on the child. Renee left them." Francine shifted uncomfortably on the chair, making it creak and shudder. "It was a blow to him. He made his way, but Roland had to set aside his work to take care of his daughter." She smiled, nodding to herself as she went on. "Roland made his way, and the child was well loved—even if there wasn't enough money for everything." Francine shook her head. "I was sure she would go back one day. I told him so. I know she would have." Francine shuddered.

Patting the woman's hand, Helen asked, "Francine, what brought her back to the U.S.?"

"She wouldn't say. But it had to be money. She never did have enough of it. Renee loved money. He couldn't help himself, the poor man. Roland took her back."

Francine, regaining some of her composure, moved to the edge of the chair. "Renee didn't mean to be poison, but she was. It wasn't too long before men were hanging around the house, and there were dreadful rumors. Roland wrote me after she left and told me. I have the letter if you want it. He said she was very jittery, nervous. He suspected something, but what he didn't say. Renee didn't scare that easy. It made him nervous." Francine clasped her hands, and her delivery deepened with color. McCain found a distant respect for her as an actress. "One night, Renee comes home late and says that she's seen someone she knew from Shanghai. Roland didn't even know she had been to Shanghai. He threw her out then. She begged him not to, but she was too wild." She nodded earnestly. "He was so worried about the child, you see. She's only a little younger than Renee was when she married. He didn't want that for his little girl. That was six months ago."

"Why here?" McCain prompted. "Why New York?"

"Doesn't everyone come to New York at some time or another?" Miss Turdik sighed. "Roland wrote me to ask if I had seen her. He knew I lived here and had a job organizing parties." She caught Helen's sharp look and said, "Well, he wasn't likely to understand our arrangement, dear." She returned to Blake and said damply, "You can have his letters if you like, but I want them back. He won't write again now she's—" A dreadful sniff choked off the rest of her sentence.

"It makes no sense, Francine," Helen said. "She could have just as easily stayed in France. Why spend the cash to come to New York?"

"But I told you, dear. Renee was broke, flat broke. She didn't have enough to pay her way on the liner. I asked her where it all came from, and she said it was from her special friend." Miss Turdik shook her head. "Perhaps she was a bad girl after all. Who can say?" She shrugged and blew her nose into her hanky.

"When did she contact you, Miss Turdik?" McCain asked.

"Well, it's like this: Renee knew I was on my uppers, and she needed a bit of a hand up. So, we had a trade," she admitted uncomfortably. "She gave me a few tidbits about people she knew, and I'd relay them on to Helen. In return I gave her names . . . addresses . . . and things like that."

"You what?" Helen was incredulous.

"There wasn't any harm in it, dearie. It wasn't anything important."

"You are justifying blackmail, Francine! She was using you to set up her next victim, using my column—*my* column—to let them know that she had the goods and wasn't afraid to use them!" Helen could barely contain herself. "And you gave her names and addresses? What were you thinking? Did you give her the Staughtons' address?"

McCain urged his note-taking to continue at a slightly faster pace.

"I didn't know what she was going to do, Helen," Francine said quickly. "I didn't know she was going to go so far that she'd marry that boy! Why, I was just as surprised as anybody when I saw them there!"

"Whose address?" Helen stamped her foot with anger. "Whose address did you give her?"

"Why, this one. I thought you knew! You could have knocked me over with a feather when you showed me the address for the party. It was this house she was interested in, these people." Francine looked at the hanky in her lap, snuffling. "I can only apologize for it, dear. I can't change it." She looked up, pleading, "The truth is that I liked the work and we make a good team. Don't we, Helen? Didn't you think so?"

"And I suppose you took a swing at Mr. Staughton because you were morally outraged?" Helen crossed her arms.

Francine dabbed her eyes. "Now, I resent your tone. I think I might deserve better than that!"

"You forget I was there. You took a swing at the groom just as he was announcing his marriage!"

"Don't be unfair! If you would just split the hair just a little bit, you might admit that they weren't married, which would mean he wasn't actually the groom, which would mean I was just taking a swing at a man, not a husband."

Helen stood up. "Split the hair?" she asked. "You abetted

a social python in a scheme to marry into a respectable family. For what purpose? Petty satisfaction? Not to mention using *Sentinel* resources to abet a blackmailer!" Having full command of the room, Helen went for the throat. "One person is dead—maybe because you couldn't resist a nickel! Did you think of that?"

"Well, it wasn't my fault, was it?" Francine squirmed under Helen's cold stare. "I didn't know what they were. I didn't realize what she was doing until I got here tonight. It was all a trick on me, don't you see? Renee knew my weakness, and she played it against me. But then I saw her, and I remembered Roland raising that little girl on his own. I guess something snapped in my head."

"You snapped?" Helen stopped herself short. Turning on her heel, she walked to the door with as much dignity as she could muster. Before she shut it behind her, she said, "Miss Francine Turdik, you will help this man find his murderer by remembering every little thing you can about Renee Strong while she was in New York. If you don't, I promise you that you will be the subject of a real column—one I write myself!" The door slammed shut. Miss Turdik stared at the shut door and stifled a cry.

"Ma'am," Blake leaned forward with earnest concentration, "can you tell us what happened after you took your first swing?"

"Well, that young man, he snatched my wig!" Miss Turdik reached up to touch her curls. "I had to do something to defend myself, didn't I? I didn't think he would be so angry. Anyone who knows Renee knows she lies. Why get angry with the messenger?"

"Then what happened?"

"It was a bit of a shuttlecock, you understand?" She wiped her eyes as she spoke, punctuating the sentences with loud sniffing. "Everyone bouncing off of one another, making a racket. Then Harry Staughton came into the room, and things got just a little worse for everyone."

"Where was the victim during all this?"

"Oh, Renee? She ran out. She always did know when to exit."

"And Charles Staughton?"

"The boy? Well, he wasn't right behind her, but he ran after her, that much I could see. He gave me a mighty wallop right here on my chin. It's going to leave a mark. I just know it."

"Has he turned up?" Blake turned to McCain.

"Charles Staughton?" McCain hadn't been looking forward to the moment. Police instructions were to search the house from top to bottom, but so far they'd had no luck. "Haven't been able to find him yet, Nathan. Looks like he's done a runner."

 19

"MOTHER," JAMES SHUT THE DOOR to the office and put his hands on his hips, "where on earth have you been? Lund and I have been searching the house for you for over an hour!" Penelope couldn't take her eyes from Lund. There was something about his stance, as though a distance had come between them. He wouldn't look at her.

Eleanor looked from James to Penelope. "*Carmen* gives me such a headache. And such a crowd! So hot, so uncomfortable!" Penelope watched as her mother glanced from the tuxedo jacket Penelope wore to Lund's shirtsleeves. "I had to lie down, if you must know. So I went upstairs and used Mary's bed. I heard the ruckus and decided I would stay where I was for the time being. It was very restful." Eleanor settled on the sofa next to Penelope. Penelope reflexively reached for her mother's hand. It gave her no end of comfort to feel Eleanor's fingers curl around her own and gently squeeze.

James said, "You missed a great deal of excitement."

"And what has been happening here?" she asked crisply.

Lund leaned a shoulder against the bookcase, his expression inscrutable. "Renee Strong is dead from a broken neck." Penelope noticed the pomade on his hair had loosened. His black hair fell over his forehead, giving him the air of a man who has just gotten out of bed.

Eleanor dismissed him. "Don't tell me what I already know! Wasn't that Kinkaid's chippy?"

"Mother!" James exclaimed.

"Yes," Penelope said, having persuaded herself that she understood her mother a bit better after overhearing her conversation with Gott.

Eleanor looked around at each of them. "And who is to thank for this happy occurrence?"

"Mother!" Penelope found her new understanding did not go far enough.

"You can't blame me. The woman was a scourge. I met

her in Shanghai when you were in hospital. I could tell just by looking at her she was a contemptible person."

"Mother, it would be helpful if you could keep that sentiment to yourself for the next two or three days." James fell back into the nearest comfortable chair.

"How long were you sleeping?" Lund cut through the three of them with little effort.

"Well, I'm sure I don't know. I didn't wear a watch this evening. I thought I would wait until Mary came to wake me."

"And did she wake you?" Lund was almost bored as he said it.

"No, I heard a noise outside the window. Someone in the street, I would imagine. I felt refreshed, so I came downstairs again."

"When was this?"

"Just now. I must say, Thom, I don't understand the necessity of these questions."

James sighed. "We will all need to answer them. The police will be here to question Penelope any moment. You might as well work your story out with us. I know you weren't in Mary's room because I checked there myself not an hour ago."

"You must have looked in the wrong room." Eleanor lifted her chin. Penelope recognized all the signs—her mother was ready for a pique. "Do you have any other questions?"

"Only one." Lund nodded to the clutch Eleanor held fast in her lap. "Where did you find the purse? I ask because the last time I saw it, Renee had it."

Penelope reached for the clutch, taking it from her mother

and opening it with one smooth movement. The two thousand dollars was gone.

20

WITHOUT THE CHANDELIER, THE DINING room was almost too dark to write. McCain had to squint to see the squiggles from his pencil. Made you wonder how they knew where their plates were. He slowly walked the periphery of the room looking for light switches. Finding one near the door to the kitchen, McCain hit the jackpot. The room blazed with light as the chandelier switched on, the warm light bringing the room into focus. The long table at the center still drew attention, but now he could see the red-silk-lined walls, the ornately carved fireplace, and the long sideboards on either side of the table. Heavy brocade curtains were pulled tight against the windows. McCain peeked through one to watch the policemen in the street. Dropping the curtain, McCain said, "This is some room. You ever eaten your dinner in a room like this?"

Blake grunted, his eyes on the notebook in his hand. He looked up. "Here she comes."

Eleanor Harris sailed into the dining room without looking left or right. She sat directly under the chandelier in the middle of the long dining table, facing Blake. She kept her hands in her lap, her back ramrod straight. She was a good-looking woman, with her blonde hair back in a becoming low bun against her neck. The neckline of her dress didn't plunge, and the dress looked serviceably comfortable and appropriately black, as she was a widow. McCain nodded to himself. A perfectly good woman. They didn't come around often enough these days to pass without a remark. "I'm sure you were well placed to give us a practical idea of the events of this evening, ma'am." McCain didn't care if Blake gave him an eyeballing after he said it. It was true enough; she was that type of woman.

"It's very simple," she replied. "This is what happened."

Blake nodded politely. McCain put his pencil to paper.

"I knew what Renee Strong was up to because I know all about her. She's been in my child's life some time now, and, for reasons I do not understand, my daughter feels an obligation. This obligation has expressed itself in many ways. The least of these was money. There is no need for me to comment about the gifts Penelope gave Renee Strong, because they were meaningless. It is my daughter's money. She made it herself, even if it was from that awful nightclub, and it is hers to spend." Eleanor pinned Lieutenant Blake to his chair with a penetrating stare. When Blake did not comment, she continued. "But for some reason, my daughter feels she owes," Eleanor corrected herself, "owed this woman the obligation of her friendship. This, officers, was too much. I've told her many times she should cut the woman dead—that is, socially, of course. A woman like Renee Strong, with the type of low character who would offer less in return than she was given? Who would woo a friend with a wink and a laugh and disappear when most needed or desired? That is what I had no time for. When my daughter was ill and needed friendship, did this woman come to her side? No. Would you like to know what she did?" She looked from Blake to McCain. "She leaked nasty stories about my daughter to the local papers. She told society gossips in Paris that Penelope had run not a reputable casino but a house of ill repute. One where Renee herself had been an unwilling slave. White slavery! Gentlemen, I ask you! There was much more, I'm sure you can guess. The gossip columns in Berlin were so outrageous that I regretted ever letting Penelope sing Mozart! Every time my daughter was ready to put down roots, Renee ensured the gossip columns made a quiet life impossible."

Blake opened his mouth to speak, but Eleanor got there before him.

"You might ask me how I know this."

Blake shut his mouth.

"It's quite simple." Eleanor gave herself a minute shake. "She told me the first time she tried to blackmail me." She turned to McCain. "May I have a glass of water? I believe my brother keeps a pitcher of water and glasses on the sideboard near the door."

McCain found a glass and filled it. Blake had moved to the edge of his seat, a hand on either knee as he stared Eleanor down. Eleanor took a long drink and put the glass on the table. The room was quiet. They waited.

Eleanor continued, "I am sure that Renee Strong was a proficient blackmailer. It was too easy for her, too smooth. Certainly, as you get on with your job you will find some sign she had done it before. When you find her trove of indecent photographs and correspondence, I hope you also find the letters I wrote each time she attempted to blackmail me with evidence that my daughter had . . ." Eleanor paused to search for the correct words ". . . lived a full life. She must have done it just to offend me. Never gave her any money, told her off every time." She paused to take another drink. "Officers, I want you to consider that my daughter eloped when she was only eighteen years old. Barely eighteen years old! She married a man many years her senior who was a gambler and a rake, whom she hardly knew but loved. When she realized her marriage was a fraud, she honored her commitment to that man and tried to set him up with a business in which a gambler could thrive—a casino. Put aside for a moment that the man was colossally inept and could hardly balance a bankbook or muster the discipline to pay his bills. Consider instead that my daughter loved that wretch enough to see him well settled—despite all he did to her in return. That is the type of person my child is—a good friend, a good businesswoman . . . She gave up her career in the opera to marry the man!" Eleanor took a handkerchief from her sleeve and dabbed her eyes. "You'll forgive me if I am emotional. I wasn't without talent myself. I taught Penelope from an early age, so I can tell you impartially. She is a notable talent." Eleanor stiffened. "*Carmen*! Really! And she knows how I hate it!"

A furrow appeared in Blake's brow. "What exactly happened this evening, Mrs. Harris?"

"When I saw Mary give Penelope that purse, I knew what had transpired. The bank president likes to call me personally to question every expense. He believes that widows are his cross to bear. If you asked him, I'm certain he would tell you our money is his responsibility. He is concerned we will be taken in by a charlatan, you see. As if it would be any of his business if we were! This is exactly the type of behavior I expect from someone who believes that my daughter's money has become his own. That man has a surprise coming next week. I plan on auditing the books myself. Mark my words: he's got his finger in the pie! I'll find it."

McCain appreciated mastery when he saw it. She was lying—and doing it so well that it would take weeks to unravel the nonsense from the fact. It took everything he had not to look at the lieutenant to see if he had picked up on the string of fabrications. McCain just didn't trust himself not to give the game away. He was enjoying himself. He couldn't help it.

Blake tugged on his mustache. "If we could return to Renee?"

"I followed her to the coatroom—Renee, I mean. She was putting on her fur. It was obvious she meant to leave as quietly as she could. I knew I wouldn't have another chance, so I did it." The lieutenant sat forward in his seat. "I told her what I thought of her, precisely."

Mesmerized, McCain asked, "And what did she have to say to that, I wonder?"

"She told me she was going to send a photograph of my daughter doing the Charleston in her French knickers to the *Sentinel*."

McCain tried to remember what French knickers were.

Blake seemed less astonished. "Then what happened?" he growled.

Eleanor blushed. "I'm not proud of myself. I tried to take the purse. I've never fought with anyone in my life. Never. I ripped the sleeve of her fur, and she slapped me." Eleanor's face turned a bright pink. Shaken but unbowed, she went on.

"She said since I had ruined her coat, she would take Penelope's. We haven't had much since my husband died, and Penelope's fortunes were reduced by her husband. That coat was a very dear present from her father. Well, Lieutenant, that was my limit. I lost my temper." Eleanor was a glorious ship sailing into its last battle. "I struck her. Next thing I knew, she pushed me back into the rack of coats. When I fell, I must have hit my head, because when I opened my eyes, she was gone. The coats had all fallen on the floor, I left them there and went looking for her. I looked everywhere I could think of, but I couldn't find her. I was about to give up when I remembered there was a garden gate near the carriage house. I was sure Renee would use it to avoid the photographers. I came through the east parlor and crossed the balcony to the stairs that go down into the courtyard. I had just reached the bottom when I heard a noise."

"What kind of noise?" McCain prompted.

Eleanor thought for a moment. "I don't know. It was almost like squawk, or perhaps a creak, like a dry hinge. It was very brief." She considered for a moment. "Yes, perhaps more like a bird."

McCain sighed. More nonsense, but it wasn't a lie.

"I called out her name. I told her I knew she was there. It was dark, and the stairs were not well lit. I'm afraid I stumbled on the last two and fell on my hands." Eleanor raised her skirt to reveal the ladder in her stocking. "When I got up, I saw a figure running through the gate."

"What did he look like?"

"He was wearing street clothes. Several men at the party were underdressed."

"Did you see his face?"

"Not at all." Eleanor gave Blake a stern glance. "I did tell you it was dark, didn't I? And that he was running away from me?"

"All right, it was dark. Please go on." Blake kept his eyes on her.

"He dropped the purse on the lawn. I could see it quite clearly. I could hear him running, so I knew there was nothing to fear. I went to the purse, opened it, and saw the money was gone. Then I went through the gate."

"Was anyone there?"

"It was too dark to see. The alley isn't lit at all. I must speak to Harry about it."

"Did you come back inside?"

"No." She seemed to have run out of words. "I can't exactly explain it, Lieutenant. I followed the alley to the street."

"And then?"

Eleanor blinked. "And then I went home."

21

"I CAN BARELY FOLLOW IT. She finds the girl dead, then goes home for a rest." Blake rubbed his face with his hand. "Then when an hour or two have passed, she gets back in a cab and comes back here. Just walks up the steps without a single man stopping her? I swear to God, McCain. Those boys will have a lot to answer for if I find out they took a bribe to let her in."

McCain allowed the insult to pass. He knew both the kids on the door. Young, sure, but not crooked. He took his time with his answer. "The thing is, the cabbie she took works the stand at the Excelsior exclusively. He says it happened just like she said. More than that, he also says that she acted confused, like she didn't know where she was or what she was doing."

Blake pursed his lips. "She had a knock on the head. It takes people that way sometimes."

"Nathan, can you picture that woman breaking someone's neck?"

"Yes, Jasper, I can. You've got a mother's love to consider. And I think if you try, you can too."

"Fair enough." McCain stood back.

"My trouble is sorting out how much of what she told us is woman's nonsense."

McCain nodded, adding, "Mother's love."

Blake fixed his eyes on a knot in the kitchen table. "Have one of the boys go around to the front and ask the photographers if they had someone on the alley. While you're at it, you can tell them we want copies of every photograph they took tonight."

"You want me to get the captain working on a warrant?"

Blake shot McCain a look that telegraphed his every private thought about warrants. "No warrants yet. I don't want anyone downtown getting their nose in our business. Just ask nicely." Blake ran his hand over his smooth head, then reached down to tug on his mustache, a sign of irritability the bullpen knew by heart.

McCain flipped back through his notes. "I haven't even

told you who we have in the west parlor yet. There's a city councilman urgently requesting we drop his wife off at Penn Station so she can get a Reno divorce, toot sweet. Oh yes, and Alfred Gott."

"Gott is still here? Dammit, Jasper! Why didn't you say so?" Blake stood a little taller. "Did the uniforms ask him the usual questions?"

McCain checked his notes. "Yes."

Blake swore. "All I need right now is a call from the D.A.'s office telling me off for making the man wait! Get all the guests' names and let them go. We'll send out some detectives to follow up. Let the boys know I'll turn their pockets out if I think they're up to something."

"Boss, not one of these boys will take a bribe."

"Just do it, Jasper."

"Yessir."

"While you're at it, send the Harris girl back to the dining room. We'll get her statement before she goes home for the night. She's got motive. Her mother said as much. I want to see what she has to say for herself before she has time to sleep on it or have a long chat with her mother."

The door to Harry Staughton's office stood open as guests filed past, some of them craning their necks to get a good look inside. Penelope sat with her back to them, her head on her hand. James touched her lightly on the arm.

"I'm taking Mother back to the apartment. Lund is

getting us a cab. Thom is staying with you." James touched her arm. "You shouldn't be alone when you are questioned by the police. Insist on him being there. Don't speak to them alone. It's the best we can do under the circumstances. I should have thought of it before they spoke to Mother," he continued as though he were talking to himself. "I won't let it happen again." He knelt beside her. "Penelope, you must consider everything you say carefully."

"I think I know enough to keep myself out of trouble."

James took her hand. "In this case, two heads are better than one, I think."

"I can take care of myself."

He sighed. "I would accuse you of being pigheaded, but as it is a family trait, I would only be admitting the same fault. Listen to me. I need to take Mother back to the hotel so she can see a real doctor and get some rest. She needs me most right now. Lund was a policeman, and he knows these people. Believe me when I say that this is more a risk to him than it is to you."

"How could that possibly be true?"

"Because at this moment, they don't suspect him." He angled his head. "How can you be so dense? The man's in love with you, can't you see it? He has motive. He has opportunity. Well, if that doesn't make you an absolute fool—Penelope, I thought better of you!"

Penelope felt her thoughts derail. "What?" The door to the room opened, and Lund appeared in the doorway.

James stood. "Thom, just the man! I need to speak with you for a moment." James patted her hand. "I'll be back in less than an hour. Keep your wits." He was gone.

Penelope listened to the quiet murmuring and shuffling of the guests as they passed through the hallway to the coat closet. She turned away, not wanting to give the gossips any more to talk about. She was sure her face was a mess of smudges and red blotches.

A policeman stuck his head through the opening. "Just a moment, miss, and you can go in. Wait here for us, if you would."

Another face appeared at the door, more strangers looking and whispering. Penelope got up and turned off the desk lamp, plunging the room into darkness. Pulling Lund's jacket tighter around her, she crossed behind her uncle's desk and parted the curtains, looking down into the drive that followed the west side of the house. It was black, the cloudy night denying even the slightest shadow. She could hardly see the pavement a story beneath the window, the darkness was so complete. A policeman stood in the light at the mouth of the drive near the street, looking left then right as he watched the people go, the drive behind him in inky darkness.

Leaning her head against the cool glass, Penelope watched the young policeman and thought of the first time she had seen Lund in his crisp khaki uniform, his British cap an awkward fit for his sharp profile and wide shoulders. The problem with Lund as a policeman was that he never suited the part. The other Danes who had joined the Shanghai police were blond. Not Thom. He was dark. Even his eyes were an unruly green instead of blue. Before that morning, she had seen him out of uniform only twice. The first time at a party in the casino a week before Kinkaid died, and the second time when he met her family at the docks to see them off.

Strangely aware of the completeness of the silence, Penelope looked around the empty room expecting someone to be there looking back at her. Certain no one was near, she placed her head in her hand and allowed herself to remember when he had been hers. It seemed like such a simple plan when she looked back, perhaps too simple. She would sign over the Jade Tiger to Kinkaid in exchange for a quick divorce. She and Thom would leave Shanghai behind, start fresh somewhere—maybe Hong Kong. Thom told her about Copenhagen and his father. Penelope described what she could remember about New York. She lay in the crook of his right arm, her skin touching his, and they dreamed the night away. A day later Kinkaid was dead and she was in surgery fighting for her life, the headlines lurid and cruel.

All at once she was aware of a crashing hope that swept the ground from beneath her. Her brother must have been wrong. He had to be. Thom didn't love her. He wasn't hers. Penelope shut her eyes and found that the harder she tried to quell her fear, the deeper into it she swam. She covered her eyes with her hand and breathed through her mouth, trying and failing to remind herself that not every man was Kinkaid. He was a man she had learned to fear. His far-reaching anger still haunted her a year after his death.

Lund and Shanghai and Kinkaid and Renee all came together in a sickening stew of regret and fear. She could hardly think of the Jade Tiger, surely the source of all her happiness, without remembering the night she almost died beneath Kinkaid's swinging fist. The same night he died. The night after she and Lund made their plan to be free.

Shanghai belonged to the memories of the life she had

dreamed and not lived. It belonged to Renee and her cruel jokes, each one designed to take Penelope to the edge of re-membering what it was like to love a man like Kinkaid and still wish he was dead. And there—mixed within the sailors and good-time girls, gangsters and high-society debutants— was Thom, around whom the memories turned until they came loose, crashed into each other, and broke apart.

It wasn't Shanghai that had done it. It couldn't have been. It was people who brought that kind of suffering to them-selves. Lifting her head, Penelope returned her attention to the alley. It was because she wasn't looking for it that she saw the movement in the darkness, a faint ripple within the inky shadows that stepped closer to the street. The figure wait-ed until the officer had stepped away, helping someone into a car, perhaps even her mother, then stepped into the light, turning up the black lapels of his tuxedo so the white of his shirt wouldn't flag attention. He made for the street with a long stride, and she saw his face.

The power of the memory came to her clearly: a man in a tropical suit who played at the Jade Tiger craps table for hours. First winning, then trying to win back his losses, Jack Rollins had gambled until he lost it all, right down to the clothes on his back. When he returned the next day with more mon-ey, Kinkaid kept him playing until it was all gone. Jack kept returning, day after day, until he had nothing left. Now he stood under the streetlight, much as he had that first night she saw him, dancing on the cusp of ruin, Renee on his arm.

As Jack broke into a run, he glanced back at the house. Penelope hoped he would get away. Someone deserved to be free. He turned up the street, leaving her view.

"The police would like to speak with you now." Lund stood in the door. "It won't take long. Then I will take you home." He came forward with a handkerchief in his hand, folded into quarters.

Penelope reached up to touch her face. Her fingertips came away wet. "I'm sorry. I'm sorry for all of it." She didn't know where the apology came from. Somehow, she thought it should be said.

Lund wrapped his arm around her shoulders, drawing her to him until she rested against his waistcoat. She sobbed as he held her upright when she barely thought she could stand. "Don't worry." Penelope felt his voice through his chest. "Not much longer now."

As much as she wanted to, she did not believe him.

22

WHILE BLAKE GAVE QUIET INSTRUCTIONS to the patrolman who led her into the room, Penelope Harris paused in the doorway to the dining room and looked around herself. The chandelier bathed her in a flattering gold light. As tired as she was, she was still a striking beauty. McCain gave Lund high marks for his taste in women. Thom followed her a moment later, pulling his shirt cuffs through his sleeves as though he had just put on his jacket. Lund nodded to McCain and remained just inside the door. As far as McCain could tell, Blake hadn't seen him. Lund put his back against the wall, leaning his weight into it with the practice of a former po-liceman. Crossing his arms, Lund concentrated on Blake, his face somber.

"How can I be of help, Lieutenant?" Penelope sat in a dining room chair, her dress pooling around her feet in rich folds of red silk and purple shadow. She didn't look at Lund. She didn't need the jolt of courage. She knew how to keep her chin up all on her own. McCain could see that clear enough. She wants this over with, he thought. She looked every bit of a soldier in front of a firing squad.

It had been a long night, and Blake was beginning to tire. McCain could easily see the signs in the slouched shoulders and heavy lean of his arm against the dining room table. It wasn't many men who could soldier through a twenty-four-hour day. Blake was no different. McCain had his tricks for never getting tired. The first was to never sit down unless you absolutely had to. Give your feet a rest before the day was over and they'd give in.

"I understand you were friends with the victim," Blake said. "What was she like?"

"Renee was the headliner at the Shanghai casino I owned with my husband, Kinkaid. She was talented, one of the best performers I had ever seen. Wiped the floor with everyone else." She had an air of defiance, as if she expected Blake to burst forth with evidence to the contrary at any moment. "She didn't have an easy life. Never caught a break, the way she told it. I suppose she didn't have many chances to get it wrong, not without consequences. That's one thing I learned from her: money does change everything. For a while, she was my friend."

"What came between you?"

"Renee never had enough money. It built up her resentment. I paid all the staff very well. She made more money than any other headliner in the French Concession, but it was never enough for her."

"Did she have enemies?"

"Renee had a strong sense of self-preservation. I would say because of that, she did not have many friends."

"Things being what they are these days, there isn't much room to make a mistake." Blake smiled. "Maybe she pulled a con on the wrong man or took something that didn't belong to her."

"What a terrible thought." Her words were flat. She watched Blake as though she could read his mind.

"The reason will come clear," he went on. "It always does. It would be helpful to know where her money came from. She was wearing an expensive necklace. Pearls, I believe."

"The necklace was a gift from my cousin Charles."

"I understand she had an apartment on the West Side. Did your cousin pay for that too?"

"They only met a few weeks ago, according to my other cousin, Mary. If Renee had been here for any length of time, I rather doubt it was his money that was paying for the apartment." She spoke with such easy aplomb, McCain found it difficult to tell if she was lying. It would be a devil proving anything she didn't admit to. Some witnesses were like that.

Blake watched her. McCain nodded to himself. Blake had heard it too—the careful step of a witness holding something back. "Is that so?"

She didn't nod. She waited. It was odd the way she watched them. McCain didn't see her blink.

"I understand she knew your husband as well."

"Yes, we were all friends." Her answer was a little too quick. "Kinkaid wooed Renee away from a nightclub to our casino, the Jade Tiger. He promised her own show, with a headline, costumes, dancers. It was well worth the investment. Renee could show great bonhomie when it suited her; she was the life of the party every night."

"Did you ever argue?"

Penelope took a moment to consider her answer. "She didn't like it when I sang at the Tiger," she said finally. "She didn't like that I actually could sing, if you understand me properly. Renee had to work hard for what she had. She did not appreciate anyone taking her spotlight. Resented it."

"Didn't you own the club?"

"I may have, but it was her stage."

"You were still friends after that?"

"Renee wasn't one to let petty jealousy get between her and a friend with money."

"A little cynical, don't you think?"

"It didn't matter to me." Penelope shrugged. "Most of the women in the British zone didn't have the time for a woman who was up all night and slept all day. I wasn't in their tennis club, and I didn't arrange flowers for the church. Seems like I spent most of my time with the chorus girls and my accountant. I was a child, really. There were some hard lessons I had to learn." She smiled. "One thing about Renee, she knew how to have a good time. She went out looking for the most trouble a girl could get herself into. There were so many men.

So many affairs. And of course, there was my husband." She paused. "Renee put all her eggs in his basket, so to speak. When he died, she didn't have anyone to fall back on."

"You mean when he was killed."

"Yes, of course."

McCain lifted his pencil to look at her, his finger stroking his lower lip as he thought. There was something. He had the distinct impression all someone had to do was ask the right question, and the skies would open. That's what it was, he decided. She was waiting for Blake to ask the critical question. Was braced for it to come at any moment. The waiting was taking a toll on her, slowly using up her nerve. McCain glanced at Lund. The man stood completely still, his arms crossed. He was like a rock, that one. There wouldn't be any reading his reactions. He knew better.

Blake went on, "When was your husband killed?"

"August 1927."

"A year ago." Blake's words were flat. "Did you know Renee Strong was in New York?"

"Yes, I saw her this morning. She wanted money."

The lieutenant whistled. "That sounds like blackmail. What'd she have on you? Your mother told us Renee had photos of you in your bathing suit."

"My mother said that?" She laughed, relaxing into the sound with something that McCain thought might be relief. "Renee never had anything like that on me. I was naïve, but I wasn't stupid." It struck McCain like lighting—she was telling the truth. "If you're looking for photographs, I'm afraid you're barking up the wrong tree. Besides, we're as close to broke as we can be without being out on the street. The money brought us here, and my father's annuity keeps food on the table, but I have to work."

Blake nodded. "What do you do?"

"I give singing lessons. I teach a few children at the Excelsior. Mother has thought about returning to teaching. And she would be much better at it than I am. She taught me. Although," she paused to think, "who knows what will happen after the papers tomorrow. I might have no students at all." For the first time in the interview, she reacted. A hard blink and a quick glance at her hands. Her concentration had broken for half a moment. Was it worry? Or embarrassment? It was gone as quickly as McCain tracked it, her face as smooth as ever.

"What about your cousin Charles? Does he have money?" McCain tried not to speak too fast or look at her when he asked. The answer would be in what she said, not how she said it.

"I have no idea, Lieutenant. I've been traveling for the last year. I only arrived in New York less than a month ago."

"Your cousin married a notorious chiseler." McCain looked up from his notebook. "You weren't concerned?"

She had come right to the edge of her honesty. He could feel it. "I was, but not enough to kill her for it."

"What about the sock on the jaw?" McCain stood ready with his pencil.

"She had it coming." Penelope smiled.

"I can see how it made you angry. Would have made a man like me angry too. Woman like that, coming halfway around the world to bleed your family dry. That takes nerve." Blake's eyes narrowed. "She'd have to have a reason to come all that way, don't you think? Couldn't have been easy, or cheap. Though I'm sure there were plenty of richer men along the way to fleece. I'm thinking she must have had a reason. Something from Shanghai." He paused. The girl stared back at him, intent on every word. He was almost there, McCain could feel it. She was ready to tell him. Blake just had to hit the right words, ask the right question. "What could a girl like that have on someone like you?"

"Lieutenant," Lund had been so quiet, McCain had forgotten about him, "does Miss Harris need a lawyer?"

As soon as Lund said it, McCain knew he had broken the thread, freed her from whatever confession she was creeping toward.

The tips of Blake's ears turned pink with irritation. "What for? What are you doing here, anyway?"

"Miss Harris's brother thought she shouldn't be unchaperoned for a discussion with the police. I don't think he realized it would be an interrogation. Miss Harris has been up most of the night, without food. She found the body, if you'll recall."

"I recall."

"She's had a shock," Lund continued quietly. "Perhaps we should continue this tomorrow. When she's recovered."

"I have a right to question this witness as I see fit, Lund. You can like it or lump it."

The girl spoke. "I understand, Lieutenant." She stood. The silk unfurled and glistened in the light. "Look at this dress, Lieutenant. What exactly do you think a person can get up to in a dress like this? The slightest struggle, and the straps would fall down, I'd trip on my hem and fall over, and this fabric would show every mark of it. Look at me!" Blake looked at the hem of the dress, the heavy silk was mirror smooth where it fell from her hips. A few marks appeared near the hem, but free of any tears or pulls. Penelope sat back down.

McCain sighed. The lieutenant had lost the moment. She was swimming up for air now, leaving Blake below her in the depths. He watched Lund, wondered what the hell the man was up to.

"My mother hasn't done anything wrong. Neither have I. Introduce me to the woman who can break a person's neck at a moment's notice without chipping a nail or putting a ladder in her hose—I'd like to meet her."

"You could have paid her off. Sent her away."

"Mary and I did wonder if we could convince her to leave Charles. If they hadn't married yet, there was a chance. Especially given how dead set my uncle was against her. But we were too late. They already married."

Blake shifted unhappily. "She had you hooked good and proper."

"Like a fish on a line," she agreed. "She was going to have a settlement out of my uncle, and support. If there was a child, perhaps more." She shrugged.

"How much did you have on you when you made the offer?"

"Two thousand."

McCain whistled.

"She turned it down?" Blake asked, incredulous. "Two thousand cash?"

"They were married, Lieutenant. She might have gotten

more than that in a month if my uncle wanted them divorced badly enough."

"Badly enough to kill her, maybe?"

"My uncle was in full view from the moment the brawl broke out to when we found her. He couldn't have done it."

"Charles wasn't," Blake added conversationally. "Have you seen him since the fight broke out?"

"What's that?" Penelope's careful control shifted slightly.

"Where were you after you sang?" Blake pressed. "Several witnesses said you followed her out."

"I didn't follow her. There was a fight. A society columnist came into the room and made a scene. Thom picked me up and carried me out when it got to be too much."

"Where did you go then?"

"I looked for my cousin Mary. I helped her as much as I could, but the crowd was exceptionally large. Too large to manage. The men had cleared out most of the brawlers when James found me and told me to get my coat. He and Lund went around the house looking for Mother. When they couldn't find her, we met at the closet and we left through the back. I didn't want to leave Mary, but I had made such a scene earlier that being here was causing her more trouble. James was going to see me home, then come back to help."

"Did you see your mother in the coatroom?"

She gave Blake a quizzical glance. "No, what a strange question! Every coat was on the floor when we came into the room. It took quite a while to realize my fur was missing."

"I understand the victim was wearing it."

"Yes."

"Did that surprise you?"

Penelope laughed. "Surprise me that she stole my coat? No, it did not, Lieutenant Blake. Sadly, it was exactly the kind of thing she would have done."

"It would be helpful if we could take a look at her things. Do you have an address where she lived?"

"I didn't even know she was in New York until I saw her this morning. I couldn't possibly tell you where she was living." A movement caught McCain's eye. Lund had lifted his head to watch Blake, his body as tense as a sprinter on his mark. Blake waited a moment, thinking, considering the girl. McCain watched as the wheels turned.

She stood slowly. "Lieutenant, it's quite late. I'd like to go home."

Blake nodded, but she was already moving, the dress flowing around her like molten ore. Lund opened the door before she reached him, his eyes flashing from the shadow.

"Can I ask you just one more thing?" Blake came around the table.

"Of course."

"Why did you sing?" Blake moved in close to her, leaning his hand on the table so his head was level with hers and only a few inches away. McCain thought it was a cheap trick designed to unnerve her, more in line with what boys they left back at the precinct would have done. Somewhere in McCain's blind spot, Lund cleared his throat.

"Isn't it obvious? I wanted to show her up." She turned to go.

Blake stopped her with a hand on her arm. "You know what I think? I think you were rubbing her nose in it. Whatever it was she had on you."

She waited. Blake held on to her just a moment too long, long enough for McCain to feel embarrassment for the man. His hand fell, he stepped back. "Perhaps you're right." She shared a rueful smile. "I have quite a temper."

"Carmen was a criminal, wasn't she, miss?" McCain pressed forward. "She ruined the young man and made him run off from his job as a policeman."

Penelope moved toward the door, the dress flowing out behind her. Lund met her just before the door, gently taking her by the arm. "Carmen was many more things than just that," Lund said. She looked up at him, her face suddenly bare of control. She softened, concentrating only on Lund. Her body shifted slightly toward him, her entire posture easing into comfort like an exhale after a deep breath. Whether she loved him now, McCain couldn't say. But she had loved him. It was there. McCain watched them go.

Blake mopped his bald head with his handkerchief. "You've heard this *Carmen* opera before, have you? What kind of woman are we talking about?"

"I would have thought the victim fit the bill more than this one. Carmen is a criminal, runs with a gang, smugglers, I think. A bad egg."

"And what happened to her?"

"She was murdered."

The lieutenant stood with his feet wide and stared at the carpet for a moment, thinking. "All right, Jasper," he said finally, "let's have a word with Harry Staughton. I want to know if he knew his only son had married a gold digger."

23

HARRY STAUGHTON AND LIEUTENANT BLAKE considered each other from across the west parlor. Harry's size made him loom over the carved mantel, his black hair and beard unruly against the sweeping line of the marble. His dinner jacket only emphasized his bulk and protruding hands, each the breadth of a salad plate. McCain took out a notebook as Blake seated himself across from Staughton and wondered how long it would take for Harry to offer him a bribe. Staughton glowered at McCain. Something about him struck McCain as out of the ordinary. It wasn't his build or his hair. It was his eyes. They had the look of a man who had lost his grip and his temper. McCain considered sitting on one of the chairs by the door, blending into the background, but he changed his mind. He positioned himself to Staughton's right instead, where the man wouldn't forget he was there.

"I'll try to make this as quick as I can. We believe the victim was killed between nine and ten in the evening. Can you tell us where you were at that time?" Blake kept a careful distance.

"I told your man outside everything I know. Why don't you ask him?" Sweat stood out on Harry's forehead, but he still shivered like he had a cold.

"I'm afraid I have to ask you all over again," Blake replied calmly.

Harry shifted uncomfortably. He stared past Blake's shoulder to the shut door. "How much longer will the body be there? My daughter is in the house. I don't want her to see such a thing! Murder." He shuddered. Taking a handkerchief from his pocket, he wiped his mouth and forehead.

Blake looked up. "Several guests have mentioned that the victim had married your son. Were you aware of their engagement?"

"No." Harry shut his mouth against the word and looked as though he would not open it again. Blake waited him out, first flipping pages in his notebook, sitting quietly staring at the man. Finally, Harry spoke with a sharp exhale. "My son has certain irrepressible qualities. He can make his mind up quickly to do a thing, then regret it not very much later. I assure you, Lieutenant, this marriage would have been such a thing." Harry's glare was so menacing that McCain lowered his notebook and took a step closer to the mantel.

"It's my job." Blake was calm. "I must ask these questions. As a man of the world, you understand they come easier from me than they do from the next man who asks."

"And who is the next man?" Harry demanded.

"The district attorney."

"I hardly knew the girl! The house was full of people. Any one of them could have killed her!"

"It is your belief, then, that someone at the party killed your son's wife?"

"Of course not, you imbecile! It was a robbery. Can't you see the truth in it?"

Blake just managed to hold his temper. "I see. Were you aware the victim was wearing a necklace given to her by your son?"

"Yes!" Harry stopped moving, planting himself on the carpet nearer to Blake, his legs wide apart. "It was a pearl necklace my son bought her, with matching earrings. Did you find them?"

"Not yet."

"Now, do you see? That's what it must have been. She was robbed of her jewelry and left for dead!"

"Expensive?" Blake asked.

"According to my son, he spent his last dollar on it." Staughton brought his fist down on the mantel. The vase at the end of the shelf rattled. "Damn that boy!"

"I understand there were over a hundred guests at the party."

"Not *my* guests! I told you! My daughter had invited family, a few work colleagues. Thirty people at the most. Gate-crashers! Strangers! That's who I had in my house!"

"Did your daughter know your son was going to announce his marriage? Was the dinner a celebration?"

"Are you an imbecile? I had no idea they were married!" Harry crossed his arms. "It isn't a wonder to me they found her dead—but did it have to be in my house?" He threw his hand in the air. "My son has the judgment of an ass!"

"You aren't surprised your daughter-in-law was murdered?" Blake watched the man from his seat, the fury breaking around him as he railed away at top volume.

"Would anything surprise me about that type of woman? I know her kind, Inspector. Trouble!" Ramming his hand into his pocket, Harry controlled himself with difficulty.

"Had you met her before last night?"

"That kind of woman has a reputation. It preceded her everywhere she went!" Harry sputtered, "He kept her from me! If I had known!" He turned away with sudden disgust and held his tongue.

"What would you have done, Mr. Staughton?" Blake relaxed, leaning on the arm of the chair. Harry was silent. "I understand there was something of a brawl during the party. Do you know what happened?"

Harry blustered, "It was the guests, not our type of people! Not our type of people at all! That had nothing to do with us. It was started by a columnist from the *Sentinel*. Trust me on this, Lieutenant, I will be making a call to the *Sentinel* to ensure they know the kind of person they have on their payroll."

"According to several witnesses, your son started the brawl when he struck a guest."

"Lies!"

"I understand your niece may have known the deceased."

"My niece is a very respectable young woman! She doesn't deserve to be dragged into the gutter by the likes of you!"

"I assure you, we are only interested in who murdered your son's fiancée."

Harry snorted and turned his back to the room. "I've told you what I know. Now, you can go."

"Understood." Blake stood. "Now, if you could tell us where we can find your son, Charles."

Harry exploded. "He's been in the room with the rest of them! You must have interviewed him by now?"

"Beg your pardon, Mr. Staughton, but he is not. I've had my men search the house. There's no sign of him. If we don't find him soon, things will begin to look bad."

Harry's face drained of color. "What could you mean by that?" His robust voice was dry, a shadow of its previous bite.

"You have described a volatile young man who just earlier this evening was seen to attack a female reporter with a closed fist. A young man who was incensed when he learned that his wife was already married to another man, and who disappeared around the time we suspect Renee Strong was killed. I am sure you can see, just as we can, how it might look to a jury."

"You think . . . you think . . ." Harry staggered, his breathing rapid and shallow. McCain moved quickly to the man's elbow, Blake taking the other. The two policeman lowered him into a wide armchair. As they sat him down, the blood drained from his skin, his lips turning an alarming color of purple.

"It's an attack," Blake said as he loosened Staughton's tie, unbuttoning the shirt collar so quickly the button popped.

Harry gasped, his hands resting lightly on Blakes arms. "My son . . ." he began.

"You rest here, sir. We'll get a doctor for you."

24

EMPTY OF ITS GUESTS, THE FOYER felt too large, as though it were about to swallow Mary and Penelope whole. Mary's dress hung limp against her, the blue fabric a note too bright next to her drained face. "It's too much." Her hands tightened around each other, then relaxed. "Where is Charles?" Her voice barely above a whisper, she ran her hands over her face, her fingers trembling. "Where could he be?"

Penelope kissed her cousin on the cheek. "I'm sure they'll find him soon. Charles won't have gone far. I'm sure he wandered away to sleep it off somewhere."

"Yes." Mary looked around them as though she expected a wayward guest to leap out from behind the bannister and surprise them both. "He was quite drunk. I've told the police he would never do such a thing."

"Of course he wouldn't! I told them the same thing." Penelope put her hands over Mary's. "I feel as though I am leaving you alone with barbarians at the gate, Mary. I feel I should stay."

"No, you go. It's all right. James is here for Papa, and the police are everywhere. Your friend Mr. Lund says he is coming straight back to help us look for Charles. Besides, you must get home to your mother." Mary drew the collar of the mink cape together at Penelope's neck and said, "It's far too short for you, but it will do for the ride to the hotel." She lost her composure and laid her head on Penelope's shoulder. "Oh! I can barely take it in! A dead woman outside and Charles missing! What will the papers say? What will happen to Papa's business?"

Penelope wrapped her arms around Mary, holding her close. "I know something about newspaper coverage. It will be bad at first, but it will get better. I promise it will."

The front door opened, giving Mary a start. Lund appeared, closing the door against the flash of camera bulbs. Penelope heard them smashing against the pavement as the photographers switched them out, getting ready for the next guest to appear.

"I've gotten us a ride to the Excelsior." Lund said quickly. "I couldn't find a cab, but one of the guests has agreed to drive us back. His car is waiting just outside." A fist wrung her stomach as Penelope considered the phalanx of photographers at the step. "The police will help us get to the car. We must be quick."

Penelope nodded. "I will come back, Mary. As soon as I am sure Mother is all right. I promise."

Mary smiled sadly, her small face tired and drawn. "I will be here."

Lund took Penelope by the arm and placed his hand on the door. "Are you ready?"

It was as though she had plunged herself into a bucket of flashing sharks, their teeth sharp, their tails lashing out to grab and push and startle. She lifted Mary's fur and covered her face against the flashbulbs, the mob's displeasure obvious at once in the tremble of the words and questions.

From the corner of her eye, she realized that more than just newspapermen stood on the step. Regular people stood alongside, shouting and maneuvering to get a better look. She heard her name from a dozen different voices. The two policemen only just held them back, the bodies pressing in from all sides as the cameras flashed and the bulbs broke against the pavement. "Was it murder?" "Who died?" "Was there a killing?" "Mrs. Ambrose! Look this way!" "Miss Harris, say hello!" The voices called out all around her while the crowd surged and buffeted them. When they reached the car door, they were at first thrown up against it by the force of the crowd. It took several seconds to open the door properly and get inside. A final yowl went up just as Lund propelled Penelope into the car, the driver pulling away before the door had swung shut.

They were away.

"I MUST ADMIT, I HADN'T considered we would meet again in exactly this way." Alfred Gott sat facing Penelope, his hand holding the strap from the ceiling as the driver took a tight corner. "But I am pleased, just the same."

Penelope fought the urge to look at Lund. "Freddy. I did not know our ride was with you."

"It wasn't." Lund growled. "I got a ride with a friend of James—a John Case."

"John owes me a favor." Gott smiled behind his white mustache. "Besides, I couldn't leave a damsel in distress. Even if she doesn't think highly of me. You must give me a chance to prove myself to you, Penelope."

Penelope felt cold down to her toes. "I know you too well, Freddy. Well enough to know you don't do anything without there being something in it for you."

"Can't I be a good cousin?" The car turned, putting Gott into a dark shadow. "You would have had a devil of a time finding a taxi at this hour, and the crowd was quite rowdy, as you saw." He expelled a quick laugh. "Of course, this would be an opportune moment to discuss some business we have . . ."

"If you don't mind, perhaps we could discuss the matter on another day." Penelope found it hard to keep the tight edge from her words.

"My dear, I wouldn't dream of it." Gott's eyes squinted—from a smile or a grimace, Penelope couldn't be sure. "I was speaking to Thom, of course. We must discuss what you will tell the police."

Penelope looked from one man to the other. "Tell them? Tell them what?"

"Thom has been following me for the New Amsterdam Bank, haven't you?" Gott smiled. "I'm sure it has nothing to do with what happened this evening. But the police might get the wrong idea, if you understand me. I want to know what you told them. Renee told me she saw you on her tail. You gave her quite a scare. Of course, she scared so easily at the end. She had a terrible case of nerves."

"I wasn't aware you knew Renee well enough to realize she was afraid," Lund replied.

"Renee and I were old friends. Weren't we, Penelope? No use hiding it from the police when they were bound to find out one way or another." Gott addressed Lund. "I expect you might have told them anything by now. We hardly had a moment to chat earlier."

Penelope stole a glance at Lund next to her. A light from the street passed the window, putting his profile in stark relief against the darkness outside. His green eyes were unblinking, his whole body focused on Gott. "What would we have to chat about, Alfred?" Penelope realized with a jolt, Lund was angry.

"Why, the investigation, of course. What will you tell the police?"

"In case you need a reminder, I don't work for you."

"That's a shame." Gott shook his head. "I could use a man like you on the payroll. You've only been in New York, what? A year? And look at how far you've come. But after Shanghai, what secrets could a city like New York hold for a man like you?"

Penelope leaned forward in the seat. Without thinking, she put her hand down into the darkness and placed it over Lund's. "No need to worry, Penelope, my dear." Gott chuckled. "Thom isn't in any trouble."

"I should say not!" She straightened. "I would think you would be more concerned about yourself! It won't take long for the police to learn about it. Thom won't have to tell them anything!"

"Renee knew a great many men. I was only one part of a large crowd—an exceptionally large, very notable crowd." He addressed Penelope. "Your husband was one, if I remember correctly."

"Kinkaid is dead and gone, Freddy. If you are trying to scare me, you'll have to try harder."

"I want to know what you told the police." Gott focused on Lund.

"The truth," Lund replied.

Gott shifted. "Go on."

"That I was invited to the party by the family because

I am a friend of Miss Harris's from Shanghai. That I was a policeman in Shanghai, and that I now work for the New Amsterdam Bank."

"That's all?"

"They asked if there was anyone at the party who knew Renee from Shanghai." Lund slipped his hand from Penelope's.

"You're making this so difficult." Gott gestured irritably. "Just tell me what you said!"

"I said that there were several men there who had known her. Including Harry Staughton—and you, of course."

Gott's face hardened. "You shouldn't have done that."

"Generally speaking," Lund replied, "I don't like hood-winking the police. Neither does the New Amsterdam Bank, if it comes to that. My boss will back me. You can call him and hear for yourself if you like."

Gott stared out from the shadow, only the white part of his eye visible. "Give up your clients at the first sign of a police investigation and you won't have any more business."

"You aren't my client. The New Amsterdam Bank is my employer. I can tell the police what I like as long as I protect the interests of the bank." Lund turned his head and met Gott's eye with an unblinking stare. The interior of the car seemed to shrink as Lund's attention to Gott narrowed. "Did you kill her?"

"Certainly not!" Gott pursed his lips with displeasure. "I saw them together at the party. Dear Cousin Harry looked as though he could murder her. I saw him give her money. I'll swear to it, if it comes to that. She gave him an envelope. I'm sure she was blackmailing him." The way Gott caressed the words was almost indecent.

"Was that what you were looking for?" Penelope shot back. "In Uncle Harry's office? What he bought from her?"

Gott rolled his eyes. "You can't blame me for trying to get something on my competition, my dear. Your uncle has been a thorn in my side for years."

"That's low, Freddy! Even for you!"

"I wasn't the only one who saw. It doesn't matter if I tell the police or not, although I do believe I will tell them—just to prove I am a good citizen."

"When did she start blackmailing you?" Penelope shot back, proud of the way she kept her voice despite her nerves.

"Trying your hand at amateur investigations? Would you like to hear my alibi?" Gott practically smacked his lips with pleasure. "I stood by in the west parlor to hear your spectacular performance, then stepped away when the fighting started. Violence is distasteful to me." He smirked. "I was in the east parlor having a lovely conversation with a brute called Mikey-boy Cernoch until the police arrived."

Penelope gave a start.

"Your alibi is provided by Renee's bagman?" Lund asked incredulously.

"Ironic, isn't it? I'm surprised you didn't see him. He couldn't have stood out more. Didn't even wear a formal jacket. Said he was there to protect her. From what, I'm not sure. The man was about as drunk as anyone I've ever seen, and that's saying quite a lot. We stood there talking for quite some time."

"An ex-con who was in prison for manslaughter isn't much of an alibi, Gott."

"So he killed a man. It was in the ring, wasn't it? It was an unsanctioned match. How could he know? My lawyers will make him look like a saint." Gott glanced out the window. "Take us around to the back, driver, where the kitchens are. There might be one or two photographers there, my dear, but not as many as at the front." The car stopped. "So long, Thom. Remember what I said."

25

LUND LED PENELOPE THROUGH A maze of kitchens until they exited from beneath the main stair of the Excelsior. The lobby lights were dimmed. A lone housekeeper on her knees at the foot of the grand stair dried the washed floors with a thick towel, a pile of used rags beside her. Beyond the front desk, a doorman stood with his hands behind his back, looking out through the brass-trimmed glass doors into the street. About a dozen photographers milled about on the sidewalk like a school of feeding fish just on the other side. They watched the oncoming traffic with unforced concentration, waiting for a taxi that would never come.

Lund stayed between Penelope and the street as they crossed the lobby to the elevator bank tucked behind the grand staircase, just out of the photographers' sights. Only the housekeeper at the stairs seemed to notice them. If she thought it was unusual to see a woman and a man arriving at the hotel at 3 a.m., she kept it to herself.

As they rode up, Penelope sagged, leaning her head

against the polished brass. "Almost there," Lund said quickly. "Just hold on a moment or two longer."

"That horrible man." She spoke to the floor.

"Don't think about him. He isn't worth your time."

"He ruined us. Gott. Did you know?" Her voice came from far away. "When my father tried to sell the business, Freddy blocked its sale to Chinese investors. Had it voided before they could take charge. It ruined us. My father's health—he couldn't take it. It killed him." The color had gone out of her face. "Are you working for him?" She kept her eyes on the floor.

"No. It's exactly what I said in the car. One of the bank's customers was being blackmailed . . ."

The elevator doors opened before he could finish. Penelope exited the small space with a long stride, her apartment key out and ready for the lock. The door opened before she reached it, a white-uniformed nurse on the other side. Leaving Lund to explain, Penelope went straight through the door to her mother, not even stopping to remove Mary's borrowed fur cape.

A small lamp on the bedside table cast a dim light on the bedspread. Eleanor lay still with her face just outside of the light, a white-blonde plait laid over one shoulder. Sleep had wiped Eleanor's face smooth of worry, making her look ten years younger. Penelope took her mother's hand and knelt. "Mother, are you awake?"

"Penelope?" Eleanor opened her eyes. "I have a terrible headache. I'm sure it was the champagne. I shall speak to Harry."

Penelope paused, uncertain. "Mother?"

"I suppose that wasn't a very good joke, was it? Don't worry." Her mother patted her hand. "James says I've had a bad knock on the head, but I will be all right." Eleanor shut her eyes again.

"He'll be a good doctor." Penelope felt the burn of tears. They would find the money somewhere, wouldn't they? She laid her forehead on the side of the bed, the tears rolling down her nose.

"Your makeup will run," Eleanor warned her quietly. "And what will Mr. Lund think?"

What was the point of keeping any secrets from her mother?

"I heard him talking to the nurse just now. James is a tenor. Your policeman is a definite baritone. Very soothing."

"He isn't my policeman." Penelope sniffed.

"Use my handkerchief, for goodness sake." Eleanor removed her hand from Penelope's and patted her shoulder. "Not your policeman? Use your brains, girl. I know you have them. Now, change out of that dress and into something warm—your hands are as cold as ice!"

LOOSENING HIS TIE, LUND TOOK comfort from the small-ness of the living room, the practical furniture and the small mementos from China surrounding him. It was the opposite of the Staughton house in every way. The couch made for comfort, not appearance. A worn red rug from the Chinese provinces clashed with the cheerful print of the armchairs.

Irregular books on shelves lined the walls in a jumble of color, a small watercolor of L'Opera Comique in Paris the only break in their stacks. And just there on the mantel, a framed photograph of David Harris standing with a pipe in his mouth and his hands in his pockets, smiling for the camera. In the midst of the jumble, the photograph clearly had pride of place. It was the first thing anyone saw when they stepped through the door. David's image did the rest. That he had a striking intelligence was clear from the photo. His eyes held the viewer with a notable charisma. Lund almost couldn't help himself when he said, "Don't worry. I have good intentions."

Pulling himself away, he moved to the window and looked down into the street. A crowd twice the size of the one in front of the Staughtons' had gathered. The *Special Edition* must have published. These are gallows watchers, he thought. The mildest rumor of murder could create the effect. Everyone wanted to see what a killer looked like. He took off his coat and threw it across a chair, relieved to have his arms and shoulders free. A crystal decanter caught his eye. From the smell of it, James or Penelope had been able to find an excellent source for alcohol. This was the real McCoy, come right through the Long Island Sound, straight from the Bahamas. He swallowed the whiskey at once and poured himself another.

When he turned back, he saw her standing there in the doorway with the light behind her. She stood completely still, her hair a strange halo against the light, her face in darkness. Penelope had changed out of her dress and into pajamas. He could see the pants peeking out past the bottom of a man's heavy tartan robe. Her face was cleaned of makeup, the glittering silk and diamonds put away. "Feeling better?" he asked.

She nodded, stepping into the room. "I won't turn on a light," she said. "It feels more peaceful, I think, in the dark." She sat on the couch, curling her legs beneath her. "It will be morning soon enough."

"How is Eleanor?"

"She seems fine."

Lund gestured to the cupboard with his glass. "Nightcap?"

She nodded.

He found a second glass and poured the whiskey, giving it to her straight. He sank into the couch with a sigh.

Penelope stared at the bottom of her glass. "Is it true, what Gott said about Renee? Was she making a fool of Uncle Harry?"

"Regardless of whatever she did or did not do, Gott is sure to tell the police as soon as he can. He and your uncle have been at each other for years."

"It will ruin Uncle Harry." Penelope took a drink. "What did she have on him?"

"Any number of perfectly ordinary crimes, I'm sure." Lund felt the whiskey doing its work as a muzzy relaxation came over him. "Renee had a strange talent for finding the weak spot in a person's character."

She spoke across him. "What will happen now?"

"The police will ask questions until they find the killer."

"But what if they can't?" She angled herself toward him. "What if they never find out?"

"Someone killed her, Penelope. The police always find out."

"Not always." She took a drink, looked away.

"Yes, but you're thinking about Kinkaid. That was different. There is what you know and what you can prove in court. They are completely different circumstances."

He could only see her profile in the dark. She was oddly calm. "How so?"

"The police knew who killed Kinkaid. They just couldn't say so. Couldn't prove it."

"That's ridiculous, Thom! I'm surprised at you! If the police had known who Kinkaid's murderer was, they would have made an arrest." Even in the dark he could see the blood drain from her face.

"You have nothing to fear anymore, Penelope. If the police had wanted to charge you for killing your husband, I would have arrested you myself when I found you passed out with your finger on the trigger."

26

"You shot Kinkaid. Four times in the chest and once in the head." Lund took a deep drink, stopped, and asked himself, "Was it four and one? Yes, it was. Because there was one bullet left." He exhaled. "It has been a long night. I'm not myself." He added after a thoughtful pause, "Kinkaid was a terrible criminal. He should have been banged up a dozen times and would have, too, if he hadn't had you to help him. You outwitted us every time. If you hadn't done that, he would be rotting away in jail in China right now. Of course, that would have meant he would have lived. And I've never met a bastard who deserved a bullet more. But that's behind us. Can't think of what might have been." He sighed, the weight of the evening creeping into the darkness all around them.

"I was on the beat when I heard the shots. I was loitering like a lovesick fool. Or maybe I just knew what a bastard Kinkaid could be. Lucky. I didn't believe in luck before that night, still don't." Lund stood, refilled his glass. "You were half-dead but breathing. I guessed you had passed out from the pain, or maybe the blood loss. I made sure you were alive. I went inside and saw the rest."

"He found out. No, he suspected," she corrected herself. Then she laughed with bitter sadness. "None of that is right." She opened her eyes and looked away from him to the windows. She took a deep breath, this one a little stronger than the last. "He was always jealous. I can't remember what I had done to make him suspect—" She broke off. "He knew there was someone. I didn't even have a chance to tell him I wanted a divorce." She couldn't finish.

"He found out about us, didn't he?" The knot in Lund's stomach tightened as he watched her.

Penelope stared into the glass in her hand. She sighed. "I've tried to think what it was. Why was it that night? There wasn't any way he could have known I was leaving him." Her voice was a quiet rustle in the darkness. "He told me he was going to kill me one way or the other. Have the Jade Tiger all to himself." Lund heard the words catch in her throat. She put her hand to the scar on her face, looked away into the shadow of the room, remembering.

"You shot him five times." Lund's words were quiet, calm.

"Yes." She struggled with the words. "I can't explain it. I thought . . . I thought he would get up."

Grasping for her cold fingers, Lund leaned forward, his words more urgent. "I took care of the gun. Made sure they would never find it." Taking her hand in both of his, he said, "I told my brother, of course. We've never had secrets from each other. Obviously I couldn't be a policeman anymore."

"Matthias knows?" Fear flashed across her face. "Do they hang women in China? I must say, I don't know."

"Didn't you hear me? I said I took care of it."

"That's why you left China. Why you aren't a police officer." Penelope covered her mouth with a hand, just catching the sound of the sob as it escaped. "Oh! What have you done? What have I done?"

His thumb ran across the inside of her wrist. "If I was meant to be a policeman, it wasn't meant to be in Shanghai. I don't regret it."

It was odd the way he could read her mind, know every thought. She took her hands away. "I killed a man, Thom. Murdered him."

"That's not how I saw it. You forget, I was the one who found you. Kinkaid beat you half to death. I still don't know how you lived to see the morning. You'd lost so much blood." Lund's logic cut through her thoughts. "But the authorities would have never seen it as self-defense. Not with all the carrying on he had done with Renee. I couldn't bear the thought of you in prison. Especially there. Someone had to help you. I was glad it was me."

Penelope took a deep breath. "Renee was there." She

wiped her eyes, which she kept on the floor, unable to look into his face or speak to him directly. "She saw it all."

"Why am I not surprised?"

"When he hit me . . . she laughed. I remember that." Penelope put her hand to her ear, her fingers hovering over the faint scar. She pulled herself together and looked him in the eye. He had to understand. She had to tell him what she had done to her husband. "Thom, he left me there on the ground. I could have gotten away. Taken the car to the police station at the docks. But I didn't. I waited for him to come back." She paused. "Father taught me how to shoot. I didn't miss." They sat there a moment, the words filling the space between them. "Does your brother know . . . everything?"

"Yes. I needed his help." He looked down at his glass. "Nothing would have saved you once the Crown set their prosecutors on the investigation. You killed your husband in a jealous pique. That would have been the story, with Renee the prime witness for the prosecution. If I hadn't done what I did, you never would have left Shanghai." He took the last drink from his glass. "Pretty soon Blake is going to start picking away at Shanghai." Lund barely recognized his own voice when he continued. "There's no reason for them to suspect anything if we're careful."

Penelope searched his face. He watched as the facts began to come together for her. He was in love with her and everyone knew it. He had covered up the murder, done things only a policeman would have known to do. He was first on the scene when the authorities came. They would have found him with the body of a man shot with precision, holding the woman everyone knew he loved, beaten half to death. Would anyone believe her if she told them the truth? That she had shot her husband? If they did, what would Lund do?

She spoke. "You're going to tell them you killed Kinkaid, aren't you? And they'll believe you, because they weren't there and they couldn't know . . ."

"Penelope . . ."

The reality of the situation settled in a cocktail of terror and anger. "You shouldn't have done it, Thom. Don't you see? It's why I left, to save you from what would come next. But nothing ever came. I've been living the same day over and over again, certain someone was about to knock on the door and take me away." She shook her head. "You should have let them arrest me. I should have stood trial. It would be better than knowing you gave up your life . . . for me." She took her hand away from his and stood up. "I must fix this. Somehow. I must fix this."

Lund began, "Penelope, I . . ." but she wasn't listening. The telephone rang from the hallway, loud even through the closed door. Penelope went to the phone feeling half-awake, the memories from Shanghai clouding her thoughts.

"Yes?" She looked at Lund from across the apartment, her blue eyes wide. "It's Mary," she said. "They've found Charles."

27

McCain stepped out into the courtyard and looked up at the morning sky slowly turning from black to a deep blue. Another hour and it would be daylight. His hands behind his back, he studied the ground around his feet and thought. "Now then," he said to the young scullery maid, "why don't you show me how you went about your work during the party?"

She looked around the little courtyard, her eyes tired. "There weren't enough glasses. We were washing them as soon as they came back. Me washing, Petey drying. The rags began to pile up some. Plus the napkins and things were coming back." She paused.

"Cook told you to take them away?"

She nodded bleakly. "There wasn't no one here when I left the kitchen. I would've seen 'em."

McCain nodded, looked up at the sky. "Of course," he said finally. "Plus, it was dark."

"Very dark," she added. "Mr. Parker turned off all the lights, so no one would see the benches and get ideas."

"So, you had your towels and things. Where did you take them?"

"In there." She pointed at the garage with a limp hand. "It took two trips. Then I had to sort the rags so the laundry could know what to do with them. The napkins need to be starched, see? But not the rags. Cook is very particular about the laundry. It took some time to get it right. I had to rub the soap into the stains on the napkins if I found them. That keeps them white."

"About how long, would you say?"

"Twenty minutes?" She screwed up her eyes when she looked at him. With something of a shock, McCain realized she was about twelve years old. "When I came out, the woman was sitting right there." She nodded to the bench. "She looked like she was sleeping. I told Mr. Parker." Her story came to a halt.

"Did you hear anything while you were in the garage?"

"They call it a carriage house," she told him sullenly. "Like they have horses in it?" McCain had the definite impression she was posing the statement as a question.

He thought a moment. "Seems fair. Engines have horses, don't they?" He made notes in his book. "Can you show me where you did the sorting? Just so I can have a clear picture of where you were and what you did?"

She led him past the kitchen garden to the garage. They had passed the Rolls and were coming up on the green coupe when McCain glanced through the car window.

It was habit, he told Blake later. There was a bum on his beat liked to sleep in empty cars when it was raining. Sheer force of habit made him look through the window of the green coupe. There, on the other side of the glass, was Charles Staughton. McCain opened the door, and Charles fell out on the concrete, limp and grey.

"Come here, girl!" McCain shouted, hoping to snap her out of it before she fainted, but he was too late. All the starch went out of her body when she saw Charles, and she fell, hitting her head on the concrete floor. Swearing, McCain dug for his whistle and blew it as hard as he could, checking all the while for any sign of a heartbeat.

James Harris came running. Blake barely kept ahead of him as they pushed through the throng of police staring at the body. James removed his jacket, throwing it aside and pushing his cuffs up over a standard army wristwatch. A shoulder shoved McCain to one side as he dug his fingers into Charles's neck. "Keep quiet!" James shouted with authority. The rumbling and pushing around the vehicle stopped.

McCain whispered, "Don't worry, son. He has a heartbeat. He's going to wish he hadn't when he wakes up."

"If he makes it through this, I'm going to kill him," James shot back. He continued rapidly, his sentences broken with brutish swearing he could have only learned in the army. "We must have an ambulance, as soon as possible. He has to go to a hospital." McCain stepped back, watching with a practiced eye as the ambulance intended for Harry was commandeered to rush Charles to the nearest hospital.

"Didn't anyone think to search the garage?" Blake shouted at the top of his lungs, swinging toward McCain with a face like thunder. "Did you search his pockets?" McCain nodded. "Find the necklace?"

"No, Nathan. There wasn't any necklace, or earrings either."

Red faced and sweating, even in the cold bite of the October dawn, Blake began to bark orders. He wanted both cars searched, two men inside the car and a third man watching to find what they might have missed. The laundry room taken apart rag by rag and the trash outside the garage gone through piece by piece and what were they doing standing there? Get on with it!

In a familiar act of defiance, McCain stood still and wrote every word of the instructions in his notebook until he was sure that every patrolman over whom he had seniority was engaged in searching the garage. Then he wandered back out into the garden and stared at the pond, arms crossed. What was so bad about going to the country to be near the water? Why did they have to go and ruin a nice paved yard to show off a few interesting fish that were going to die in February? He remembered the stone bench and stared at it, sucking his bottom lip while he thought. Finally, he called over two of the younger beat cops and instructed them to lift it off the ground. It was part lunacy, part seniority that made him do it. The younger man trapped in McCain's body had a hunch.

It took more of an effort than he had expected. The men couldn't hold the bench in the air but had to place it a small distance away. McCain got on his side and peered into the stonework that the bench hid away from plain sight. The first thing he found was a black suit button trapped in the crack just below the bench, quite clean of dirt. He set it aside with a delicate flourish that telegraphed importance to the other men. The courtyard went quiet.

When Blake came up, he found McCain flat on his belly, using his penknife to tease something from between the bricks. "Look at this," McCain said. "It's in this crevice here. Someone must've pushed it back with their finger trying to reach it." McCain grunted, and the penknife dragged its prey out into the light.

"Don't touch it," Blake said. The policemen stood and

stared, the once-delicate gold wire scraped and mangled by McCain's penknife, but the diamond at its center still brilliant and unbowed. "Have any other brilliant ideas, Jasper?"

 **28**

THERE WERE A HUNDRED QUESTIONS to ask her, but not one was uttered aloud. Penelope retrieved a suit from James's closet and made a call to the front desk for a cab as Lund changed out of his tuxedo. His mind a jumble of unconnected details, he dashed down the eight flights of stairs as though the devil himself were at his heels. Truth be told, Lund was angry with himself. He had never meant to tell her, but now that he had, he couldn't decide if he had done the right thing. He was grateful for the interruption, happy to have a moment to rush away from her and absorb his mind in some other problem.

Lund could barely remember what he had said to Penelope when he left, or what she had said to him. What he could remember was her face. Had he kissed her as he left? He realized that he had. His face burned with the memory that she had kissed him back. What was it she had said? Oh yes, he could hear it now. She said, "It will be all right now." She had looked at him with the firm conviction of someone who knows because the worst has already happened.

Lund wasn't so sure. To him it seemed as though the worst was yet to come.

"WHAT ARE YOU DOING HERE?" McCain gave Lund a quick once-over as he came up the front steps to the Staughton house. In the morning light, the patrolman looked older. "A little late if you were looking for the family. They've all gone to the hospital. Did you hear about the son?"

Lund nodded. "Mary called Penelope. Does he look good for it?"

"I wish I could tell you different, Thom." McCain came down the steps. "It looks bad for the kid. If he pulls through, more than likely Nathan Blake will be waiting with a pair of cuffs."

"Listen, McCain, I know these people. If Blake thinks that Charles did this thing, he's going in the wrong direction."

McCain pursed his lips, looked left and right, up and down the street. "Can't say what Nate is thinking. Keeps it to himself until he's sure. Won't be too much longer in any case. Found an earring. Lab boys think they might be able to find a fingerprint on it. If they do, we'll go through everyone we know was in the house until we find a match. Could take a long time, usually works in the end."

Lund heard heaviness in the words, caution. He fell into step beside McCain as the man started up the street. "Coming off shift?"

"Not yet." McCain checked the time on his watch. "There's a problem at one of those addresses you gave us for the victim. Seems the place had already been tossed when we got there. The super was paid off to look the other way."

Lund felt a gnawing discomfort he hoped didn't show in his face.

"They had some news at the station." McCain took off his cap, smoothing his hair with one hand. "Alfred Gott came in this morning, smooth as you please. Said you had been doing a piece of investigative work for him. Following up on a blackmail job, he said." McCain peered out at Lund from under the brim of his police hat.

"What I told you is true. I was working for the bank, not Gott. He's trying to push you onto me."

"Why would he do that, I wonder?"

"He thinks I'll back him up, that's why."

"I stuck my neck out for you, Thom. I have good instincts, but I'm old enough to know a man can be wrong. You are the only person we know of that knew where the victim had been holing up. Did you give Gott a tip-off?"

"You know where I was all night, Jasper. I didn't give Gott the tip-off on anything. I've got no interest in being bought off by a man like him, or anyone else for that matter."

McCain nodded absently and put his hands in his pockets. "That reminds me. Beautiful girl, Miss Harris. How well did you know her in Shanghai? You know, back when she had a husband? Before he was killed in a, what was it you said, a robbery?"

Lund was silent.

McCain sighed and looked down the street. "I should tell you the lieutenant was all set to call the police commissioner in Shanghai half an hour ago. I hope you told him everything he needed to know, or there'll be hell to pay. He's already got it in for you about Gott. Thinks you might be hiding something else."

"I told you the truth about Gott." Lund's bad mood clipped the words.

"Doesn't matter." McCain studied him. "Truth is, son, no one's a friend when the game's murder." His eyes narrowed. "You were a policeman once. You should know that as well as I do."

Lund nodded. He knew. He knew too well.

29

"Lieutenant, I must take exception to your methods!" Harry's bulk filled the small office, his voice shaking the glass in the window. "Just down this hall my son is fighting for his life!" He pounded the desk with his fist, making the lamp shudder and switch off.

A nurse opened the door and looked in, causing the three men to turn and watch her with silent intensity.

"Is it my son?" Harry took a step toward the door, his fingers stretching out toward her so suddenly that she straightened up and took a step back.

"You should be in a hospital bed, Mr. Staughton. All this exertion isn't good for your nerves."

"I'll decide what's best for me, woman!" Harry shouted, his face turning red.

"There's a man here for the inspector, and a phone call."

Her face froze into an expression of active disapproval. "The doctor will need this room presently," she added coldly. "This is a hospital, after all."

"All right, nurse. This won't take long." Blake nodded toward the door as he spoke. "We won't keep you long, Mr. Staughton."

Harry was silent as he sank into the nearest chair. Blake thought the man looked sick, shrinking into his overly large coat. "What do you want to ask, Lieutenant?" His booming voice barely lifted above a whisper.

"A witness came to the station this morning. Told us you knew a good deal more about the victim than you admitted last night." Blake took a small notebook from his pocket, un-hitching the pencil hidden between the pages.

Harry stared at the floor between them. "I met her for the first time last night. I told you that earlier today."

"I'm afraid that won't do, Staughton." Blake was calm, but only just. "Had you met your daughter-in-law before last night? Please consider your answer."

Harry rubbed his eyes with a massive hand, bringing it down over his face until it pulled hard on his beard. He stiffened and spoke with a harder edge than Blake had recollected. "Who told you? Gott? No, it wouldn't have been him." Harry's eyes wandered around the room as he spoke quietly to himself. "Too obvious for Gott. He does all of his work in the dark."

"Sir, I must ask you again—"

"Yes, I knew her. Damn it all, I knew her." Harry's massive bulk slumped in the small chair. Covering his eyes with one hand, he leaned on his knee with the other. "In China," he said bitterly. "I knew her in Shanghai."

Blake nodded at another police officer, who brought out a notebook and began taking notes. "When was that?"

"Summer . . . 1925." His words were tired. For the first time, Blake saw the grey in his black beard and hair. "My son and I traveled to Shanghai to see about some business dealings we had there." Harry looked up. "She was performing at the Jade Tiger. Singing, dancing, that sort of thing." He asked suddenly, "Have you ever been to China?"

Leaning an arm on a cabinet, Blake was silent.

"It's a strange sort of place, quite unlike anywhere else. It has a special intoxicating enchantment. You would know what I mean if you had been. Everywhere you look there is color, life. So alive and vibrant—like a dream. I've never seen any other place like it. It was a long way from home, Lieutenant. I am ashamed to say that I forgot who I was."

"How well did you know the girl, Harry?" Blake asked.

"About as well as you think I did."

"Well enough to be blackmailed by her?"

"Yes, well enough for that." Harry sighed. "I suppose I should be ashamed of myself. But I can't even manage to find that much regret. Renee was something special in that regard. She could convince you to go wrong, guide you right off the righteous path, and make you feel good about it."

"A witness at the party has made a statement that you threatened her—Renee, I mean."

Harry's eyes narrowed. "It was Gott, then, was it?" He swore loudly. "That bastard!"

"Our witness says you exchanged envelopes with the victim. Did you pay her off?"

"With what? I ask you! With what?" Harry laughed. "My

children have cleaned me out! All that was left was my house, the clothes on my back, and my children's trusts! I've only just come back from the brink of ruin. Did Gott tell you that? There was nothing to pay her off with unless I chose to ruin myself and my children in the process!"

"Then what did you give her?"

"I thought I could trick her. What a fool I am."

"What would you have paid her with? If there was nothing left . . ."

"I am ashamed to admit it, Lieutenant. My niece Penelope gave me a cash loan a year ago, just after she sold the casino. I don't know where she found the money. To be honest, I was damn glad she did. It's keeping me afloat. When my daughter told me Penelope was coming tonight, I thought I would ask her for another loan. But James told me they are broke, maybe even a little worse off than we are." Harry sighed. "I couldn't believe it when she offered the loan in the first place. I wouldn't have blamed her if she had never spoken to me again."

Blake shifted. "What do you mean by that?"

The large man shrugged, making the chair creak. "I introduced her to her husband, Kinkaid Ambrose. I was the reason they met. God help me. A thoroughly bad lot, that man."

"I understood Kinkaid Ambrose is dead."

"He died in Shanghai. He and Penelope were coming home after a late night at their club and were set upon by thugs. When they found Penelope, she was badly beaten and cut along her neck and face. She lost a great deal of blood, but she made it through. She couldn't remember the attack, or even why they were there."

"They ever find who killed him?"

Harry shook his head. "Shanghai might be an intoxicating dream, but behind the façade is some very dirty business. Kinkaid had backroom deals and gambling debt all over the city. Among other things," he added darkly. "After Penelope paid them off, she had herself to worry about. She spent months in a clinic in Munich," he gestured around his face, "for where they cut her. The surgery must have cost her a great deal of money. After what they did to her, you can hardly tell now. I'm not surprised she's broke."

"Are they broke?"

"As close as they can be to it," Harry grumbled.

"Not sure I believe anything you just told me, Mr. Staughton. Unless your definition of broke is different from mine. You must have had a lot of cash lying around to have a party like this one. Not sure if you realize I can get a warrant for your bank records."

Harry's mouth moved wordlessly until he shifted away from the detective uncomfortably and cast his eyes away. "All right. I have money. But I'm not made of it, dammit!"

"They're your family, aren't they? You could help them." Harry didn't answer.

"Followed me? Why on earth would she follow me?"

"Why else would she come halfway around the world? You were paying her off, weren't you?"

"I told you, I had nothing to pay her off with!" Harry broke off as the door to the office opened. A young detective's face appeared around the edge.

"Is it my son?" Harry was across the room in a moment.

"No, sir." The detective nodded to Blake.

"Lieutenant, I must get back to my son. Is there anything else?"

Blake shook his head. Harry stood and hurried from the room without another word. "Who was on the horn?"

"McCain. Says he's got the flatfoot from the bank down at the precinct. He said he's going to wait to go off shift until he hears from you." The detective put his hand in his pocket and smiled.

"That strike you as funny?" From his position against the filing cabinet, Blake gave the detective a look that could make hair go straight. "A little old man busted down to the night shift who comes in every day on time and leaves late? You could do a damn sight worse than looking at him as a model, O'Hara. Fix your damn tie. I don't like slobs in my bullpen." As O'Hara fumbled with the tie, Blake stood straight. "Call him back and tell him to meet me at the M.E.'s office."

"But, boss . . ."

"You have something to say?" Blake stepped up to the younger man. A half head taller, he looked down into O'Hara's face. "You're new around here, so I'll give it to you right from the shoulder. After that it's up to you. I run a clean detective squad—no kickbacks, no free meals, no bribes, and no free passes. You know who I learned that from? That little old man you think is a joke. I didn't want to be in this precinct, but you Joes got yourself in trouble and someone had to bail you out. Every man jack of you but him." Blake put his hands on his waist. "You ever want to know a little bit about Patrolman McCain, you take yourself down to the library and read up about Detective Sergeant McCain in the newspaper stacks. Maybe you'll learn a thing or two about policework!"

He leaned in so their faces were just inches apart. "You know what he did to get busted down?"

O'Hara swallowed his gum. "He made an arrest."

"That's right, Detective. He made an arrest. God help you have as much integrity one day."

30

"It's kind of early for your report, isn't it, Phil?" Mc-Cain had a leisurely posture, his hand in one pocket, his cap pushed back on his forehead. "Lieutenant Blake will be along in a moment." He nodded toward the hallway. "He's washing his hands."

"Early? What do you mean early?" The medical examiner exhaled sharply. Phillip Mercer was a stocky man, but with his cheeks puffed out, the rest of him diminished behind bushy white whiskers and bright pink cheeks. "Didn't the precinct call me up and tell me it was an emergency? Didn't they interrupt my breakfast and tell me I had to do it right away?" McCain was certain he could smell Canadian whisky from the other side of the room.

"Wait for the old man, would you, Doc?"

"Here I am." Blake closed the door behind him and took three steps into the room.

Mercer sat down behind his desk, moved some papers, glanced at Blake from under bushy white eyebrows. "Well, it's murder," he said sullenly.

"No takers, then?" Blake chewed the words off and spat them in the M.E.'s face. McCain found the effort to keep his face blank almost impossible when he heard Blake's tone. He pulled his hat down over his eyes and took out his notebook. Blake's mood had turned black, and once that happened on an investigation, anything could set the man off. It didn't matter how many times McCain reminded him to keep his temper. When Nathan chose his moment, there was no going back. It was going to get him fired one day or busted down like McCain, walking a beat with green cops just graduated from the academy. McCain had managed his demotion through fine Irish stubbornness and the distant memory of his mother crying when she saw him in his uniform. Blake had darker devils chewing away at him. He'd never make it without a lieutenant's badge. Never.

"What do you mean by that!" Mercer stood up from behind the desk, his cheeks puffing in and out feverishly.

The lieutenant smiled. It was a long, slow event that spread out and made itself comfortable. "Well, it's just that I'm surprised, that's all." Blake removed his hat, dropping it on the M.E.'s desk with a flourish that said he didn't believe a word the man said. Spreading his feet and crossing his arms, he continued, "I would have thought a family like the Staughtons would have made a sizeable contribution to the widows and orphans fund by now. He says he's broke, but I bet the niece would put in for a packet."

"I will have you know I am the agent of justice in this city!" Mercer hopped on the balls of his feet, his glasses tilting slightly on his nose as he banged his hand on the desk.

Blake laughed. "Don't get sore."

Mercer glared at the lieutenant. "We disagree once, and you act like it's the end of the world."

McCain cleared his throat. "All right, Doc. All friends here. When did she die?"

Mercer looked warily from Blake to McCain. "I didn't find anything to contradict the window already written on the report. Someone snapped her neck between nine and ten last night. It matches the witness reports the orderlies dropped off." He handed a few pieces of paper to Blake and sat back down.

Holding up the paper, Blake read. "This doesn't say anything about any other injuries. Any bruising anywhere else on her body? Arms, maybe? Her back?"

Mercer sighed, flicked at some of the papers on his desk. "Yes, those will be in the longer report. He hit her once in the abdomen, once on the neck. There's a handprint on her arm where he grabbed her."

"A handprint?" McCain felt a cold surprise.

"He grabbed her hard enough to leave an impression of all four fingers."

Blake put the report back down on the desk. "Raped?"

"Her underclothes had been disturbed, but I don't think he got anywhere with it. Killed her instead." Mercer's voice was quiet. "I swear, Nathan, there are days I wish I never came to work." The little man blinked hard. "She tried to fight back. I'd say it's a good guess she scratched him. She had something under her nails, looked like skin to me. He pulled off her earrings and the necklace after death. One of the earrings ripped the lobe. He was in a hurry."

"What about her? Anything you can tell me?"

"No old injuries; her hands and face were in excellent condition . . . I'd say she was a fairly pampered female about twenty-five years old."

"That definite?"

"Pretty definite—especially after we washed off all the war paint. If she had any ID, that would confirm it."

"Toomey and O'Hara are searching her apartment now." Blake looked up from the paper. "That all, Phil?"

"Nate," Mercer said coldly, "someday you and I are going to have a drink and a long talk about how not all medical examiners are your enemy." He took a breath. "I put it all in the report. You have a copy of it in your hand, so you know nothing is going to change." He added with a flat determination, "I'll testify—if it comes to that."

McCain picked up a copy of the report and began to read the top sheet. A small item caught his eye. "What's this? A button?"

"I found that one up her sleeve," Mercer said. "That's the only button we logged during the examination. I'd say she pulled it off the killer's sleeve while he was attacking her. It's the only way it could have gotten in there." Before Blake could ask, Mercer added with certainty, "I'm sure of it."

"Could it have come from a woman's dress?"

Mercer raised an eyebrow. "I'm no expert, but I'd say it's too plain for that."

"Maybe a man's coat, then." Blake held up the sheets of paper. "All this in the report you just gave me?"

Mercer sucked in his cheeks and shouted, "Of course it is! Why wouldn't it be?"

Blake looked at him ruefully and crossed his arms. His blue eyes were sharp. "Anything else?"

"Only that he's strong, stronger than average, I would say," Mercer held his hands out in front of himself with the fingers stretched out, "with largish hands."

"What about the jewelry we sent down, where are you with that?"

"Do I look like the fingerprint lab, Nathan? For God's sake! Doesn't anyone know their job around here anymore?"

31

THEY STEPPED INTO THE MIDDAY sunlight with the air of men coming up from deep water. McCain pulled his jacket straight with a quick tug and glanced at his boss.

Blake smoothed his mustache with his left hand. His face flattened, and for a moment he had the appearance of a much younger man, taking McCain back fifteen years. Then, blinking, Blake took a breath, the years coming back fast. His heels striking the pavement with crisp insistence, he put his hands in his pockets and started down the street, McCain coming alongside him with an easy stride. "Leave it to me to catch a case about a dirty blackmailer. I was back at my desk for half an hour this morning and got three calls from the district attorney's office. I had to leave just to get some peace!"

"Think it's made someone nervous?"

"You know the blackmail racket in this city. If Renee

Strong had a secret talent for it, she could have made any number of unfriendly people unhappy. Especially if she was edging in on someone else's game. Her apartment was tossed, did they tell you?"

"They did." McCain watched the crowd around them.

"Must have been someone looking for her stash. Get your head out of your notebook, Jasper. I'm not saying a woman did it. All it would take is someone thinking Miss Harris was being hurt or taken advantage of—someone like her brother, for example. Or her uncle."

"What about Charles Staughton?"

"Him!" Blake snorted. "Couldn't have a better suspect! Renee stood him up in front of the world and humiliated him! Charles Staughton is either guilty as sin or a fool. I can't decide which. Maybe both."

"The whole party saw him roughhousing with Mrs. Anthony Stone." McCain tucked his notebook into his pocket and thought it over as they walked along. "Wouldn't be the first time a dopehead put his hands around a woman's neck."

"Or the last," Blake added darkly. "If one of the family killed her, why take the necklace? Strikes me it isn't the kind of thing they would notice."

"Could have taken it to make it look like robbery."

"With all those people around? There wasn't much time to get the deed done, and once it was done, even less to fix things."

"Times are tough all around. You never know what a person will do."

Blake nodded and moved on. "Then there's the victim." Blake stopped, making a sudden movement with his hands.

"By God, I think about the planning she must have put in to have them by the hair the way she did!"

"Couldn't have been clearer. Once they announced the engagement, the whole family would have to work to keep Strong's past quiet to save themselves. That's enough motive for all of them. That's motive enough for me."

"That's the thing." Blake punched the air with a finger. "It's eating at me. Renee Strong could have stayed there after the performance. She already had them over a barrel. All she had to do was stick around and introduce herself to a few people as his fiancée. Instead, she gets a coat and leaves the back way . . ." Blake let the words trail off into nothing. "Why?"

"Doesn't seem in character to slip away unnoticed," Mc-Cain agreed. "Especially with the crowd so rowdy. Things were just getting exciting."

Blake grunted. "Do we have a complete list of the guests yet?"

"It's not going to be easy. There were gate-crashers and invitations sent out by the victim that the Staughtons didn't know anything about. We've got the list from the sister, though. The boys are making calls now. Listen, Nate, could be worth it to follow up on the name Lund gave us last night: Mikey-boy Cernoch."

"The boxer? Gott mentioned him too—even used Cernoch as his alibi. What the hell was he doing there?"

"Thom said he was muscle for Renee Strong and pinned him as her bagman for the blackmail. He saw them together yesterday morning in the park."

"And Lund was tailing Strong?"

"That's what he said."

"Wait a minute." Blake held up a finger as they walked forward in silence.

"What are you thinking?"

"That Lund might feel a little responsible for the Harris girl. He might not take it so well if she's being blackmailed by a woman he knows is a crook. What happens if he sees them together? Maybe he loses his cool . . ."

"You mean Thom?" McCain snorted. "I've never seen the man get angry."

"Doesn't mean he can't, Jasper."

McCain grunted, his eyes on the pavement in front of them. "We already know Mikey-boy was at the party because Alfred Gott mentioned him too. Gott said they were speaking to one another between nine and ten. Kind of hard to miss the man. He wasn't wearing a boiled suit, and, you know," McCain pointed to his head, "he's missing part of his ear from that fight with 'Fighting Ray' Rohm. Thom says the girl hired Mikey for protection." McCain eyed Blake. "If Mikey-boy knew she had two g's in her purse," he shrugged, "who knows what he'd do? Could be we're overthinking it. What if this was a simple robbery?"

"You think he's good for this?"

"He was locked up for manslaughter, wasn't he? And that wasn't in the ring either. Beat a man to death in a street fight."

"That was manslaughter. This was cold murder. That's a different kind of animal, Jasper."

"Not for nothin', but two thousand dollars is two thousand dollars."

"What about the way he worked her over before she died? It was personal."

McCain pursed his lips. "Okay. So, it goes like this. Miss Harris sings, and Renee Strong leaves the party. She helps herself to a coat, leaves the back way. Our lad sees her, follows her. Wait a moment. Do we agree it's a lad?"

"Can't see it any other way."

"All right then. It had to be a split-second decision to follow her. Why? Could have been the money, could have been she was blackmailing him. Couldn't have planned it. There was too much in the way—Mrs. Anthony Stone, Miss Harris singing. He must have decided right there to chance it."

Blake picked up the narrative. "He catches her in the back, just before she gets away. Grabs her by the arm."

McCain nodded. "Okay, she fights back, and he gets mad. He loses a button. Two of them."

"Mad enough to break her neck?"

"Sure. Maybe it was an accident. Or maybe he meant to do it. But he does it. Now it's done. She's dead."

McCain shifted his weight. "What does he take first? The necklace? Or the cash?"

Blake stopped walking. "Necklace first, grabs the earrings, drops one. Then the cash."

McCain was thoughtful. "Unless it was the kid—Charles Staughton. He might have followed her out, seen she was leaving, and lost his temper. But it doesn't figure for the money. He didn't have any on him. Or the jewelry."

"Or his father, Harry Staughton." Blake laughed to himself. "My money is on him if we're talking about an act of passion. Renee Strong was holding onto the dynamite, would've sunk him."

"Witness statements place him at the front of the house at the time of the murder."

"Easy enough," Blake said placidly. "He comes from the front to the back through the alley, sees the girl, and loses control." Blake stopped walking for a moment. "I can't get my mind off your boy Thom Lund. Seems to me he's the one we should be considering. It's as plain as day: he's in love with the Harris girl. He doesn't have an alibi, but he does have one hell of a motive."

McCain frowned. "Why would he do it, a man like that?"

"Love, if he wasn't practical. Blackmail if he was. Maybe the victim was blackmailing him on the side, keeping him on a tight leash. Lord knows more than one good man has made a mistake he had to pay for. It would pay well for a woman like that to have a former policeman on her list." Blake sucked his teeth. "They're all lying. I can feel it."

"I can't bring myself to believe Lund would do it. It's just a feeling. Call it gut instinct."

Blake gave his full attention to McCain, stopping in the middle of the sidewalk. "Gut instinct, huh? Well, how about this for a scenario?" Blake pushed the hat back on his head and looked down at McCain. "He'd been watching Renee, hadn't he? What if she saw him and decided to work him over as a mark? They were both in Shanghai at the same time. Makes sense she would know things about him. Left suddenly, didn't he? Maybe there's something there, something only she knew? When she sees him at the party, she makes her play and he kills her. When you think about it, it makes sense. After he kills her, he takes the jewelry and the money to make it look like a robbery, then disappears down the alley, drops the money and the necklace in the garbage, and reenters the house at the front. He's a former policeman. He'd know what to do."

"See here, Nathan," McCain protested, "what could Thom have done to be in so deep to a woman like that?"

"I don't know. Murder the Harris girl's husband, maybe?" Blake watched McCain carefully. "If I were a betting man, I'd say your man Lund did it. He was first on the scene the night Kinkaid Ambrose died, remember? He admitted it. He also said they never found anyone for the crime."

"If he did kill Renee Strong, he was a pretty cool customer, to do something like that, then hang around the body for another four, five hours, talk to the police like it's nothing, even offer up evidence that incriminates him. He led the bunch of them right to the body when they walked through the house. Why would he do a thing like that?"

"He didn't have a choice, did he? Mary Staughton was leading them to the back of the house herself."

"Nathan, I'm not saying I've never been wrong, but I know the man and I'd bet my badge he wouldn't do any of those things."

"I don't like it. I'd like it better if he was held for questioning until we heard back from China." Blake exhaled so his cheeks puffed out. "You believe he had nothing to do with it?"

"That's what I said." McCain waited.

"All right, he's your baby, Jasper," Bake said finally. "You're responsible for him from here out. Make sure you know where he is and what he's doing until I make up my mind about him."

McCain shifted his weight and sighed. "All right, he's my baby." They began moving again, slowly making their way downtown. "Anything else you want done while we're at it?"

"Yeah, I got a list." Blake waited a moment while McCain retrieved his pencil and the small notebook from his pocket. "Okay. Tell one of the kids to take that button you found down to Phil. Ask if it's a match to the one he has. Then get some of the boys to start comparing them to the boiled suits. Start with Charles Staughton. It's a cert the nurses kept his clothes when they brought him in. Then I want you to ask around and see if you can dig up a lead on where Mikey-boy is holed up. If you find him, take a couple of the boys to bring him in. If he was keeping an eye on the victim, he might have an idea of who wanted her dead." Blake shoved his hands into his pockets and picked up the pace, lengthening his stride with energy. "I'll put O'Hara on the victim's apartment. Although there isn't much hope there since Lund gave the game away to that heel Alfred Gott."

"Lund said the girl did her banking at a savings and loan downtown. Had a box. He gave me the number of it and a couple of other places to look." McCain did not look up from the page.

"That means a warrant. I'll take that one." Blake thought for a moment. "Better circulate a drawing of the necklace to all the usual places."

"If the murderer hasn't already used the two thousand to get out of town."

"Put someone on making sure the report includes a photograph of the button Phil found. Then I'll meet you back at the precinct at four to question Penelope Harris. I have a few more questions for her. " The lieutenant looked over McCain's shoulder at his neat writing. "Well, that enough for you?"

"I'd say so. Where are you headed?"

"To get a warrant, what do you think? Listen, Jasper, you still on nights?"

"In perpetuity," McCain shut his notebook with a flip, "as you know very well, Nathan."

"Well, you're on this until I say otherwise. You been up all night. Can you handle that?"

McCain thought a moment. "If I need it, I can get a couple of hours on the cot in the locker room."

Blake nodded. "Sure, after you find Cernoch."

"Sure, Nathan. After I find Cernoch."

32

ELEANOR SAT WITH HER BACK straight and her heels crossed, her hand on Harry's right arm. Beside her, Harry Staughton looked away toward the wall, his face a mask of despair. He covered his face with his hand. He spasmed and shook like a man who had been poisoned—his mouth in a grimace, his face wet with silent tears. Penelope found it unbearable to watch.

James was asleep in a chair next to Charles's bed, his hand loosely touching Charles's wrist as though he had been checking the man's pulse when he shut his eyes. Mary sat beside him, her valiant hat quivering as she stared at Charles, willing him to live. In a spontaneous gesture, she reached out her hand for Penelope, who took it, kneeling beside her chair with relief.

"The doctor said we have to wait now," Mary whispered. "They've pumped his stomach. He must have had something before he came to the party. I told the doctor it couldn't have been the champagne," she added earnestly. "It was French. I had to explain to the man we've had it since before Prohibition began." She patted Penelope's hand. "Thank you so much for coming. It's good to have a friend here."

Penelope leaned forward. "Is there anyone you would like me to call? Any person who would be helpful to you?"

Mary expelled a quiet, bitter laugh. "All my friends disappeared as soon as the *Sentinel* was published this morning. You can't expect much when your new sister-in-law shows up murdered, I suppose. I had calls all morning canceling lunches, fetes, parties, fundraisers. It seems that a cold is striking down all my close acquaintances. I expect there will be more when I go home."

"But, Budgie, they couldn't think you murdered Renee! That isn't possible."

"No, but they think Charles might have, which is as good as the same thing, if you think about it. Let's be honest. I would have killed her myself if I had it in me!" Mary talked on, just shy of hysteria. "My first thought was how relieved I was! That narrows the distance between me and what the murderer must feel, don't you think?" She turned to look at her brother lying perfectly still in the hospital bed. "Once the afternoon papers are out, we are finished socially. I couldn't care less, but it's bad for Papa. Will he have a firm to go back to by the time the afternoon edition runs?"

"Budgie, dear," Penelope whispered. "I am so sorry."

"I should be the one apologizing, Penelope." Mary grasped her hand. "I shouldn't have ever made you come to the party. I suppose we are lucky she didn't take the money, after all. At least there's that."

Penelope glanced at her mother, leaned forward, and whispered, "What are you talking about, Mary? The purse was empty when Mother found it."

"Was it?" Mary's face drained of blood, and for a moment Penelope thought her cousin might faint. "A robbery? Oh, my dear! If it was a robbery, then they can't suspect poor Charles, now can they?"

Penelope tried hard not to show her surprise. It made perfect sense that Charles would have taken the necklace back if he had spent his last nickel on it. And two thousand would have been more than enough to pay for a couple of years hiding out in South America. "I think we are all under suspicion," Penelope whispered. "At least, that was my impression."

The blood flowed quickly back into her cousin's cheeks. Mary pulsed with fresh energy. "No, you'll see. One of those miscreants she invited as a joke attacked her and made off with the money. Makes perfect sense." Mary returned to her brother. "If only Charles would wake up. The doctor said we must wait. Did I tell you?"

It was all her fault. Watching Mary stare at Charles, waiting to see if he would wake up, Penelope couldn't shake the conviction that they wouldn't be there had she kept her troubles to herself. Charles would have never met Renee, and they wouldn't be in the hospital waiting to see if he would live or die. If Charles killed Renee, wouldn't that be Penelope's fault too? If she hadn't eloped, she wouldn't have gone to China with Kinkaid, bought the casino when she came into the inheritance from her grandmother, or met Renee. If only she hadn't done any of it. Her fault. It was all her fault.

Penelope held her cousin's hand fast and whispered urgently, "I wanted to protect you from what happened in Shanghai, Budgie. With Kinkaid. Please believe me." The words were coming easier now. Penelope wanted to tell Mary, explain everything that had happened. Penelope took a breath as Mary looked into her face.

"Penelope," Eleanor's voice punctuated the silence, making both women jump, "I think I will be staying here tonight." She stood and opened her purse. Taking out a small card and a pencil, she wrote on the back of the card and handed it to her daughter. "Could you please go home and get me some things? I don't want to leave Harry."

Penelope thought of half a dozen things she could say but bit them all back. She took the card, embraced Mary and her uncle Harry, then kissed Eleanor on the cheek. Eleanor squeezed her arm and gave her a nod, then sat down next to Harry. James slept through it all, his quiet breathing too faint to hear, his skin the color of milk. Penelope kept her head up as she passed the policeman at the door and hardly looked at his counterpart at the nurses' station.

Penelope walked down the hospital hallway a thousand miles away from the staff who bustled around her. She paused to look at the card in her hand and almost laughed.

Written across the back were two words: *Go home.*

33

When McCain shook him awake, Lund was dreaming about a cedar that grew near the precinct house in Shanghai. Lund walked past it every shift and wondered how old it was, how far the roots went into the ground. He woke from the dream with the sensation that he had forgotten something important behind, the details of the dream disappearing except for the gnarled bark of the cedar hard against the touch of his hand. All around him, locker doors slammed shut like a volley of empty shot.

"I see you've made yourself at home." McCain tipped his hat back and put his hands in his pockets. Policemen in various stages of undress surrounded the cot, their suspenders bright against the blue of their pants. "One of the boys show you back here?"

Lund swung his legs over the side of the cot and smoothed his hair. "They said it was better than sleeping in a cell."

"Not by much. There was a bit of a scuffle last night near the boatyard. We're down a few uniforms. I wouldn't ask if I didn't need someone. I figure I can rely on you." McCain straightened his hat. "Feel up to lending a hand?"

Lund stood and pulled on his suit jacket by way of an answer.

"ALL RIGHT, YOU'VE ALL SEEN THE PHOTO. He's six-two, short hair, with a nose that's been broken more times than I can count and a missing ear. You'd think he'd be hard to miss, but we're in Hell's Kitchen now, gentlemen, so all those things are par for the course. Blow your whistle if you find him, and for God's sake don't shoot the bastard. The lieutenant wants him alive enough to answer some questions. The wagon will stay here while we fan out. Anyone see the man, give the signal and the rest will come running." McCain glanced at the men gathered around him on the sidewalk, putting the faces to names as naturally as he could count. "Poulhaus, you take Macklerow and head down to Sister Red's. See if our man has paid to rest his head on one of her satin pillows. Brown, you take Lamb and head to the Anchor down on the corner. Sully's got a couple of beds in the back that rent out from time to time. If Mikey-boy isn't there, ask around—politely. We're looking for a murderer, not booze, so keep your priorities straight. And if you find the man, don't take him on without the rest of us. Blow your whistle to let the others know. He's a mean cuss when he has his blood up. Warner and Dunn will stay here with the wagon. Keep your eyes peeled and your fists up." McCain nodded crisply. "All right, boys, let's go."

Lund leaned against the paddy wagon for the speech, his hat low over his eyes, his arms crossed. While McCain spoke to the others, he took in the filthy sidewalk piled with trash that overflowed to the street, the faded signs of failed commerce plastered with *Closed* signs and papered-up windows. He doubted that they could see through the glass there was so much grime built up.

"You're with me." McCain was beside him walking past

the wagon, a young patrolman with ruddy pink cheeks coming up alongside him. "This is Patrolman Mike Skinner. He knows this street, so he's coming with us."

Lund glanced at the patrolman as they all walked and wondered how old he was. Twenty? He was wondering what good an inexperienced pair of hands would be when the kid met his glance and grinned. Lund saw a dozen years of street smarts flash by, followed by a hard wink. He didn't worry about the kid after that, falling into step beside them and removing his hands from his pockets so they swung free. He was suddenly aware of the street around him, the detail falling into a crisp image that would haunt him from that day forward.

"Listen, Thom, this is Hell's Kitchen." McCain kept his voice low. "They don't like the law coming down here, so we're walking a line with the local criminals. We're here for Cernoch and that's all. Do what I say and stick close to me." McCain stopped, nodded to Skinner. "This the place?"

The kid slowed his step. "Yeah, Sergeant, this is it."

"I told you not to call me that, Mike. I'm a patrolman now."

Skinner laughed with a squint that told Lund it didn't matter what McCain said. The kid said, "Two entrances, back and front, and an emergency exit through the basement that comes up next door. Mabel keeps a shotgun behind the counter for when things get rowdy. Last I heard, this was Shannon's gang's territory, but no way they'd be here now. Too early in the day." Skinner added, "Shannon always eats lunch with his mother," and chuckled.

"God love a gangster who loves his mother." McCain

stopped walking. "All right, Thom, here's where you pull your weight. This is the only speak that stays open at this hour of the morning. If Mikey's drinking, this is the only place he could buy a bottle. We need someone to go in there and have a look, see if he's there. Skinner will go with you. I'll wait around front in case you flush them out." McCain looked at their faces and nodded. "Well now, get to it."

34

LUND WALKED DOWN THE ALLEYWAY to the rear of the building, the buttons on James's jacket pulling where the fit was too small. When he got to the heavy metal door, he knocked with a free hand and waited in the damp shadow of the building, his mind a disciplined blank slate. There was a knock from the inside of the door. A muffled, heavy voice, rich from a lifetime of tobacco, said, "Yeah, what is it?"

"Applesauce." Lund consciously deepened his accent as he leaned toward the door.

"What was that?"

"I said, applesauce."

A long pause followed, for which Lund stood perfectly still and thought of nothing at all. He was about to knock again when he heard the lock shift and the door opened a crack. An eye and a nose appeared. Lund was carefully appraised. "I don't know you, brother."

The hair on the back of Lund's neck stood on end. Instinct

pushed his foot through the opening in the door, forcing it open. His left grabbed the smaller man by the shoulder as his right pushed past to hit the man once on the chin, knocking him out.

Swinging open, the door revealed a small storage room stacked floor to ceiling with crates and boxes. In their midst was a narrow cot, an ashtray where a cigarette burned alongside a folded racing sheet, and an army blanket. Holding the man up by the collar, Lund laid him down on the cot and covered him up, pushing the ashtray out of the way of the blanket with his foot. Replacing his hat, he nodded to Skinner and started down a narrow hallway that smelled intermittently of piss and mold and damp earth. Ahead of him was an unlatched door, the sound of someone changing the channels on a radio coming from the other side. Lund had been to speakeasies before, but none of those had left him with the impression that he was blithely walking into someone's living room. They crept closer to the door, listening to the conversation just on the other side. He heard Skinner whisper, "Looks like I figured wrong. That's Jack Shannon behind the bar." Lund nodded.

"You've been drinking smoke in the Bowery, Mikey-boy." They could just see Jack Shannon through the peephole. He was almost the size of Mikey, with arms the size of jackhammers. If size wasn't his advantage, his sobriety was. Shannon crossed his arms and leaned back out of their sight. The rest of the room was blocked from view. Lund wondered how many men could be sitting there watching.

Mikey groaned. "I feel like I'm dyin', Jack. Feels like my insides are turnin' inside out."

"Then you need a doctor. Run along and get yourself a quack down at the city hospital, why don't ya? I can't make you well with what I got!"

"I'm gonna be sick." Mikey followed this declaration with the act. The small room filled with the scent of gasoline.

"Jesus! You're stinking up the place!" The bartender leaned over the edge. "That's it. I want you out of here." He threw a rag at the drunk man's head. "Clean that up!"

Mikey reached into his pocket, his fingers too numb to find the opening easily. "I'll make it right, Jack." The words slid together until there was no room between them. Mikey pulled money from his jacket and put it on the bar, slapping it down with a bang. "See that? I bet that makes it right." Mikey leaned an elbow on the bar and swayed. "I gotta get to the hospital. I need help, Jack. I can pay you."

Jack looked at the money. "Where'd you get money like that?"

"She gave it to me," Mikey replied with a shaky smile. "C'mon, be a pal. I can cut you in. Just get me to the hospital."

Shannon picked up the hundred and came back into view. Lund felt his gut twist into a knot. Jack Shannon had a hard, hungry look. "No dame gave you a hundred bucks, Mikey-boy. You ain't done nothin' worth that much money since you quit the ring." Jack picked up the bill and held it to the light.

"It's good." Sweat stood out on his forehead as Mikey appeared to collapse into his coat. "She gave it to me. As good as gave it to me."

Jack leaned down toward Mikey's face. "What kind of racket is this?"

"It's clean, I swear it." Mikey shuddered, his face a hard

mask. "I swear to God, Jack, I'll give it all to you if you get me to a hospital."

"How clean is it?" Jack was at ease behind the bar, one hand on the wood, the other at his shoulder holding onto the towel he had just used to wipe down the wood.

"Clean enough. Renee was a good earner. She had a shakedown racket going on the Upper West Side. She took a girl for two thou." Feet and chairs shuffled and groaned as everyone turned to listen. Two thousand dollars bought a lot of attention.

"You mean to tell me that a punch-drunk asshole like you has two thousand bucks when a working stiff like me doesn't?" Jack laughed and looked up into the room at someone just beyond their sight. "Isn't that a kick in the pants?"

"They're going to kill the poor sap." Skinner breathed the words in the darkness of the hallway.

Lund leaned down to Skinner's ear. "Get the rest of the boys. We're going to need them all."

Skinner looked up at him in the dark, his youth bright in the shadow. "And you?"

"Go on." Lund turned his back to the darkness behind him and cleared his head. Loosening his hands, he put one against the door and walked forward.

"Who the hell are you? Where's Paulie?"

Lund put his hands in the air and affected surprise. "Hey, hey!" Widening his eyes, Lund allowed a thick Danish accent to color every word. "Paulie said I could come back. I have password, what the hell? Applesauce, dammit!"

Jack Shannon stepped back. He stood behind a makeshift bar of what was little more than pieces of scrap wood resting on top of two huge beer barrels. Near him, the radio sputtered with static, filling the small room with unconnected words and a hissing emptiness. Three street toughs stood or sat between Lund and the door. As he came into the room, one of the men stood and passed him to the door. A fourth man in the corner slept with his head on his arms, so still he might have been dead. Leaning on the bar, using both hands to hold himself up, his feet kicked out behind him and his head down, was Mikey-boy Cernoch.

"Hey," Lund kept his hands up but craned his neck out, "what the hell the matter with him? He sick? I heard you have good beer. I don't want to get sick."

Jack Shannon straightened. "Aw, him?" He swung a hand around with a dismissive wave. "He didn't get that liquor here. He got it someplace else, where they don't discern like we do."

He put his hands down on the bar, mirroring Mikey's posture from the other side.

"I'm gonna be sick." Mikey heaved. Lund looked at the mess on the floor and saw blood.

"Jesus, Mikey!" Jack leaned over the edge. "That's the last straw. I want you out of here. Boys!" Two toughs stood and came forward.

Lund was counting off slowly in his head, trying to think through how long it would take Skinner to get the others against how long it would take the tough who went to check on Paulie to make it back and tell the others. "Hey, what you do?" Lund made himself indignant. "What this man do? He sick!"

"What is he? A kraut?" one of the toughs asked the other.

"Sounds like one."

Jack Shannon studied Lund. "What are you, mister?"

"Danish, dammit." Lund kept his eyes on the toughs.

"I don't know you, friend. How'd you find this place?"

"Sully told me. He said you had work."

"He said? That's interesting, since Sully was a girl the last time I checked." Jack laughed. "We've got a live one, boys. Go ahead! Show me how fast you can take him apart."

The two of them came at him. One with a knife. Lund relaxed and let his restraint fall like a glass shattering against stone. Skinner had gone back to meet McCain. The police were still a whistle away. The bank was so distant it might as well have been in a vault ten miles underground. Lund smiled. No, it wasn't a smile. It was a grin.

He put his boot into the first one's abdomen, kicking him back into the wall hard enough to make him bounce, the second man just missing him. Lund moved forward, coming in close. He kept his breath even as his open hand made a wide arc down across the second tough's face first, hitting him with the front of the hand, then around with the back. He hardly broke a sweat.

Picking himself off the floor, the first tough countered to the indignity with wrath, which was fine with Lund. Deep in his temper, he made himself promise not to kill the man. It would be enough that the tough would remember Lund every time the weather turned cold. Lund broke his wrist easily, then went for the knee with the heel of his boot, the man falling back in a faint against the wall. The second tough was older, smarter maybe. Lund pulled his chin close to his chest and put up his hands, loose and open.

"Nobody slaps me, mister." Taking a step back, the second

man pulled a knife from his belt, the blade honed down to just a sliver.

Lund dodged the first feint easily, jumping backward into a table he drew in between them as he struggled out of James's too small jacket and wrapped it around his hand. Time was moving too fast. In a moment, the third man would be back from checking on the door and there would be four of them, including Shannon. Lund didn't see an opening, so he made one, lunging forward, one hand wrapping the jacket around the knife, the other hitting sharply in the throat. The man crumpled to the floor, his hands at his neck as he writhed. Lund crouched down and said, "The secret is to not try so hard to breath. You have about six minutes to learn how." The kid spat at him. Lund was laughing when the arm came around his neck.

Shannon pulled him close, pinning Lund down where he couldn't break free. He saw stars. He felt choked and gasped for air and heard Jack begin a low giggle from somewhere deep in his chest.

Then he heard the unmistakable click and roll of a Smith & Wesson .38-caliber police-issue revolver.

"I'd stand very still if I were you, Jack. I'm getting a little creaky in my old age." The pistol butt came down hard on the back of Jack Shannon's skull.

McCain had arrived.

35

"YOU'RE A LUCKY MAN, you know that, Lund? There's nothing Jack Shannon likes better than strangling a man. Isn't that so, Jackie my boy?" McCain nudged the recumbent bootlegger with a foot. "He's faking. Doesn't want to tangle with Poulhaus. Did you hear me, Jackie?" McCain put his hands on his knees and bent down to shout, "Your old friend Poulhaus is here. Ready to have a chat with you about the girl you worked over on Forty-Ninth. Oh look, Lund, he's interested. The man's woken up. A miracle. Yeah, that girl, Jack, remember her? Poulhaus remembers." He jerked a chin over his shoulder to the a big red-headed policeman who was just coming through the door.

McCain cleared his throat. "All right, men. I want you all to know that I am willing to shoot any man who tries my temper in the next five minutes." Looking over his shoulder to speak with Poulhaus, he added, "Two policemen at a time—one to cuff 'em, one to give 'em the boot if they resist."

Poulhaus nodded once, a grim smile on his face as he looked down on Jack Shannon. "You can count on me, McCain."

"Poulhaus," McCain's voice held a warning, "I want them at the station alive." He glanced at the ice pick on the ground, kicking it away after he stared at it a moment. "And in one piece."

Skinner knelt beside Mikey and felt for a pulse. He looked up at Lund. "He's alive. Help me get him up."

Skinner and Lund each took an arm, lifting Mikey

easily between them. Mikey wobbled like a limp doll, his feet dragging on the floor. "I wasn't drinkin' no smoke, Skinner." Mikey fell into Lund's chest, his voice muffled against Lund's shirt.

Skinner snorted. "Whoever you were drinking with wasn't a friend. You got alcohol poisoning, clear as the nose on your face. Wood alcohol, maybe worse." He patted Mikey down, reaching into a pocket and removing a wad of money. "What the hell, Mikey? This is a lot of dough!"

McCain glanced at the money in Skinner's hand. "That look like two thousand to you, Lund?"

"Just about." The aftereffect of the fight was sinking into him. He felt slow, heavy. He pulled James's jacket on one sleeve at a time. Distantly, he thought he felt pain. He pushed it away, allowing adrenalin to hold the answer to every question.

"C'mon, we'll take him on to the station and get the police surgeon to have a look at him." McCain looked down at Shannon on the floor. "Don't worry, Jack. I'll tell your mother where you went. You got him, Poulhaus?"

Satisfied, McCain walked out into the light, pulling the front door shut behind him.

❖

THE AMBULANCE ROCKED BACK AND FORTH, sirens screaming as it raced out of Hell's Kitchen. From the sound of it, Warner was running every red light while Dunn hung out the window shouting for people to get out of the way. Mikey lay on the floor. His powerful frame barely fit on the long bed. The three men sat around him on the narrow benches that lined the interior. McCain sat on one side of the wagon looking down at the prostrate boxer, Lund and Skinner on the other. Lund reached down to feel for a pulse. "He alive?" McCain asked.

Lund nodded and was silent.

Skinner sat back against the cold wall and crossed his arms over his chest. "You ever seen alcohol poisoning up close?" His youthful face hardly moved as he spoke.

"What's smoke?" Lund asked.

"Gasoline—well, any kind of fuel—mixed around with whatever makes it taste good." McCain glanced at Skinner, then back to Lund. "That's what Prohibition has brought this city to—draining a gas tank and drinking it like it was god-damn water."

Lund swore fluidly in Danish. "Will he live?"

Skinner leaned on his knees, looking down at Mikey, thinking over his answer. "Can't say. If he lives, he might be blind or crazy—or both. Nobody comes away from drinking smoke with nothin' to show for it."

"Mikey! Mikey!" McCain slapped the man's face gently.

"Where's Renee?" Mikey mumbled. "Where is she?"

McCain cleared his throat. "There you are, Mikey-boy. You had me worried."

"McCain?" The boxer opened a bleary eye, the other one too swollen to open. The way the eye ranged around the ve-hicle. Lund wasn't sure the man could see them.

McCain was firm. "Where'd you get the money, Mikey? Where'd you get two thousand dollars?"

Mikey rocked back and forth as Warner took another corner on two wheels. "I don't feel so good."

"We're going to get you to a doctor, but you have help me too." Lund watched McCain's face as he spoke. There was something in the words that didn't fit, wasn't right. It dawned on him that McCain did not believe Cernoch would live. "I need to know some things. Where did the money come from?" McCain spoke quickly, as though time was running out. Lund was concerned. The boxer's face was a damp grey, his lips white, the blood around his mouth a glaring red.

Mikey's face screwed up like a child's. "She's dead, ain't she?" He looked like he was about to cry.

"Renee had a lot of money with her last night. Did you take it?" McCain took the lead, Skinner and Lund settling back away from the dying man.

"I didn't steal from her. It wasn't like that."

"Are you trying to tell me she gave you the two thousand?"

"No—" Mikey began to cough, then rolled over onto his side and was sick. The nauseating odor of fuel and blood filled the small wagon, red standing out against the white floor grate. McCain banged on the partition. "Speed it up, boys!" Lund was thrown against the side of the wagon as the vehicle lurched and swayed. "Mikey, did you kill Renee? You can tell me, son. I'll make sure they know you were sick when it happened."

Mikey lay on the floor on his side and panted, his blood-shot eye fixed on the wall behind McCain. Lund was sure he couldn't see him. "I didn't kill her. She was dead when I found her." He spoke as though he was forcing each word out.

"I saw her leave the party. I knew she'd want me to drive her somewhere. I thought I was right behind her, but I wasn't. I got lost trying to find a way out. McCain?"

The patrolman leaned over the boxer. "Yeah, Mikey?"

"You ever seen a house so big?"

McCain leaned forward. "What about the money?"

"I came around the side of the house, down the stairs. I heard her call out. It was cut off, but it was her. I knew it was her." His breathing became more labored. The words came at longer intervals. "There was a man. He ran off." The labor in his breath began to clear. "Her purse was right next to her. Right there on the bench, full of money. Her money. I ain't never seen anyone who could run a grift like her. Honestly, McCain. I ain't never seen it before." A grin tugged at the corner of his mouth. "She was a good girl."

"Who was it, Mikey. Who did you see?"

"He killed my girl." The words made the blood in Lund's veins run cold. Mikey coughed, a long string of saliva trailing from his damp lips. He took a breath. "He ran right past me. Saw him clear as day. It was the guy that followed her everywhere. He went everywhere she did."

McCain swore.

Lund found he was surprisingly calm. He asked, "What did he look like? Did he look like me?" He took off his hat and leaned forward.

Mikey looked in Lund's direction. "I can't see you," he said. He laughed. "I can't see anything!"

Skinner cleared his throat. "So what'd he look like then, Mikey-boy? This man following your girl?"

Mikey coughed and thought through the words while

the ambulance swerved and bounced. "Taller than me," he said finally. "He was big. All over, like. Big feet, big hands, big head. He could swing, that man could. Clocked me but good." His chuckle sounded more like a deep wheeze. "I used to hit like that, back in the day. When things were good."

Skinner thought a moment. "Did you talk to the man?"

"Sure, told him to clear off his patch. That's when he hit me."

"Was he foreign?"

Mikey was lost in the rocking of the bus. His body swayed. "He was just an average Joe." Every word came slowly. "She was a good girl. She wouldn't say it, but I could tell. She wasn't afraid of no one but him. Just him. You know what it's like to see a smart woman like that afraid? When she wasn't afraid of nobody?"

"What did he want, Mikey? Why was she afraid?"

"All of her. He wanted all of her. It's what they all want after a while." Bleary eyes focused on nothing. Mikey waited a moment, his breath wet and heavy. "I loved her, you know that? I never loved no dame before. Not like that." He blinked as though he was surprised, and sighed.

A few minutes later, McCain banged on the partition. "You can slow it down now, Warner. The man's dead."

36

PENELOPE SAT IN THE LIEUTENANT's office by herself, the sounds of typewriters from the bullpen filtering through the thin door. An occasional burst of laughter made her jump. She concentrated on the view ahead of her: a bleak expanse of red brick slowly growing dark as the afternoon gave way to evening. Behind her, the sounds of the police floated through the crack under the door—shouted commands, faint laughter, footsteps. She was cold, and suddenly frightened, her imagination running away with her.

The nice patrolman with the kind eyes had met her at the apartment door not an hour before, his smile gone, a somber mask in its place. The warrant allowed the police to search the apartment for James's suit as well as Lund's, but somehow they managed to make a mess of all the rooms in the process. They asked the cook all kinds of questions, flustering the poor woman to the point of hysteria. A good deal was made of the trash chute in the hallway. McCain sent a policeman down to the bottom to have a look at what was there. She expected an officer to appear at any moment with a telegram from Shanghai. Then where would she be? All she knew was she had not been arrested. This fact surprised Penelope, as it struck her that the little man was standing on the verge of a decision with every word he spoke.

At least they had allowed her the privacy of the kitchen exit when they took her out, the men's clothes wrapped carefully in paper under the patrolman's arm. The sudden awareness of dancing along a wire fifty feet from the ground struck her somewhere between when the cook was questioned and when the police wrapped up James's suit to take it away. Penelope sank into the wool coat she had forgotten to put back in the armoire, turning up the collar to the draft, and went with them quietly.

She didn't like lawyers—boring, officious men, the lot of them—but she wished she knew one whom she could call to ask why the officers were so subdued despite their industrious searching. She was unable to bring herself to ask the question herself. Not after she saw how carefully they wrapped the suit. So she sat, and she waited. Fingers twined in a tight grip, her eyes trained on the darkening red brick, the click of the radiator warming in the near distance.

She tried hard not to think of Shanghai and failed.

She waited.

"You don't know what the man meant, Nathan. You can't say you know for sure." McCain kept his voice neutral. "You base it off exactly what he said, but he said the man was an average Joe. You know Lund. He's got a hell of an accent. No one would mistake him for an average Joe. It feels wrong."

"Well, what did it feel like, then?" McCain was certain that Blake was loud enough for the desk sergeant to follow every word. "Why don't you let us in on it, Patrolman McCain?"

If the dig hurt, McCain was determined not to let it show. "I think someone else was following her around. Someone who she was afraid of."

Blake crossed his arms, quivering with rage. "And who would that be?"

"Gott maybe—or some other no-good man she picked up somewhere. God knows a woman like that would pick up a few here and there. Makes perfect sense!"

"She knew Lund in Shanghai, didn't she? Maybe she picked him up."

"Now, Nathan—"

"Lieutenant, Patrolman McCain!"

McCain thought he heard Skinner suck his breath in through his teeth, and couldn't blame the kid. He straightened and said, "Yes, Lieutenant, sir," just stopping himself before saluting. "I was going to ask you, Lieutenant, when in your experience did you know of a woman like that who was willing to admit she was afraid?" He kept his eyes front.

"You're guessing!" Incandescent rage made Blake spit, his finger jutting out to ram McCain's badge. "You willing to bet that on a guess?"

McCain kept as still as he could. "I am."

"What do you think?" Blake turned to Skinner, his hands moving to his hips.

By McCain's recollection, Skinner had a sister, a mother, and the motherless baby who survived a difficult birth to look after. If he wanted the food and medicine that a growing family needed, he had to make money, and if he wanted to live long enough to see the baby play his first game of stickball, he had to get out of Hell's Kitchen. McCain waited on Skinner's words, keeping the facts of the matter well in mind.

"He was blind drunk, Lieutenant," Skinner said slowly. "I wouldn't trust a word of what he said. Beginning to end."

"That's not how a court sees it, Patrolman. A court of law says a dying man's declaration is considered the truth. Now what did the bastard say?"

Skinner blushed. McCain couldn't blame him. A good Catholic boy like that didn't like the dead being spoken about in such terms. "He said the man was the one following her around. But he didn't say a name."

"See that?" Blake said. "That's all I needed to hear. He didn't have to say a name. You and I both know who he meant. Lund admitted he was trailing her for the bank. She recognized him and told Cernoch."

"Lieutenant." McCain kept his eyes front. He had been dressed down by louder men than Nathan Blake, and given his savings, time spent in Hell's Kitchen, and a godson with ideas, McCain found himself ready to lay his career on the line. "You're wrong."

Blake crossed his arms and leaned down to shout at McCain. "I don't care about your gut! It can't testify in open court! I've got a fingerprint on the earring, and I've got the suits—all I need to match those up to our boy Lund!"

"You don't know if it's his fingerprint or his buttons." McCain's placid reply was a stark contrast to Blake's fury. "He's got no motive at all," he said clearly. "None that we can find."

"He loves her!" Blake pointed in the general direction of the waiting room. "He was doing it for her! Don't you wonder what that woman had on the Harris girl? Want to know about how her husband died? The consulate sent a transcript of the file over an hour ago. Would you like to know what your boy Lund did to cover up how she murdered her husband?"

McCain exhaled ruefully. So that was it. Nathan was disappointed. It all made sense now.

"He found her in the alley all right, badly beaten and her face cut open to the bone. But what he didn't say was that she had been moved." Blake picked up the folder and shook it. "It was a setup, Jasper! First class! He had plenty of time to make it look like a robbery. Just enough to cover her tracks." He threw down the folder hard enough for the papers on his desk to spill out across the blotter and scatter across the floor.

McCain lowered his voice. "Don't do this, Nathan. You'll regret it."

"I don't have a choice." Blake walked around his desk to collect the papers back into a stack. "The D.A. called a half hour before you came back. The whole investigation got kicked upstairs. Our pal Alfred Gott gave him a visit just after we left and made it clear he wanted to see justice served."

"And his photos found . . ." McCain said under his breath.

"Not to mention putting the knife in one Thom Lund. Gott's story now is that Lund was obsessed with the victim, kept following her long after Gott told him to stop. Put that together with this file, and his goose is cooked."

"How much time do we have with the evidence?"

"Not enough." Blake rubbed a hand over his bald head. "As soon as it's logged and I talk to the girl, it's done. A couple of hours to type up the witness statements . . ." He sighed, his temper winding down as quickly as it had sprung up. "Midnight maybe? Might as well prepare your friend for the worst, Jasper."

"The fingerprints on the earring will clear him. I know they will."

"That will take days. You know it. First we have to get the fingerprints. Then we have to match 'em."

"The papers will have the story an hour after you give the file to the D.A. The man will be ruined, Nathan. And he didn't even do it!"

"Listen to you! You don't even care that the man was a dirty cop! I never should have let you have your way and take him with you to bring in Cernoch."

"He tried to save the man's life. Sure as Christmas, Jack Shannon was about to kill Cernoch for the two thousand. We recovered the money and the statement because Thom Lund stuck his neck out. He was alone in there with three armed men. Would he have done that for a man who would implicate him?"

"He didn't know Cernoch had seen him kill Renee Strong."

"That's not what Cernoch said, Nathan."

"It was close enough for me."

"It doesn't make sense."

"We're going to find that necklace at his apartment. His fingerprints are going to be a match. And it's Lieutenant, Patrolman McCain. I'd thank you for remembering that." Blake stood straight and looked around the bullpen at the men in the room silently watching. "Get back to work!"

As he turned, Blake saw Penelope standing in the open door of his office, her face an ashen white. "Lieutenant," she said, "have you arrested Thom Lund?"

"Now, Mrs. Ambrose," Blake leaned forward on his desk, his hands clasped together, "I'm going to be honest with you. I'll admit, I had my doubts to begin with, but we've learned a few things since we interviewed Thom early this morning. I think you may know something about the matter, and I'm going to ask you a few questions. Do you want a lawyer?"

"But, Lieutenant, it's not possible. Thom wouldn't do a thing like this."

" I think you will find, as I have, that for the right reasons murder is quite easy. I think Thom Lund had good reasons for killing that woman, and what's more—I think you know it too."

Penelope could hardly believe him. She gripped the edge of her purse, knuckles white.

"All right." Blake sat back and looked at the papers in front of him. "I made a call early this morning. Asked for the report on your husband's death. I was curious but got a bit of a surprise. You didn't say Mr. Lund was the policeman who investigated the crime when we spoke last night."

"It wasn't important! It was a coincidence!"

"A man who's in love with you just happened to be the one who investigated your husband's murder?" Blake said. "Seems a little bit of a stretch to me."

"There was too much crime to go around those days and too few police." Penelope glanced over her shoulder at Mc-Cain, who leaned against a filing cabinet behind her.

"Policemen don't like coincidences, Mrs. Ambrose. We don't believe they exist."

"My name is Harris now, Lieutenant. If you don't mind."

"I don't blame you, changing your name. Your husband was a first-rate heel. The report," he held up the paper, "goes into detail on what happened to you that night." He peered at her across the desk. Then, his hand moving quickly, he tugged on the bonnet of the desk lamp, shining the light directly in her face. "Okay, I see it now. You must have paid a packet to get that fixed." He looked down. "Says here you had been cut on your neck. Plus there was the beating." Blake lifted his head, cocking it to one side. "Doesn't look too bad from here." He squinted. "Where'd you go to get the work done?"

Penelope swallowed the hard lump in her throat and tried to breathe. "Munich. There were doctors there who had some experience from the war."

"They did a good job." Blake tapped the page with a blunt finger. "You were an awful mess when Lund found you. Beaten, cut up." He looked her in the eye. "Raped."

"Lieutenant . . ." McCain warned.

When Blake parted his lips to speak, there was a snap, as though a dog and broken its leash. "You want to know what I think?"

"No." She was certain she was about to be sick.

"I think this wasn't a robbery at all. I think your husband beat you within an inch of death, assaulted you, cut you. Money could have been the reason, or maybe you had ideas about leaving him. Yes, the risk makes sense for a man like Kinkaid Ambrose. He'd have to have the money. Then your man Lund comes along and loses his cool. I'm not saying it wasn't justified, but he did shoot the man five times. I'd say he has a problem with his temper, if I'm being honest. Then again," Blake's eyes met hers, "I can't imagine what I would have done if I found the woman I loved like that. I'd want to kill someone. I know I would. I think that's what your friend Thom did. I think he was doing his rounds and stumbled on the scene. Your man killed your husband and cleaned up the scene. Then, and only then, did he let anyone know something had happened."

Penelope sat motionless, staring ahead, no clear thought in her mind but that night. Every part of her vibrated, an extended shiver that ran from her hair down to her feet.

"I'd say, if he had come clean with it right there, it would have been justifiable. Maybe. I don't know how the courts work in that part of the world, but I imagine that an honest policeman would have the same chance there that he does here. But your man didn't play it that way. I think he shot your husband, blew his damn head right off, then went about covering it up so it didn't look that way to his fellows. What do you think of that?"

"I think a lawyer would say that's slander." Penelope was surprised she could speak. "I think you're guessing because you aren't good enough to do your job properly and find the man who really killed Renee. I think you'll dig through the past to make an innocent man fit the crime instead of looking for the real killer."

"And who would that be? Your cousin Charles, maybe? Or your uncle?"

Her thoughts were desperate as they scanned the night's events, searching for any detail she had forgotten. "There were a lot of men there who had known Renee before. Is this all you can come up with? A former policeman who has done nothing but help you? A man who was placed in a crowd by dozens of witnesses at the time of the crime? And a drunken fool who no one believes was physically capable of the crime?"

The lieutenant couldn't contain his sarcasm. "Or it could have been James Harris." He looked up at her. "McCain and I heard him talk about the body. He knew an awful lot about what had gone on with her. Too much."

"James is in medical school. He was a navy medic. He knows a great deal about it." The words were quick and hot, almost as quick as Blake's. She forced herself to match him. She had to match him and beat him if she could. It was all she could think to do. "Besides, he was with me in the coat closet."

"The entire time? Are you sure about that? McCain here thought he overheard you both getting your stories straight with Lund before you were questioned. That ring a bell? Maybe James knew so much because *he* killed Renee Strong. After all, he couldn't possibly approve of what she was doing to you, or what she planned to do to Charles."

No, no. It was a bad dream. It couldn't be real. Penelope stood, leaning forward over Blake's desk, her words desperate. "What about Jack Rollins? He was there! What did he see?" She searched the lieutenant's face.

Blake looked at McCain. "Who's this Jack Rollins? Ever heard of him?"

"No one mentioned him to us," McCain said slowly. "What kind of person was this Jack?"

She rooted in her purse, her fingers trembling. "Look, he gave me his card. That's where he is. Jack was at the party last night. He knew Renee in Shanghai." Penelope looked from one man to the other, pleading with them both. "He worked for my husband as a ship's captain. He knew her. He knew Renee. I saw him in the alley after she was dead. You should find him, talk to him."

"I have to caution you against lies like that one." Blake put a finger on the business card and pushed it back toward her across the desk. "It will get you into trouble you can't get out of, Mrs. Ambrose. You tell a person one lie, and you can't help telling another. Even if it means dragging a perfectly innocent bystander into the matter."

"If he even was a bystander," McCain added with dry cynicism.

"True enough!" Blake nodded at McCain. "This Rollins fellow might not even exist at all. Jasper, what's the penalty for wasting police time?"

"Alfred Gott!" Penelope called out desperately. "He was her lover in Shanghai. He never forgave her when she left him for Kinkaid. He said he'd kill her!"

"Has an alibi."

"What about her driver, Mikey?" She could feel tears on her face, but she couldn't stop trying to convince them. "He's her bodyguard. He must have known she had the money on her. He killed her for the cash. Two thousand! It was too tempting. He must have done it! Have you spoken with him? He would know something, surely!"

"Cernoch had an alibi. Besides, he's dead."

She flinched, momentarily struck dumb.

Blake smiled to himself, jabbed at the papers on the desk with a finger. "You want to know what this report from Shanghai says about you?"

"No." The word strangled in her throat.

"Okay. Maybe I'll tell ole McCain there, since he needs to know the type of criminal class he is seen around town with." He smiled at the man behind her. "Do you know who this little lady was back in Shanghai?"

"Stop."

Blake laughed. "She wasn't just a casino owner; she was a heavy. Big enough to have a name they called her. Want to know what it was?"

"No." She could barely speak.

"The Jade Tiger. Can you imagine that, Jasper? This little girl right here was called the Jade Tiger. It wasn't just the name of her nightclub—it was *her* name." Blake laughed again, the sound landing like a body blow on Penelope.

"It's better for everyone if you tell us what you know," McCain said to her. "Lund will get a fair trial. We're known for it around these parts. No one has to know what you were into in China if that's how you want it. Just tell the lieutenant what he wants to know."

She shook with the effort it took to speak. "But it didn't happen like that. It wasn't like that at all!"

"You have any proof to that effect, young lady? More than just your word?" McCain crossed his arms.

"No," Blake said. "She won't help you, Jasper. You think the man's innocent. I know he's not. Whatever she knows, her skin is more important to her than his. Poor sap's fallen in love with a stone-cold criminal."

"I'll clear him, Lieutenant, if you won't." She clenched her hands against the trembling and tried to prepare herself. What was jail like in America?

"Going to confess, are you? Well, it's a little late for that."

Blake ripped the ground out from underneath her. "We have a witness, see? He says he saw Thom Lund running from the scene. All we need is the necklace he stole and a match to the fingerprint that's on the earring."

"I don't know who your witness saw last night." Penelope fought to clear her thoughts. "Whoever they are, they're lying. Thom wouldn't have done such a thing."

"Even if she was blackmailing him? Even if she was blackmailing his girl? See, I think you haven't considered how angry a woman like Renee Strong could make a man like Thom Lund. It wasn't enough that she was blackmailing him. She was blackmailing you as well!" Blake stood up. "Take her down for fingerprints, Jasper. Just in case she knows how to break a woman's neck without breaking a nail or tearing her dress." He grinned, the shadow falling across his face, his teeth a slash of white in the shadow from the lamp.

McCain nodded and turned. The redbrick wall grew cool and dark.

Night closed in around them.

37

PENELOPE STOOD IN THE DOORWAY to the apartment, light behind her, darkness ahead. Looking past to the row of bedrooms, taking in the untidiness the police had left in their wake, she hardly noticed as she locked the door behind her, a final click in the heavy silence.

The weight of the day lay on her shoulders like a yoke. Penelope had not felt such misery since Shanghai. There had been so many long nights spent waiting that she had lost count. Sitting up to watch the street through the darkest parts of the morning. Praying Kinkaid would not have lost so much gambling. Hoping that Renee had eased him out of a foul mood with flattery and lovemaking. They had been so much alike, Kinkaid and Renee. She wondered if they were together now that their lives were over. If Renee had found peace, would it include Kinkaid? Penelope couldn't help but wish something better for Renee than a man who could barely keep up with her train of thought, let alone make her happy. It came to her like a jolt of electricity. After everything that had come between them, after all the terrible things Renee had done, she missed her. She missed Renee.

There had been good times. There had been laughter before the jealousy settled in. All her memories jumbled together in a rowdy cacophony of jazz, gin, and rolled stockings— Renee in the center of it all like a glittering jewel. Penelope could hardly fathom that she was dead and she would never see her again. In the quiet part of the night, when no one was listening, she hoped there was a nightclub just for Renee. A little place with an endless volley of booze and music and French cigarettes. A place where the dawn never made you fear for your sins and the night never wore your terrors like a coat. Penelope prayed for it fervently, standing in the hallway, tears running down her cheeks. When the moment passed, she straightened and took a deep breath, the terrible heaviness increasing as her thoughts turned slowly back to the practical, the reliable, the mundane.

She unbuttoned her coat and took off her hat, laying both on the chair next to the phone. She got down on her knees and began to clean the mess the police had left in the hallway, happy to have something to keep her occupied. Memories of the evening glided past, mixing fluidly with her memories of Shanghai as she worked, lost in a labyrinth of roads not taken, every imagined result better than the one at hand. The papers would come for all of them, but especially her—because of the lost inheritance, because her husband was murdered, because Renee had been so much larger than life. Ruin was so close at hand. Penelope could hardly believe it hadn't already happened.

Her logic just skirted that this was Renee's doing, the woman at the center of the glittering gambling trap singing in a loud, garish shout, "Who's sorry now?" in good time with the band. Renee's affair with Kinkaid must have begun at once, or perhaps they had known each other before. Penelope sat up on her knees. She had never considered it before. How long was it before Renee had slipped into Kinkaid's bed? Wandering through the memories from the Jade Tiger, she ticked off Renee's beaus. Uncle Harry had been simply too embarrassing, his booming voice cascading across the casino as Renee sat on his knee. Poor Charles barely deserved thinking of. There were so many others who were more energetic or wealthier. Alfred Gott was there, his long white hair combed back behind his ears, his mustache scrupulously trimmed, his eyes as hard as stones. He kept Renee the longest, paying for every precious minute. Renee had gone against her own interests there, cutting Freddy off without a thought when the crack appeared in Penelope's marriage.

Freddy could have killed Renee easily if he only had a motive. But he didn't. Men like Freddy didn't kill for women like Renee. They might kill for money, but when it came to women, they just got down to buying another one.

The men shifted one behind the other as Penelope racked her brain, trying to think who would have wanted to kill Renee. Who could have hated her that much?

It was almost too easy to think of Kinkaid, as though the memory had been standing behind a door waiting to reach out a hand as she passed by. She fought the madness that raised his specter from the dead with everything she knew. The first time they met, their first dance, first kiss, the breathless anticipation of their elopement. Then, finally, the first time he hit her, the apologies, then the next. The slow, inexorable crawl toward her death or his, moving with certainty in the same direction until there could be no mistaking his intentions, no matter what he promised in the dark.

When the beatings became too much, Penelope had put on her hat, covered her bruises with what makeup she could find, and gone to the police. They took her report with dutiful zeal, then called Kinkaid to come take her home again. In an alleyway near the station, he pushed her back against the brick and put his hand over her mouth. "No one will believe you." Covering her eyes with her hands, Penelope gasped as the memory swung out and struck her. "Not now, not ever."

Four years of hell married to a man who was only just smart enough to know how to hit a woman where it wouldn't show. Abetting his criminal activity had been a kind of self-defense—if she had value, perhaps he wouldn't beat her. A balance was arranged: Kinkaid would have his affairs, and

Penelope would quietly fund his criminal activity. Kinkaid played at being a criminal like a child at a costume party, but that wasn't enough for their partners. They'd started to notice how bad he was at it. Penelope had to do something or they would both die. It was pure chance that she had been good at it. Good enough to make a packet for their partners. Good enough to draw the attention of the police. Good enough to sock away enough cash to run away from Kinkaid and start a new life.

The arrangement held firm until she met Lund. By then, Penelope was too far gone to worry what anyone thought, and Kinkaid was too afraid of the police to object to their friendship.

She was struck by the sudden memory of the dress she had worn that night, soaked in so much blood the silk turned black. She had to go back for the money, the damned money. She had thirty thousand in the wall of her office, having taken her cut of the profits before Kinkaid ever knew. Without it, they would never get away, never be free. Kinkaid would come after them—kill Lund, then her. He found her in the office, the money in a case she used for stage costumes. Kinkaid had been so drunk, the thought it was full of money didn't even occur. No, it was her he came for, her he was angry about. He had heard a rumor in the bar below. Someone had seen her buying two train tickets west. Someone had come to tell him before she could get away. It must have been Renee. No one else would have had the guts to tell Kinkaid when he was drunk. But even Renee could not have predicted how Kinkaid's temper would explode.

The fear came. Penelope curled into herself on the floor

in the New York apartment with the yellow wallpaper and
the Chinese mementos, her eyes shut tight, and waited for a
window in the anguish.

How many nights had it replayed in her mind? Every
time, she searched for another way it could have happened.
But Kinkaid was too angry. It was all-consuming.

While Kinkaid was in the offices above, Renee must have
emptied the bar, must have gotten everyone out. Penelope had
the distant recollection of Renee's face in the office doorway,
her face slack with fear and astonishment before she quietly
shut the door on what he would do.

By the time he dragged her downstairs to the bar, Penelope knew he was going to kill her—but not at the nightclub.
Wasn't it Renee who had mentioned it? Not at the Jade Tiger.
It was a whisper that hung just above the memory. Not at the
Jade Tiger. If she could get to the car, Penelope knew she
could kill him with the .32 in the glove box. It was logic, not
terror. She was a good shot, and he would be five feet away—
hard to miss. It was a plan, not self-defense. All she had to do
was live that long.

The coupe shone bright in the moonlight, and Penelope
staggered to it, Kinkaid's hand in her hair. She swung out
at him, loosened his hand just enough for her to reach inside the door for the gun he didn't know she had, the gun
she usually carried with her everywhere. When she stood, he
came toward her laughing and reached for the gun. He was
surprised when the first shot caught him in the shoulder. The
second came for his heart. He balanced on his knees, and she
shot him again and again, certain he was about to stand up,
about to take one more swing. She shot him until the hammer

clicked. Misfire. There was a sound and she turned the gun on Renee, the hammer coming down against an empty chamber.

On her apartment floor, Penelope covered her head with her arms and cried until she thought her head would split. When the clock rang out ten, she pushed off from the carpet and staggered to the bathroom, where she discovered that her tears and mascara left the impression of inky raindrops all around the collar of her French silk shirt, ruining it. She washed and began the march back from the brink, her mind slowly surfacing from the lake of memory. She had to pull herself together. She had to help Lund.

It was then that she remembered: Carmen never cried. Not one tear did the gypsy shed for anyone, not even herself. The gypsy didn't understand misery, and even if she did, she would never succumb to it. There were too many men to love, too many beautiful things to steal. When Kinkaid beat her, it was Carmen who survived the cruelty. When Renee hit her pride, it was Carmen who dealt from the bottom of the deck to get herself back. When her father had died, it was Carmen who held Penelope's head up with an indomitable spirit. She would not give in. She would never give in.

The melody came to her lips unbidden. She sang.

"*L'amour est enfant de Bohême. Il n'a jamais jamais connu de loi.*" Love is a gypsy's child. It has never, ever, known a law. Penelope felt her way through the music, her memory of the crowd and the party crowding in around her thoughts with sudden firmness. *Love me not, then I love you. If I love you, you'd best beware!* She could see them all from where she stood on the chair, looking up at her as she sang: Mrs.

Anthony Stone, Mary, James at the piano, even the Amazing Gilberto from his position on the floor. *The bird you thought you had caught beat its wings and flew away.* Gott stood by Helen Mayfield, gloating, she was sure of it. Charles, barely on his feet, weaving as he watched her sing. Nearer to him, Lund looking up at her, waiting. Even in the memory of it, her heart beat faster, and she wanted to restore the Habanera, to sing a love song instead of a dirge, to hope instead of hate. No, this Habanera was for Renee. She tore herself away to look at Renee, her grief tainting the memory of her anger with regret. *Love stays away. You wait and wait. When least expected, there it is!*

The music stopped. Penelope fell into the silence, unresisting, remembering Renee. She had humiliated the woman with the song, jeering at her with the lyrics. It was a final confrontation between them—war, if you like. But Renee had not turned to look. She had not seen Penelope. It was as though she were a thousand miles away, unable to hear her. No, Renee stared across the room at someone else. Penelope was sure she had not seen such terror in her face before. The moment took hold of Penelope as she followed Renee's eyes, silence interrupted by the roll of the roulette wheel and the distinctive click of the ball spinning, spinning, looking for red while the beggar bet on black. His future winding down as the ball slowed to take his last nickel. Renee's high giggle speckled the memory with her curious delight at ruin. Another man, another day at the wheel, another ruined wreck for Renee to record on her tally. She saw the man as Renee saw him. She stood in the bathroom, her bare feet cold against the tile, the music silenced, and knew who had killed Renee.

It was no use trying to tell the police. They wouldn't believe her. They had their man. They had Lund.

Penelope had wasted too much time trapped under the blade of a knife thinking there was nothing she could do. She was at the end of the tether. She could feel it, and it was time to snip herself free. She had only one debt left to pay: Lund's.

She walked to her bedroom, pushed aside the suitcase that held a fortune in cash, revealing a locked box just behind it. Cradling it on her lap, Penelope stared down at the pair of Beretta .32s nestled in their green velvet beds and wondered at how many nights she slept with a gun in her hand. The guns steadied her, her hand hardly shaking as she picked up the receiver and rang the operator. There were words, then the ring on the line. When she heard his voice, it was as though hardly a minute had passed since she had left Shanghai, the danger and misery were that close at hand. "I need to see you."

Penelope returned the receiver to the cradle. There was silence all around her as she experienced a vivid recollection of the Jade Tiger, the peal of Renee's laughter ringing out across the empty floor.

She had done a hundred bad things since the day she married Kinkaid. She couldn't blame every one of them on him, as much as she wanted to. Killing him hadn't wiped all that guilt away, no matter how hard she tried. She had lied, she had stolen, she had broken so many laws.

She took the safety off the Beretta.

There wasn't any getting away from who she was, or what she had to do.

38

"Your effects." The desk sergeant emptied Lund's wallet, watch, cufflinks, and all of his pocket contents onto the high desk in front of him, then pushed a card and a pencil across. "Sign here."

The jumbled disorder of the ruined things he had held in his pockets looked as much like trash as it could. Lund wouldn't have to look inside the wallet to know all the cash he had carried there was gone. One of the cufflinks was bent in half, while the other had lost the enamel insignia of his initials. The watch face was smashed, the hands stuck at six thirty, about twenty minutes after he was booked and taken to questioning. And his handkerchief looked as though someone had used it to clean their shoes—only their shoes, if he was lucky. He hardly blinked as he stared at the desk sergeant, a simmering rage making English words difficult to remember. He had forgotten what bastards the police could be. Lund exhaled, his ribs aching from the breath he had been holding in.

"Go on. It's all there, present and accounted for—all of it." The desk sergeant leaned heavily on one arm. "You hear me all right?" He raised his voice. "Sign here."

"And if I don't?"

The desk sergeant straightened, narrowing his eyes. "You want a doctor for that hearing problem?"

Lund sighed and picked up the pencil. When he was done with the paper, he took the wallet and the watch and pushed the rest into the bin.

"Got a little careless, did you? I'd be more careful next time." The officer snorted.

Lund pulled his jacket on, gritting his teeth tight against the bruising on his ribs. He wasn't sure if it was his work with the D.A. or his accent that had gotten him the special attention. In either case, the officers had been careful to note any new injuries as ones he got from the brawl in the speak. He hadn't minded the beating. There had been others in his past. New York had nothing on Copenhagen. Lund knew how to take a beating.

No, the worst part was keeping his temper when the sergeant in the bullpen used the boot. He could have killed the man. Quite easily killed him. Even now, keeping himself from knocking out a few of the desk sergeants' teeth was taking special effort.

"Hold on there, Thom. Look where you're going." McCain grasped him by both arms near the shoulder, unknowingly wrapping his hand around some of the worst bruising. Lund gasped from the sudden pain and struggled to release his arms. Lights burst and floated across his vision. McCain caught him before he collapsed completely and lowered him back onto a bench. "Take it easy there, son. Take a deep breath." The officer kept his hand on Lund's shoulder.

Lund tried to stand and fell back again.

"Thom, you been drinking?"

"Yeah, with a blackjack and a pair of brass knuckles." He almost laughed.

McCain pulled his jacket down smartly. "Which one of them worked you over? Little guy? Never takes off his hat?"

"I'm fine." Lund straightened warily. "I've had a shock, that's all."

"Is that Danish you're speaking? Sorry to say I don't know it." McCain waited.

"I'm fine," Lund repeated in English.

"Nathan won't be happy about this," McCain said, his face turning a deep red. "He didn't want them to work you over. Come to think of it, I don't like it a bit either."

"I don't care what he thinks. Get out of my way."

"Now, Thom, let's not have any hard feelings."

Lund felt the surge of his temper, hot and strong like a loaded pistol at his fingertips. "Hard feelings? For what? For arresting me for a crime you know I didn't commit? For sending in your goons to work me over? For the petty theft of my belongings? I thought you and Blake had a straight precinct, McCain. Now I know better."

"We do run a clean precinct."

"Doesn't look like it from here." Lund stood up and turned toward the street, pushing through the entrance hard enough to send the door back with a bang.

Following close behind him, McCain matched his quick step as he glided down the precinct steps and started up the street. "Listen to me, Thom. Nathan never meant for you to get worked over. They were only supposed to hold you for a while, keep you tied up with questioning."

"Until what?" Suddenly alert, Lund stopped. "Where is Penelope?"

"Well, that's what I wanted to talk to you about. But if you don't mind, maybe I could do it on the way?" Lifting a hand, McCain whistled, drawing a taxi out of the shadow. The car pulled up slowly, and the passenger-side window came down.

"I ain't hauling no drunks tonight, McCain," came the surly voice as it pulled up. "I've had enough of you cops putting drunks in my cab!"

"He's not drunk, Sam. He's a paying customer. And just to make sure he doesn't cause you any trouble, I'm coming along with you."

"Now hold on a minute!" the cab driver protested as McCain opened the door and took a visibly unwilling Lund by the elbow. "Who's payin'?"

"Nathan is." McCain pushed Lund across the back seat before getting in next to him. He took off his cap and smoothed his hair. "I hope you don't mind, Thom, us sharing. It's been a long day, and Nathan and I are having something of a disagreement. I think it's a bad night to play games. He disagrees." The car pulled away from the curb with slow finality.

"What kind of games?"

"Oh," McCain put his hands on either knee, "tag."

The casual language of police officers reached Lund from a long way away. "He brought her in for questioning, didn't he?"

"He did." McCain stared straight ahead.

"Is she still here?" Lund put his hand on the door handle.

"She isn't, and if you don't mind, I'd like to get moving in the right direction. I don't like the look of it, Thom. Nathan would just call me an old woman and take my badge, but given the way this case has been from the beginning, I figure we've got to catch up to her before she gets in over her head. She seems like the type. Does she strike you that way?"

Lund reached forward to grab the driver's shoulder. "You! Cabbie! I'm paying double. Put the pedal down."

"With a cop in the car?"

Lund grabbed the cabbie's collar, and pulled him back. "Get moving."

The driver put the pedal down, surging through traffic to the sound of braying car horns.

"Say, Sam, any chance you can keep your eyes on the road?" McCain was unnervingly calm. "I don't want to have to arrest you for disorderly driving."

"There is no such thing as disorderly driving, McCain!"

"Says you." McCain folded his arms.

"Why'd Blake let me go?" Lund leaned back against the seat. His whole body felt like a bruise.

"Fingerprinting cleared you and James." McCain reached up for the leather loop above the door as Sam took a corner on two wheels. "They're going through the guests now, getting everyone to hand in a clean set so they can review them. You ever try to match a fingerprint?" Lund didn't have a chance to answer before McCain continued, "Dull stuff. They'll spend days on it and never catch a break. By the way, you can be proud of your girl. Nathan gave her the works, and she never broke a sweat."

"Why that—"

"Keep your temper, Lund. The way I see it, there wasn't anything the lieutenant can't take back when the time is right. He's got a lot on his mind. See here, whoever killed Renee Strong has the necklace, which means they could already be on their way out of town. We have to catch the man fast if we're ever going to catch him at all. Every second that ticks by is another second he's ahead of us." McCain added darkly, "Then there's the D.A. to worry about. There's been

all sorts of calls turning the screws on this investigation."
Lund could feel McCain studying him in the darkness. "I'm
not saying Nathan is right, Thom. But you aren't standing
in his shoes trying to run an investigation either. New York,
she's a tough city to love. She wants to do wrong to you every
time she gets a chance, but she's still your girl at the end of
the night."

The taxi took a hard left across traffic and came to a halt.

"Sam, why's the car stopped?"

"We're here, flatfoot! Didn't you tell me to step on it?"

"Why, so we are." McCain turned to Lund. "Listen, I'm
going up to the corner to talk to the two uniforms. I'm not
doing myself any favors bringing you along like this. But I
want you to know what I think of you. I think you were a
good cop and you're a decent man with a hell of a problem
on your hands. I don't think you're dirty, or a murderer. I'm
trusting you to stay right here and not warn her." McCain got
out of the back of the cab, walked down to the corner, and
popped his head inside a car. Then, after crossing the street
to the Excelsior, he disappeared inside. Lund could see him
through the glass door speaking with the doorman.

A second later, McCain had pushed through the door and
was running to the corner. Lund grabbed the driver by his
jacket. "Catch him! Get there!" He shook Sam like a toy. The
cab pulled away from the curb with a squeal, catching up to
McCain just as another patrolman pointed up the street to
the taillights of a car. McCain popped the driver's side door
open. "Move over, Sam!"

"But she's my jalopy!"

McCain was shouting "Move!" just as Lund pulled Sam

up by his collar and deposited him on the passenger side like a sack of potatoes.

"Go on!" Lund shouted. "They'll be out of sight soon. You'll lose them!"

"That's enough of your Danish-speak, Lund. Speak English like the rest of us foreigners." McCain laughed at his joke. "Don't worry, Sam. I have to commandeer this cab, all right? For the police." He put his foot down on the accelerator so the wheels spun and screamed.

"No you don't! Not my cab, you don't! This is my livelihood, McCain! You can't just take it like that."

"Sam, have I ever lied to you? Have I ever steered you wrong?" McCain blew through a red light at twice the speed limit.

Sam's red face was looking increasingly suspicious.

McCain snorted. "Listen, you can't take that kind of talk seriously, Sam. Now, you can stay in the front seat the whole time if you want. I just can't let you drive."

"There she is!" Lund spoke in crisp English. "Hurry up or you'll lose her."

Slipping the clutch, McCain steered the car into traffic and went through the alley toward the back. He was silent, his general joviality fading into the same hardness Lund felt tight in his gut.

"You do know how to drive, don't you?" Sam asked plaintively. "I'm all for helping the police, but if something happens to my jalopy, I'm sunk."

"Of course I know how to drive." McCain used the particular inflection that struck fear into the heart of anyone who knew him.

Lund leaned forward. "Jasper, do you know who she is going to meet?"

"A killer, probably." McCain looked in the rearview and watched Lund sink silently into his coat. He addressed Sam. "Ain't love grand?"

39

"You sure you want to go to this address, lady? The docks ain't a place for a woman to be this time of night."

"I'm meeting someone." Penelope's voice barely made it past the fur collar.

"You in some kind of trouble?" the taxi driver pressed.

She stared out the window, feeling the car gently rock her back and forth. She said no but knew the cabbie didn't believe her. She didn't need a hapless do-gooder on her tail, not where she was going—straight back into the past. Penelope was cold, and she found that she did not want to finish what she had started. Inside her muff, her hands clasped each other, her skin warm against the cold metal of the guns strapped to the lining of the fur. She imagined what running away would feel like. More than anything, she wanted to tell the cab driver to take her to the train station, where she would buy a ticket to somewhere else, anywhere else.

"This is it." He had to say it twice before she heard him. She handed some cash through to the front seat and stepped out of the car. "You want me to wait?"

"That's not necessary." Penelope stared up at the warehouse.

"No skin off my back if I do," he said with a friendly smile.

She didn't answer him. She could feel him watching her as her practiced hand opened the heavy door that acted as a flood barrier. There wasn't any sound at all from behind the dark windows and abandoned loading dock. It wouldn't be much longer now.

IT TOOK LONGER THAN IT should have to flag down the cab as it left the docks. They chased it down an alley and around in a circle without knowing if Penelope was still in the back seat. In the end, McCain had to drive Sam's cab across his path to get him to stop.

Sam leapt from the passenger side to the driver's window. "Tim, the girl you just had in your rig—where'd you drop her?"

A man slowly rose from the driver's side. He looked from Sam to McCain. "Back there at a warehouse. Who are these men? You okay, Sam?

McCain got out and came around the car. "Police business. Can you take us back there? It's important."

Tim became taut with energy. "I thought there was something! She went inside. She's a queer thing, and I don't like it. If I didn't know better, I would say she's going in there to harm herself. I've seen it before. There's the docks right behind us. She goes in the water this time of year, and she's done for in less than a minute. You've got to do something."

"It's not as bad as all that. Not yet, anyhow. Can you take us down there?"

Tim nodded, and McCain put a foot on the running board, his hand coming in around the window to hang on. The drive was quick, Sam coming along behind with Lund in the second car.

At the entrance to the warehouse, both cabs stopped, and McCain, Tim, and Sam stepped out. McCain unsnapped the cover of his holstered pistol and checked the load. "We could use you. One thing we do know: he's a strong one. But he might be armed. It's up to you."

Both cabbies straightened, but Tim stopped Sam with a hand on his shoulder. "Not you, Sam. You got a wife with a baby on the way."

McCain looked for Lund, who was standing slowly from the car as though every joint was dry and hard. "I'm going." He took off his coat and hat and carefully laid them on the seat of the cab.

"Wait a moment. Lund, you stay here a minute." McCain kept his voice low so the sound wouldn't travel. "Sam, you go back and call my precinct. Tell them I'm here. They'll send someone. You have a gun?" Sam shook his head no. McCain turned to Tim, who also shook his head. "Thom, what about you?"

When McCain looked for him, Lund was already gone, the heavy metal door swinging shut behind him.

Now that she was moving, Penelope felt better. All her mind seemed to hold were the directions he had given her over the phone, winding her turn by turn into dark rows of crates and equipment. It was dirty and unkempt and smelled of wood rot and mold. All the usual signs of industry and success were absent. Trash settled in every imaginable place. When she heard the rats, she made a quick decision not to look down. It was clear to her as she made her way through, no one had worked that part of the dock for some time.

Penelope turned the corner. The clutter of empty crates gave way to a wide, tall room. She looked right and saw the huge gates that swung open to the river when the boats were to go out or come in, depending on the business being done. A lighted metal box stood at the top of a flight of steps. A door with a wooden board that read *Office* stood open and spilled light onto the concrete floor around her feet. Penelope stopped, stared up at the yellow windows. She had an instinct to run away. She could feel it clearly, screaming at her to go. It wasn't easy to ignore, but she managed it.

She climbed the stairs. Every step against the metal sounded like a bell to her ears. There was movement against the light and the sound of papers sliding across the floor.

Pausing on the landing, Penelope tried to catch sight of the man moving against the back wall of the office. She stepped out of the darkness, her hands holding each other tightly inside her heavy fur muff. He stood up from behind the desk, a whiskey in one hand and the light behind him, the shadow hiding his expression. "Hello, Penny," he said, his words dry and empty against the darkness.

"Hello, Jack."

40

"I DIDN'T EXPECT YOU TO ACTUALLY COME." Falling forward even as he seemed to try to stand himself up, Jack Rollins had the appearance of a man coming apart at the seams. The easy charismatic smile Penelope had caught at the party, the curly hair swept behind his ear, the neat suit—all of what she had seen of him was gone. Jack swayed on his feet, the suit he had worn to the party undone at the neck and wrists, the tie gone, his hair a damp mess of sweat and alcohol. She saw the scratches up his arm first. Once she knew what to look for, she found more at his neck. Renee could fight like a wildcat. Penelope could smell him from across the room. Jack made a loose gesture with his glass. "I've been getting drunk. Been working on it all day. A good long drunk." His words slurred around the edges. "Want a drink?"

One step into the room and the trash was up to the straps of her shoes. Newspapers, torn ledger entries, letters, and invoices spread across the floor, covering every inch. Dangling from its cord, the phone receiver emitted a series of strange clicks and whirs as it swung and turned. The room stank of sweat and booze and something else that Penelope resolutely ignored.

"I said, want a drink?" He was momentarily loud in the way drunks are when they think they might be funny. "Or do you drink whiskey?" He laughed. "What shall we toast to? Prohibition maybe? How about the Yankees? No, I know! Let's toast to the Jade Tiger!" He leered.

"We could toast to Renee."

"Bad luck!" Jack took a long pull from his glass and considered her as he swallowed, his eyes closing, disappearing into the hollows of his skull. For a moment, Penelope thought he was about to reach out to her, but instead he gave himself a shake and fell back into a chair with a laugh.

"You killed her, Jack. I know it."

He laughed, slamming the glass down on the desk so hard that it broke. The office filled with the smell of sour alcohol and inexplicably of kerosene. "And what kind of proof do you have of that? What about that Staughton kid, her fiancé, huh? Maybe he did it. Maybe he's going to fry in the electric chair." He wiped his mouth with the back of his hand. "The papers said they found him in a car in the garage. Trying to leave town."

No, her head said, not him. You, you bastard. It was you. A terrible fury began to climb up from the soles of her feet, rooting her to the floor.

"How much did she take you for, when it was all said and done?" Jack's words slurred and slipped.

"She had two thousand in her purse when she died. Did you know that?"

Jack hung on the words, his eyes focusing and unfocusing on an unseen point between them. He began, "She didn't have that kind of money . . ." and stopped.

"It was business between Renee and me, and I don't lie about business." Her hand tightened on the concealed gun. "I went straight, Jack. Do you know how hard that was to do? To leave everything behind and try for something else, something better? Maybe take all that bad I did and make something better. Take care of my family." Penelope took a deep breath. "Why did you have to kill her? At my uncle's house? Why?"

She stopped short. She could feel the silence moving around her through the warehouse—there had been a change. She sensed that someone else was listening. She pivoted toward the windows, looked down at his desk, her body in profile to Jack. Within the fur muff, one hand held the gun, her finger on the trigger. It wouldn't be easy to miss at this range, but if someone came through the door, she'd have her hands full. With her back to the windows, the Beretta in her right hand could take a man on the stairs while she held the other one in her left steady on Jack—if it came to that. She was sure Jack couldn't see the muzzle hidden within the fur, as drunk as he was. Not until she fired. Penelope stared straight ahead into the heart of the shadowy warehouse, letting her eyes unfocus. There was something. She was sure there was something moving just outside the light.

Jack laughed again. "What do you care? Didn't she have you dangling from her string? She was going to have all of it from you, one way or another. She was on you for life! She was going to have it all, one nickel at a time!"

"She was a fool to waste her time," Penelope replied. "I told you. There wasn't anything left." She lowered her voice. The door to the office was shut. The windows as well.

"I see you checking the windows, Mrs. Ambrose. There isn't anyone here but us."

Penelope shivered, tightened her hands on the guns. Jack leered at her, his head low, his eyes bleary. She had seen the same look in Kinkaid's eye, felt it in her memories not so long ago. She had never forgotten it and never would. Jack rode on the cusp of a murderer's luck, defying every minute that it might run out.

"I guess you think you knew Renee pretty well. I knew her too. Don't forget. I was there from the beginning. I was there the night you met. You had cash, you had looks, and she had style." Penelope kept her voice steady, conversational. "How long did it take for her to strip you of everything? I can't remember. Was it a month?"

"That's not how it happened."

"Roulette was your choice. I remember that." Penelope nodded. "You played it like a man who lost his mind. I can see Renee there alongside, pressing you on to gamble more. Kinkaid paid her for that kind of thing, but I think she would have done it anyway. She liked to see how far she could drive a man. I knew Renee for four years, and I can guarantee you one thing about her: whatever she felt for you, it wasn't love." Angling her head to take him in, Penelope waited for him to answer. When he didn't, she added, "I remember the first time I saw you at the Jade Tiger. I thought, Renee will have that man for breakfast, and everyone will know. And she did. And we all knew."

"If you were a man, I'd knock you down!"

Penelope met his eye and held it. "Kinkaid told me he couldn't keep you away from the Tiger. You were like a bad penny, always turning up. Waiting in the alley for the chorus girls, talking up the muscle we kept around the door. That was all right with Renee. She liked to have a man or two around. When Kinkaid died, she must have needed somewhere to lie low. She wouldn't have wanted to talk to the police just then. Even Dai Li was looking for her, but he couldn't find her." Penelope smiled. "Did she run to you? Did you show her your greasy little billet down on the wharf and promise you would always take care of her? She would have thought that was sweet, then gutted you like a fish. But you didn't have any money left, did you? Poor you if you did. She took whatever you had left and ran."

"You always were a snotty bitch, weren't you? Nosy, smarter than everybody else, busybody—"

"She ran to Paris after that. I should have known she would come to America. Did you see her here in New York? Could she even remember you?"

"It wasn't like that . . ." Jack slurred. "You wouldn't understand! She wasn't like that with me." He straightened himself, smoothed down his shirt with a dirty hand. "She loved me!"

"Just out of curiosity, because I have to know . . ." Penelope took a breath, looking down at the desk. She caught a glimpse of the necklace, the heavy, garish setting almost swamping the pearls. The diamond clasp sparkled in the stale yellow light like water through a gutter. Renee was wicked, sometimes cruel, definitely crooked, and Penelope's enemy for life—but she hadn't deserved a man like Jack Rollins. She had not deserved to die like that. Penelope swept her eyes up from the necklace to his face. This man, who was nothing. This man who stole from his father, gambling away money that never belonged to him. Who drove a successful business into the ground. This man who thought a wild thing like Renee could belong to him—owned like a suit or a necklace. No, Renee did not deserve this careless fool.

"Did she even have to con you to get her hands on your father's money? Or did you just give it to her outright? What did you do when you saw she was already married? To a rich man. A man you could never be. What did you do?"

"I killed her, that's what I did. I put my hands around her filthy, greedy neck and I strangled her until her bones broke. And you know what? She had it coming, she did! She had it coming!" He was at the top of his voice. His face, an unnatural shade of purple, crumpled into a grimace, and he shuddered with laughter until tears ran down his cheeks. Leaning on the desk, he looked down, an agonizing cry coming from deep inside. "I loved her," he said. "I loved her."

Collapsing into the chair, Jack laid his head down on the desk and sobbed. "I bet you think I'm just a mug. But I wasn't before I met her." He wiped his face with his shirtsleeve and took a shuddering breath. "You wouldn't know me from who I was then. I was something. I went to college." He considered the blurry distance and talked as though she wasn't there. "It was my idea, going to China. I told Dad we could build up a new route, create a whole new trade route. He sent me with a lot of cash. She could always tell who had it, who didn't. Cash, I mean." He leaned his head in his hands and tried to laugh but couldn't. "She wasn't always bad. Only later when the money ran out." His voice got louder, as though every word he spoke caused him physical pain. The tears ran down his cheeks freely and onto his shirt. "I ran guns and drugs and did things I never thought I could or would. All because of her. For her."

He looked at Penelope, daring her to speak.

"I knew she was using me," he continued. "I didn't care. I liked having her around." He lifted his face into the light. "I thought she would come back after Kinkaid died. But she didn't. I waited for a week before someone told me she had taken a freighter west. I couldn't get her off my mind. Even when I knew I wouldn't see her again. Even while I was in prison. I couldn't stop thinking about her. I knew what she didn't, that we were just exactly alike. That she was meant to be with me and no one else. I just had to find her again and explain." He put his hands flat on the desktop and tried to gain some equilibrium. "I've been . . . I've been trying to make it right, save Dad's company. There is still some life in her. Even with just one ship, I know I can make something out of it. I would have done anything to save the company— even go to work for Alfred Gott. He told me she was back in town. Gott told me where to look, and I started following her around town. Caught up with her once and tried to tell her I was back and making good. She laughed at me. So I gave her a little love tap, to let her know I meant business. Maybe I took it too far, I don't know. I was drunk. She had a man with her after that, made sure I couldn't get to her. I told Gott she wouldn't see me. Freddy said he would take me to her if I got dressed up like a swell. I thought he might be lying to me. But there she was, palling around with some rich swell. Getting married . . ." The word caught in his mouth.

Jack rocked his chair back and leaned against the wall.

"You couldn't understand what it's like to love a woman

like that, a woman who is everything to you, then rips it all out from under you. I was just coming to my feet again. Just beginning to make headway." His hands fumbled across the desk, moving the papers. "Where's the whiskey?" The blood drained from his face, his lips turning a pale purple. "I knew from the moment I saw her stand in front of that piano, I was all set to be a fool for her again. She saw me too. I could tell. She knew me." His words came faster as though he were pushing them out of himself and as far away as he could manage. "I followed her to the hallway and saw that old woman take her on. I had to get to her alone, talk to her, tell her how things were. She practically ran from me. It made me angry." Jack's eyes slid upward. "It wasn't my fault. Two g's . . ." His words faded away. "You wouldn't lie to me about that, would you?"

Penelope shook her head.

"Two g's. When Dad died, he told me I was no good. He knew it all. I don't have anywhere left to hide. No more money to go there if I did. I can't even hock her necklace. It's too hot!" He brought himself to his feet, swaying. "I guess I'm all outta chances, aren't I?"

Penelope knew the look. She drew a gun from the muff, pointing it at the floor. "Think it through, Jack. We could go to the police. I know you weren't in it alone."

Jack lunged at her with a wordless shout, grabbing her by the shoulder with one hand, easily knocking the gun out of her hand with the other. Swinging around, she peered out into the darkness of the warehouse, looking for someone, anyone. There was a figure, or a shadow, between the empty crates, his arm raised.

Jack shifted, holding her close until there was no space

between them, his fingers fixed around her throat. Penelope's free hand clutched at his as she stared into his face, her left hand emerging from the muff with the second Beretta pointed at his waist. She dug her fingers into his, so frantic she hardly noticed his grip. "I loved her." The words were harsh in his mouth as Penelope felt all his anger and loathing. His eyes teared, and he collapsed inward, aging years as she watched. "I loved her," he said.

For a moment, he held her to him and they stared into each other, searching out what was left in Renee's wake. If his painful grip wasn't enough to remind her, the wet agony in Jack's red eyes stared back at her like a mirror into her past. Kinkaid laughing with delight as he hit her. The shock of the knife on her face, then her neck. Her blood covering the front of her dress and hands. The sharp retort of the gun.

Shoot, she told herself, shoot. Shoot now.

Kinkaid's face loomed up in front of her, his cold eyes shining straight into her. The gun was one with her hand. Her finger was the trigger. She couldn't do it. Penelope told herself to, commanded herself. Light flickered around the edge of her vision as Jack exhaled damp gasoline into her face. They were fools, she thought, all of them fools. Fools to believe in something like love. It was a sucker's game.

Penelope heard a door slam, and hot pain shot through her side. Papers on the filing cabinet flew up as another shot rang through the office. They turned away from the office windows like dancers waltzing on a high stage, the audience just a glimpse over her shoulder. She turned her head just as they fell, and saw a man holding a gun in the shadows between the empty crates. Jack's hand loosened, and she gasped for breath, relaxing against him as he collapsed forward onto the ground, pulling her down with him. Her ears were full of shouting and feet clanging up the metal staircase, every sound muffled and distant as she tried to turn Jack over, calling his name. Blood spread out from a wound in his chest, staining her knees and hands as she struggled with his shoulders. Her hands finally turning his head toward her, she watched his eyes flutter and settle until there was nothing left.

Penelope felt the floor shake and heard someone say, "Get her out of here."

When she looked back, she saw Blake standing there with a gun in his hand, looking down at the dead man on the floor.

"Where did it come from?"

"Who fired that shot?"

A whistle blew high and pierced the rumble of voices.

The little policeman was beside her trying not to shout. "Did you see who fired that gun?" Her answer was drowned out by the shouting all around them.

"Get around to that exit, son! Catch that man!"

"Penelope!" Lund's hand beat against her cheek like the wings of a bird. "Penelope, can you hear me?" He picked her up like a rag doll to lean her against the wall. "Penelope, are you shot?"

Penelope opened her eyes and looked up past her feet to Jack Rollins, his blood pooled around him. A shudder began in her abdomen as she looked at him, her hands cold as she tried to push Lund away.

"Penelope, what were you thinking? What were you thinking?" She looked at Lund and saw his green eyes searching hers, his hair rumpled and careless from running.

"Look at me, Miss Harris!" Blake bellowed. "Who fired that gun?"

"It was Gott. Alfred Gott." Penelope let her head fall back against the wall and shut her eyes. As she sank into the darkness, she heard Lund shout, "Over here! Get a doctor! She's been shot!"

41

"THOM!" ELEANOR STOOD UP FROM the uncomfortable hospital chair but did not come toward him. "It's good to see you."

Lund took off his hat. "Is she awake?"

Eleanor studied the figure in the bed. "Not yet. The surgeon says she should be coming out of the ether soon." She fidgeted with the sheet but did not leave the bedside. "He said the bullet went in and out of her."

"A full recovery then?" Lund took a step closer to the bed.

"Aches and pains, but nothing too serious. The doctor says she will be able to continue her singing. I know that will be the first thing she asks about." Eleanor glanced at the door, then back to him. "Thom, what will they do with him?"

Lund looked at the hat in his hand. "Jack Rollins died at the scene."

"No," Eleanor faltered, "I meant . . . I meant Alfred. What will they do with him? Alfred is more than just the black sheep of the family; he's a reprobate and a liar. But is he a killer? Would he, did he, murder that man?"

"Gott had a license for the gun. The rest—I can't say. The papers are already calling him a hero. I think he's rather counting on public sentiment to see him through."

"You've seen him?"

Lund nodded. "At the station. They have to hold him in custody. He killed a man." When Lund had seen him, Gott had his head up for the cameras, his mustache immaculate, his eyes sharp and calculating. He hadn't missed an angle when he made his statement. As far as Lund was concerned, Gott was set to walk free. He didn't like it. He couldn't put his finger on any proof to explain why.

"He was defending Penelope. Wasn't he?"

"You have doubts?" Lund asked.

Eleanor looked down at Penelope again. "I suppose I know him too well." She sighed. "Alfred makes an unlikely hero."

Gott claimed he had gone to the warehouse on a hunch, arriving just in time to see Jack attack Penelope. But the whole story felt contrived. He hadn't mentioned seeing Jack at the party and had no easy explanation for how he had known where to find him. The police interrogated him for hours, and Gott didn't change a word of his story. But there was something unbalanced about it. If there was more to the story, proving it would be almost impossible. "It doesn't matter what I think," Lund said finally. "It's down to the police now. If they suspect Gott is lying, they won't admit it to me. I'm out of it now." He felt a twinge of unhappiness as he looked down on the figure in the bed. It dawned on him that his life had not felt emptier than it did that moment, knowing he would shortly leave when all he wanted to do was stay.

"It doesn't make sense." Eleanor bit her lip.

She was a bright woman, too bright to stay in the dark for long.

"Alfred never did anything that didn't benefit him somehow," Eleanor continued. "Thom, did Alfred murder that man? Did he go there to kill him?"

It was an interesting question, one Lund had been thinking through for most of the night. Gott had given several good reasons to be at the wharf, had a license for the gun he used to kill Jack Rollins, and had no clear reason to want the man dead. But there were holes. First, why had a man like Gott, used to comfort, left his car and walked a half mile in the dark? Why had he arrived without announcing himself? And why did Gott deny knowing Jack Rollins before that day, a man with whom he surely would have had business dealings in Shanghai? "It's up to the police now," he said, knowing Eleanor wouldn't accept this answer.

She put a finger to her lips. "That woman, Renee Strong, she wasn't an easy woman to give up."

Lund felt an unfamiliar surprise. Eleanor stared back at him, her intelligent eyes studying him. "Oh?" It was the best he could manage.

"I think Freddy was involved with her. Didn't want to let her go. She was that kind of woman, the kind a man never wanted to give up on. I think he was infatuated with her, and when he heard Charles say they were married, something snapped. Someone had to pay her way to New York. It must have been Freddy. Harry has been broke for months."

Lund's interest focused. "Alfred Gott didn't kill Renee, Eleanor. Jack Rollins did."

"Well, I didn't say it happened right then, did I?" Eleanor retorted.

Lund's interest grew.

"You would have to know my family as well as I do to see it all," she said plainly. "Freddy shot Mr. Rollins because there was something in it for him. That's the only way to see it. I know it's cold and heartless, but my poor girl doesn't have any money that Freddy would be interested in. At least," she added shrewdly, "none that he could know of. I think he killed Jack Rollins because the man could implicate him."

Lund was fascinated. "Why would Gott want her dead?"

"She could have been blackmailing him, or maybe she didn't want to go around with him anymore. It comes down to Charles." Eleanor rolled her eyes. "Charles! That poor boy thinks he's Don Juan. And him with hardly the brains of a fresh loaf of bread! I was so sure he told Alfred they were married that I asked him first thing when he woke up. I said, 'Charlie, did you ask Freddy Gott for a job?' Charles told me he went straight to Cousin Freddy after his father refused to put him on the payroll. Told him straightaway that he needed the money to keep his new wife." Eleanor leaned in, intent. "Charles told me that when he told him, Freddy lost control. Threw him out. Now what does that say to you?" She waited.

Lund blinked slowly. It was fact by fact what he had pieced together himself. "I'd say we don't have enough motive."

"We don't, do we? Well, I've known Freddy all my life, and there are only two things that get him going: money and women. Charles certainly wasn't going to get close to his money, so it had to be the woman. Freddy must have fallen for her. Hard. Why else would he show up ready to kill Jack

Rollins? It wasn't to save Penelope, I can tell you that. Freddy hates the police. You were investigating him for money laundering, weren't you?"

Lund looked at his floor and tried hard to hide his disappointment.

"I've gone wrong somewhere, haven't I?" Eleanor clucked her tongue. "Now where could it have been?"

"You aren't wrong. That's the problem." Lund thought through his words. "None of it can be proved. Unless he confesses, and I doubt that very much."

"Go on, tell me, Thom." Eleanor nodded.

"All right," Lund began. "Freddy knew Jack in Shanghai at the Jade Tiger. Renee was a good-time girl then. Alfred Gott was paying for her time those days, keeping her in an apartment near the French Concession." He checked Eleanor's face for surprise and found none. He continued, "It took me a bit to remember why I felt so sorry for the kid. Then I remembered—Renee's fling with Jack was all business. Gott paid her to get information about Rollins Shipping and, barring that, to get Jack to spend all his money at the roulette wheel. Gott wanted the shipping route, you see. When he couldn't do the job with Renee, he paid some police to pick up Jack and rough him up. Thing was, Jack Rollins was already in jail. He'd met a man in a bar who didn't like Renee's nightclub act. Jack knifed him."

Eleanor gasped. "Prison? How on earth did he get here?"

"I wouldn't be surprised if we found out Gott told Jack's father how to negotiate the bribe and the release. It must have cost Rollins the earth to get his son out. It certainly ruined the business. Gott can buy it for a song now if he still wants it."

"But I don't understand how this pertains to what happened."

Lund shifted uncomfortably. "The rest is conjecture. Gott knew Jack Rollins was on his last dime. He wanted to buy Rollins Shipping outright, but Jack wouldn't sell until he was down to nothing. I think he must have convinced Jack to come to the party and see if he could sell a partial interest and keep the firm going without having to sell. When Rollins saw Renee, well, he was finished."

"But how could Gott know Rollins would kill her?"

"I don't think he expected that," Lund admitted. "I think Gott wanted to make her afraid, maybe change her mind about sticking by him. Or maybe—" He stopped.

"Or what?" Eleanor prodded. "You can't just leave me hanging."

Lund shrugged. "Or maybe Gott intended to kill her all along, hanging it on Rollins." He looked at his hat. "Like I said, it's just conjecture. We'll never know for sure. Unless he confesses."

"I rather doubt that," Eleanor replied. "Freddy was always the most obstinate little prig."

Lund put his hat on. "Will you tell her I came by?"

"Wait a moment, Thom." Eleanor reached out with one hand, taking him by the arm but otherwise remaining still. "Would you stay here for a bit with Penelope while I run up to Charles's floor to tell Harry and my niece what the surgeon said? It will only be a few minutes."

Lund nodded, reaching to pull up a chair.

Eleanor gestured for him to stand next to her. "Look." Eleanor carefully pushed back the covers to show Penelope holding Eleanor's hand tightly. "She gets restless if I let go. Here, you take her hand. That way she won't wake up."

"I couldn't possibly . . ." He took a step back.

She clasped him by the arm. "I must tell you," Eleanor kept her voice low and firm, "when we left Shanghai, Penelope was very afraid. Of shadows, of anything, really. She could hardly sleep. Then one night, she crawled into bed with me, held on to my hand like she is now, and went to sleep. When we met you at the hospital a year ago, you were holding her hand just like I am right now. Thom, I know it's none of my business, but in Shanghai you and Penelope, you were friendly, weren't you?"

Lund looked into Eleanor's eyes and saw something of her daughter there. He found he couldn't lie. "Yes."

"Perhaps a little more friendly than Kinkaid would have liked?" She urged his words forward, nodding.

"Perhaps." The admission was difficult.

"Thank goodness." She relaxed abruptly, letting go of his arm and just catching herself on the edge of the bed. "Thank goodness."

"Mrs. Harris? I don't understand."

"I was so worried that she hadn't had any happiness in her life." Eleanor put her free hand to her head. "Then I saw you talking at the party. I could see she loved you, a mother knows. I just couldn't tell if you felt the same." She reached for his hand. "Here, take hers so she can sleep. I won't be long." She took his hand and led it to Penelope's. Eleanor covered their hands with the blanket and left as Lund slowly lowered himself into the chair to wait.

42

PENELOPE LAY ON HER SIDE, the starched hospital gown a bright white against her skin. In the unforgiving light, the scar on her neck was in high relief. In the Shanghai hospital, her neck had been so heavily bandaged that Lund had not seen the scar. But here, the path of the knife stood out plainly against her skin. He had forgotten. She had been lucky to survive, let alone sing.

It all came back to him, every decision, every footstep. His last night walking a beat, as far as he knew. He went past the Jade Tiger out of habit. It was his last beat. He was nostalgic. Penelope should have already been waiting for him at the station. If only he had been a moment sooner, he would have caught Kinkaid and shot him in the act. That wouldn't have been a crime, just a policeman doing his duty. Just a moment earlier, and no crime would have been committed except for what Kinkaid had already done.

"You're squeezing my fingers." The drowsy voice from the hospital bed spoke the words slowly. "Oh, now you've taken your hand away completely. Who's that? Thom?"

"Yes, it's me." Lund leaned forward.

"I should have known it was you. Your hands are always so warm." She exhaled, satisfied. "My hands are cold." Her fingers reached from under the covers and took his hand back, their fingers intertwining until he could not tell where her hand began and his ended. "That's better."

"Let me get your mother."

Her hand tightened. "Please don't. Just the two of us for a

moment, do you mind?" She opened her eyes briefly, the blue appearing then disappearing as she shut her eyes tight.

He did not mind. Laying his hat at the foot of the bed near her feet, he sat down on the edge of the mattress.

"Thom?"

"Yes, Penelope?"

"Oh," her breath caught, "I forgot."

"What did you forget?"

"What it is like to hear you say my name." She grinned, her eyes opening gradually, the blue peeking through her eyelashes like a slash of the horizon. "Last I remember, I was in the ambulance."

"You were shot," Lund answered carefully.

"Where was I shot? A distillery? I feel drunk." She laughed, then clutched a hand to her head. "Oh my! Did I get a bang on the head too?"

"That's the ether. It won't last."

"That's too bad." Her eyes were wide open now, her pupils large. "I might like feeling this way." She laughed again and put her hand over her eyes. "Ouch! Perhaps not."

"Your mother wanted you to know, the doctor said the bullet—"

"I don't care," she said with a drowsy slur. "You aren't gone?"

"No." Lund couldn't help the grin that began with relief. "I'm right here."

She settled against the pillows as she slowly became more lucid. "Jack died, didn't he?"

"He did."

"He never had a chance."

"Murderers like to play it like they don't have a choice, but they do. Jack killed Renee with his hands. He was doing exactly what he wanted."

"I had a choice."

"No, you didn't."

It was quiet for a moment, the stillness comfortable. When he looked at her face, Lund was astonished to see she was crying.

"Did you come to New York for me?"

He fished his handkerchief out of his pocket. "Arrogant girl!" He laughed. "I came to New York to get as far away as I could!"

"Well, it didn't work." She laughed too. "Ow." She put her hand to her head. "I feel as though I've been on a three-day bender with a dodgy orchestra and a case of medicinal whiskey."

"Haven't you heard?" he asked dryly. "All the whiskey in America is medicinal."

Penelope laughed despite her headache, her mirth gathering up until she began to cry again. Lund sat on the edge of the bed and held her gently in his arms as she cried into the lapel of his suit, her shuddering apprehension expelling as she rose through clouds of grief and guilt.

"Don't cry, Penelope. None of it is worth crying over. It's all finished. It's in the past. Kinkaid is dead and gone. He can't hurt you anymore. No one knows but the two of us, and I will take that secret to my grave."

She pushed back from him. "I'll cry if I like," she said with a wet sniff. "Nothing wrong with crying."

"It's making your nose red." He laughed as she reached for the mirror on the bedside table and winced.

He handed it to her. "It's official—you have been shot exactly the same number of times that I have."

"Well, that might be." Penelope blew her nose into the handkerchief and sat up straight. "But can you sing?"

Lund sat on the bed. "I sing in church, does that count?"

"It does." She wiggled. "Can you sing like this?" She took a breath and breathed through a single note.

Lund wrinkled his nose. "I think I might."

She punched him in the arm. "It wasn't that bad! Besides, I've had ether. I should have more than one chance to get it right."

"Then take your chance." Lund smiled.

"I think I will."

Penelope sang.

Acknowledgments

When you choose to write, there are so many people to thank that forgetting one or more is all too easy. But there are a few without whose encouragement at crucial moments I would not have written these words or finished this book.

Without a doubt, I owe a debt of gratitude to my parents, who have supported and encouraged my dreams. Without their steady belief in me, I'm sure I would have given up long before I finished this manuscript. I also owe a debt to the love of my life, without whose help I never would have sorted out how to write and be a meaningful parent, partner, and author. And of course, to my children, who embrace adventure and inspire me every day.

A book does not come together without the aid of a team of professionals. My editor, Sione Aeschliman; cover and interior designer Lindsey Cleworth; and proofreader Ellen Hornor each made an indelible positive impression on the quality of this book. Any part of *The Jade Tiger* that you do not like is due to my mistakes, not theirs.

Still others I must acknowledge and thank: Kathleen White, my first writing teacher, who used the strike of her boot heels to mark the rhythm when she read aloud; author and friend Marina Scott, who was never afraid to tell me to work harder, make it better, and get back on the horse; author

May Cobb, whose generous friendship to a virtual stranger showed me how to leap into writing without fear and be bold; and all of my beta readers—from author Kelly Brackenhoff to Priscilla Smith, Blythe Wilson, and Charlotte Weathers—all of whom were honest about what they thought and pushed me to become a better writer.

For all of these and many more, I offer my gratitude and thanks.

Historical Notes

While it may seem extraordinary today, in 1928 opera signers were the megastars of their generation. Propelled by operatic theatrical breakthroughs from composers such as Bizet, Puccini, and Wagner, as well as the widespread popularity of radio, opera was accessible to many more than just the wealthy. Grand opera, from heartbreak to soaring heroism, soothed a world torn apart by modernity. Opera composers, musicians, and stars were recognizable by name, mobbed in public, and in as high demand as vaudeville, Broadway, radio, and film stars. The 1915 silent film of Bizet's *Carmen* was a popular success for Cecil B. DeMille, the music so well known that some audiences sang along to the accompaniment. The star of DeMille's film, Geraldine Farrar, was so admired when she retired from the Metropolitan Opera in 1922 that the streets around the opera house were mobbed by thousands of "Gerry-flappers." Her fans would not allow her car to pass until she put the convertible top down, stood on her seat, and addressed them with an aria from *Manon*.

In addition to the art form, the style of operatic singing was popular and slowly shifted prevailing styles of singing. When aspiring soprano Helen Morgan arrived in New York in 1924, she waited out her time between auditions singing in speakeasies. Her capable operatic voice and stage presence (as well as her habit of draping herself across the lid of the piano) developed a new style of music—the torch song. While her operatic career never took off, Morgan became a famous Broadway star whose vocal talents inspired Kern and Hammerstein to pen the musical *Sweet Adeline* especially for her.

Across Europe, the scene was the same. Vienna and Berlin opera seasons lasted all year, with hundreds of performances. Other cities released their actors for a sunny vacation in Monte Carlo, where every casino offered a daily fare of grand opera in opulent theaters for their wealthy guests. Farrar notes in her autobiography that travel to Monte Carlo was an extravagant holiday for some but could also be dangerous for singers' careers, should their managers choose to gamble away their contracts at the tables.

For Penelope, a career teaching children or aspiring sopranos would be good, steady work, especially with some credentials for the career that stalled when she married Kinkaid Ambrose. As a reluctant nightclub owner, she would have been unable to resist the lure of the stage to sing and revisit a happier time in her life. Should a reader be interested in hearing what Penelope's Habanera might have sounded like as she sang it in the Jade Tiger, they need go no further than the recordings of the great Jessye Norman. Norman's live recording of the Habanera in Berlin in 2009 inspired Penelope's raw performance in this book.

Before concluding my historical comments, I would like to take a moment to address the setting of Shanghai for Penelope's past.

In addition to immigration from rural China, Shanghai saw increasing immigration from Britain, America, Russia,

France, and many Western nations in the early twentieth century. The city was preparing itself for a renaissance of ideas and art, everything from women's independence to exploration of intellectual freedoms to a fast-growing film industry. Chinese political leadership embraced the confluence of cultures, becoming the "Paris of the East." Between the insatiable Chinese thirst for fine art of all kinds and the immigration of Westerners familiar with opera, Shanghai was precisely the type of place where a young soprano with a gifted voice would attract attention and an audience of admirers—even when she sang jazz.

At the same time, Shanghai was a free port, where no visa was required, attracting immigration of an international criminal element. Although this was a small part of the city's history, it is one that noir filmmakers and authors have grasped as the perfect setting for unfolding drama.

As Christopher Huang discusses in his excellent book *A Gentleman's Murder*, Orientalism in the 1920s and '30s was a thin veil for overt racism against Asian immigrants of all kinds. The fetishizing of Chinese women and demonizing of Chinese and Asian men was the subject of popular pulp books and movies, horror, and noir. While the Jade Tiger casino resides in the French Concession, the fact remains that almost every visitor from the West who came to see Penelope while she owned the Jade Tiger ended up committing acts that made them easy prey for a blackmailer. I have no doubt that at the root of my characters' actions is entitlement and the firm belief their bad behavior will not be remembered when they return to the West. They were wrong.

I thought long and hard about whether I wanted to

comment on the behavior. Ultimately, I believed that to allow it to pass without comment was to take part in fetishizing.

—E. W. Cooper

QUESTIONS FOR DISCUSSION

1. Why do you think Penelope sings opera and not jazz?

2. Middle-class women in the early twentieth century were not expected to work. However, Penelope is determined to earn a living. What do you think motivates her to keep looking for a paying job?

3. Renee Strong pursued Penelope across the world to blackmail her. Why is she driven to ruin Penelope and her family?

4. Why do you think Eleanor hates it when her daughter sings the role of Carmen?

5. In what ways do we understand Penelope's motivation as her past is revealed?

6. During Prohibition, speakeasies became clandestine meeting places for scofflaws and criminals. Are speakeasies still relevant in the twenty-first century? Can you think of any modern speakeasies people use today?

7. Penelope clearly believes herself to be a criminal. Is she? Does Lund believe she is?

8. As we learn about Penelope's past, we gain a deeper insight into why Lund left his career as a policeman. Do you believe him when he says he immigrated to New York for a job? Or did he travel there because he knew her mother's family lived there?

9. Why do you think Penelope left Lund in Shanghai after Kinkaid died?

10. Penelope and Lund are both willing to make sacrifices to protect each other. What does this say about their friendship? What developments would you like to see in their relationship?

11. The book ends as Penelope begins to sing. Do you think she can look forward to a career as a soprano?

12. Which opera do you think has the best plot for a murder mystery?

Even if they did, no one at this club would sell gossip to the papers."

Lund stared. Rask's ability to read his mind unnerved him, as it always did.

"All right, you can have your privacy." Rask's smile was thin and hard. "I can't imagine what on earth would keep you from telling me your troubles. You've known me long enough. I have half a mind to get you drunk and worm it out of you." Rask laughed. "Don't worry. Now we work." He pushed back his chair so Scratch could jump into his lap. Once settled, the mongrel gave a deep sigh and closed his eyes. "No one at the bank can know anything about it." When Lund didn't speak, Rask added, "What do you say to that?"

"Sounds fine. You want discretion, and you don't want it dealt with at the bank." The thought of work gave Lund relief. A problem to solve was what he needed, something to keep him from thinking about her every waking moment.

"One of the board members, Wallace Peters, wants some information about a death." Rask leaned back. "Have you met him?" Lund shook his head. "Wallace was auditing the books for his father when I started. There were a lot of late nights working shoulder to shoulder. We became friends." It was firmer praise than Lund had expected from Rask. It was emphatic. "His matter is a private one. It could take several days to settle. I expect you can manufacture a cover story that will be good enough to explain the time away."

"Is he in trouble?" Suspicion colored the words more than Lund intended.

"No, no! Nothing like that!" Rask replied crisply. Scratch shifted, looking up at Lund with a reproachful air. "Wallace is straight as an arrow and about as hard as a soft-boiled egg. I've got to find a reliable investigator who won't take him for every penny. I thought of you, of course."

"What kind of information are we talking about?"

"His sister-in-law died in June of last year. He has some questions."

"Murder?" Lund's natural caution made the word clearer than he had meant it to be.

"A boating accident, as I understand it." Rask sighed.

Lund took a long breath, waiting while the shadows of the past lengthened, paused, then retreated. "I understand."

Rask nodded, returned to stroking Scratch's ears. "I've told him over and over that he won't learn a damned thing, but it's no good. He can be quite determined when he has decided on a thing. He wants to know why she did it." Niels looked up to watch Lund. "He may be a fool, but I know Wallace—he's persistent. If you don't give him a hand, he'll go out and take his chances with the first charlatan he finds in the phone book."

Lund was cautious. "I'm not a licensed private eye in the state of New York. I don't even have a car."

"Just ask a few questions and see how far you can get. You shouldn't need a license for that, should you?" Rask reached into his inside jacket pocket and removed an envelope. "Here, take these."

Lund looked inside. "Opera tickets?"

"I had to make it worth your while, didn't I? Your lovely songbird can't have found tickets. The performance sold out months ago. Go on. Call Miss Penelope Harris and have a night out while you're at it. Have some fun for a change." Rask nodded at the envelope in Lund's hand. "Wallace insisted on the discretion. He doesn't want his wife to know about it, says it will upset her. He'll will find you before the curtain. You can talk things over with him, decide if you'll investigate the matter. If you still don't want to take him on, fair enough."

Putting the envelope in his jacket, Lund nodded. "Of course." He stood up.

"There's another matter, Thom. A bank matter." Rask stopped stroking Scratch's ear. "I want you to take a quiet look at the books. June of last year to now."

"That's quite a bit of ground." Lund turned his head to study Rask. "Am I looking for anything specific?"

"Fair question." Rask's smile disappeared, the mask of a bank president pushing the familiarity aside. "Everything William has worked on, April '27 to the present."

William Bird. The only investigator left at the bank since Lund's first investigation had put the other two with their hand in the till. Perhaps Bird had a motive or two, given how freely he spent money. He liked a good party and a pretty girl, but he wasn't a thief. A fool for a good time, perhaps. But not a thief.

"Spread it around with a few other accounts and years. I don't want him to know what you are looking at. Keep it as quiet as you can." Rask stroked the dog on his lap.

"I investigated Bird with the others. There wasn't any sign of impropriety," Lund said.

Rask gave him a careful look, pausing a moment before he said, "Things change, Thom. Sometimes they change very quickly. You know that better than any other man I know, other than Matthias."

Lund nodded. Time to go to work.

Made in the USA
Monee, IL
08 January 2022

88366953R00163